Migration

JONATHAN LOVEJOY

Armageddon Publishing
All rights reserved.

Cover: *The Snack*, 1901
William Adolphe Bouguereau (1825-1905)

ISBN-10: 0692663738
ISBN-13: 978-0692663738

For every Meredith

Surely in vain the net is spread—

In the sight of any bird

Job 6:16

Part One

Jonathan Lovejoy

Season of Death

*I*n the first days of June, the weather is cold. All the flocks have been restless since returning from winter feeding grounds, and from the Northern Islands to as far south as the Yukon, many have not bothered to return at all.

Those that remain are strangely reserved. Feeding disinterestedly, not mating or brooding. Water fowl ignore every fishing trawl. Along the shores of Newfoundland, seagulls hover in alarming numbers, making it hard to see any part of the sky not flecked white with them. Complacent locals around Hudson Bay coo in awe at the swan ballets, wedged together to the horizon.

Black-headed loons swim in enormous gatherings, peering with red eyes, having put away yodeling and laughing voices. Holding long, plaintiff wailings in reserve. Big, white snowy owls sit judgingly, congregated across the southern borders of Saskatchewan, blinking yellow eyes coldly. Sand hill cranes, with their long gray necks and red heads, are thousands of miles from their summer arctic places. They glide over the North beaches of Lake Superior, spreading 6 foot wingspans. Flapping down to awestruck onlookers.

But the greatest shock had not come from the news cameras leering coldly. It had struck like lightning from a simple video camera image. From her bedroom widow, on a small dairy farm in southern Ontario, a young girl had recorded the interior of the boiling, black Hell descending on the world below.

It seemed that confirmation had been given, that the people had a new concern. A devil other than themselves to fear. Every few days it happened, and each time it reached farther into the skies. Closer towards distant horizons.

Across the southernmost regions of Canada. From the Pacific coast to the Great Lakes. From Prince Edward Point to Brier Island, the ground is covered with species from every part of the northern and middle territories. Millions of them have settled in from Vancouver down to the streets of Seattle, across the windy mists of the Chicago cityscapes, all the way to the eastern shores of New York City. Through Central Park and Times Square, across Manhattan to the Brooklyn Bridge and beyond, the city is alive with the hustle of the living. Not the narcissistic strivings for beauty, jogging and racewalking themselves to exhaustion. Not the carnal cravings for capital, perpetrated by the suits and skirts, skittling to and fro in the jungle madness. This is the dawn of new life in the city. Perched on every sign, on every rooftop, on seemingly every inch of railing, curb, street and meter. In every size, every variation of the pattern, and every dark and light color of the rainbow.

The raptors sit in easy command at the top of the tallest buildings. Feeling at home in the dizzying heights, having no fear of gravity, watching the low morning clouds drift casually in front of them. Eyes focused. Curved talons like razors, expressions evil with hunger. Knowing already which tiny prey will be taken from the yellow flock on the rooftop so far below.

The yellow billed flycatchers, the goldfinches and red winged blackbirds, the white throated sparrows. Colorful scratches on a dark surface. Tiny chips from the top of an iceberg, beneath of which is a mountain of feathered creatures. All out of habitat, out of time. Defying every law of seasons. Every code of animal behavior known to man. And many people fall witness, because this city never sleeps, having heard the earth shattering clamour of chirping, and the thunderous beating of too many millions of wings. The people had been warned, but how could they have really known? There were simply no references. Nothing to comprehend except for the venerable movie images, and nightmare words from a story told ages ago.

The sun rises now over the Atlantic. Orange rays of brutal realization. Casting light on a hopeless reality. Fear has dawned the dread of millions, and the terror of millions more. Rulers of Creation, hiding from the truth fluttering in every corner of the eastern city. The people sit dumbfounded in their office buildings, their cafés and restaurants, their brownstones and apartment houses. Marveling untold apocalypses. Trembling their season of death.

"*How* long will they be here Mom?"

I gaze out the window. Meredith, I am called. Gray business suit, crème blouse. Bitterness in short blonde hair and 35 year old prettiness. Voluptuous curves bound in community. Entombed in repression.

"Mom, how long will it last? Mom, how…"

"I don't know, Kathy," I snap at her. "The news said they might be gone any time… they said it wasn't supposed to happen like this …"

"We're not going out today, are we?"

Cool, early summer winds drift through the city streets. Calling the flocks into restlessness. Uncertain breezes carry the smell of feathers and dung aloft. Wafting nature's warning into windows that dare be open. Currents swirl among the unwelcomed visitors, to ruffle their colorful feathers.

These winds blow whispers to the bravest bird lovers, who stroll in pretend joyfulness between the calm flocks, wielding tiny cameras and little video recorders. The air floats upward, unseen to the sky, where raptors sit at uneasy rest. Eyes blinking alertly with a new craving.

"It was just little Kathy. She wanted me to say Hi."

No she didn't

I sit comfortably on the huge sectional. Meredith Van Scoy. Jabbering away, on my favorite yellow phone.

"Oh, you want to…here Kathy, Ms. Weinberg wants to talk to you."

"Hello Mrs. Weinberg…yes…some of them are kind of pretty…"

Kathy glances towards the white window blinds. I sit with my arms folded, staring at her, a fiercely happy smile stretching my lips.

"Is Jenny in New Jersey with Mr. Weinberg this week?" she asks. "Can they go outside there?"

"Okay, Kathy. Tell her you'll talk to her later."

"I love you too Ms. Weinb…Aunt Julie."

I take the phone from Kathy, face nearly red with embarrassment.

"I know. I keep telling her to call you Aunt Julie. She really loves you, you know. She talks about you and Jenny all the time."

Julie Weinberg

"I know. I've never seen anything like this, Julie…"

Judie Wine Bird

"…there's not an inch of my yard that isn't covered with them, and you know how big our back yard is… yes, all the way to the woods. Even the pool is full of…yeah, all kinds, but mostly blackbirds… they look like crows, but some of them are huge. Julie they're perched across every wire, every street light. The trees are packed. The cars are covered…I know…it sounds like we're inside a giant aviary over here…I think they're waking up…

"…Honey, I don't care if I have to eat macaroni and ketchup for a year, I'm not going out there…I don't know what they're going to do about it, but if they want me to leave this house they'd better… What the Hell does Pinder, Lane and Garrett have to do with it? I'm just their secretary anyway…look they don't have to fire me, I'll quit before I… sweetie, this is worse than that movie. They're packed in like black rats out there. At least there was some space between those…"

Kathy has retreated to her room. She watches the strangely colored things in the tree just outside her window, and the fluttering mass of black things moving on the back lawn.

No school today

"...Look Julie, anybody dumb enough to leave the house while those things are here deserves to be eaten. Early this morning I saw a bunch of white, stork things with black legs stepping around like they owned the place...what do you mean it's not that bad, Julie? Have you looked outside?... You saw a beautiful flock of bluebirds, huh. Have you gone out to sing to them yet?... That's what I thought...Well, they're saying it goes from here all the way to the Northwest and up into Canada..."

3

From along the fences and railings at the Staten Island Zoo, across to the skyscrapers of Manhattan. On the roof and steps of St. Peter's Church, to the inner city streets of Brooklyn and Queens, to the eastern shores of Long Island. It seems that dawn has awakened their will again. They all flutter and fly noisily about. In alleys, along the beaches, over the landfills. Every species slowly loses touch with the boundaries governing past behavior. They begin to forget their different shapes, sizes and colors. They only flap and hop about, aware only that their bellies need to be fed, and that soon, they will take to the skies again. Individual flocks have grown smaller. Mixing, merging with one another. Melting into a single force of doom. A voice of calamity.

Migration

The morning sun shines brightly on the sea of shiny feathers. Illuminating cold, heartless eyes. Giving color to beaks and claws. Little redbirds, brown sparrows chirrup. The squawking bravado of crows fills the air. Blue jays screech. Orange breasted robins hop about, opening yellow beaks to the sun, halfheartedly pecking at the earth. Kingfishers and white egrets step about bewilderedly. Inner city children stare out their windows in delighted fright, to watch birds of prey swoop between brick canyons, descending upon the accursed pigeons. Alley cats hop and run in terror as they are chased underneath buildings in flurries of beating wings. It is as though an eternally large cage has been opened, and the birds have escaped and settled into the city.

A few hopefuls are brave enough to open their doors, briefly marveling at the sights and sounds of a bird kingdom. Screams are heard, as small numbers of them become agitated. Flapping and clawing their way through a foolishly opened door or first floor window.

One or two little blackbirds at a time. Fluttering. Pecking tiny knife beaks at eyes, scratching arms and hands with tiny needle claws. Three or four birds, subduing whole families, drawing deep screams from stalwart, poverty hardened mothers. Children squealing, parents flailing at the confused, lost feathered things…

Killing them. Forcing them back through the open windows. Panting, gaping at the angry red claw marks on their arms, amazed at the amount of pain such small wounds have inflicted.

And now, midmorning noises drift from the busy flock. Hundreds of northern migrating and non-migrating kinds, so many having never been this far south. Their dusty, woodsy, feathery smell saturates the muggy morning air. It wafts into windows low, then higher up, as all kinds of people look on in nervous awe.

Millions. Tens of millions, halting buses and cars. Subways are filled with the homeless, blessed because hardly a single bird has gone below. The streets are deserted by life and technology. Where people march in flawed condition every day, the flock has gathered in amoral purity, ruling in many times the pitiful 12 million human population.

They cover the beltways and parkways and freeways, spreading onward as the highways lead north of the city. Along the grassy fields and in the forests, chirping rises into dense air. Whole groups move about in bright colored clouds. Long stretches of fence posts and power lines bear the Great Horned Owls and tiny screech owls, having not fed upon the mice and rats who have barely moved a muscle in their hiding places. A great distance away, the beaches are painted white with the bodies of gulls and every water fowl imaginable.

All along this north road, trees are speckled red. Some blue. Some yellow. Even the so-called experts and bird-lovers have conceded, as not a single person is now brave enough to be outside. There are simply too many. A resting swarm. A nesting storm of devastation. Nature's beauty. A promise of dreadful prophecies fulfilled.

This road leads north to New Castle. To the upscale world of Chappaqua, 35 miles from the edge of the city. Wooded, winding roads. Pristine parks filled with death. The privileged residents look outside their million dollar palaces, holding on to their frightened sons and daughters. Praying to a God they never believed in before.

I am one of them. Meredith Van Scoy.

"Katherine, you can't tell me…okay, *Mom* then. How can you say I don't respect you, Mom? I named your granddaughter after you, didn't I? Okay, I'll call you *Mom* from now on. Look, you can't tell me different from what I'm looking at with my own eyes… look you're in Oklahoma watching it on television. If you were here, you'd know what I meant. As bad as it looks on TV, I can promise you it's ten times worse in person…*What?* A stroll among nature's *what?* (laughter) There is a swarm of hummingbirds in our flower bed that a lion would be afraid to run into. A stroll…of course I've already called the school. What difference would it make anyway? Nobody I've called has even left the house…No, I don't think anybody's been killed here, but there have been some attacks...Yes, I know. One family died in Ontario...A farmer and his family, all except the little girl. They said it looked like they were caught in one of the bigger migrations....several large migrations from the north. It's happening all over the world. Haven't you been watching the news?... Well, they think that maybe the weather might have caused it. Confused them or something. Yes, it's happening in the southern hemisphere too, but the flocks aren't as big as these...well, believe it or not, they're amazingly calm. Almost peaceful. But I get the feeling it's because they're not being disturbed... no, not yet... yes I keep the door and windows closed, Kath—Mom, I'm not that stupid..."

"Mom?"

"Yes, Honey?"

"When is Dad coming?"

"In a few days, Kathy."

I stand engaged on my canary yellow phone again, unconcerned with Mr. Corporate Offices. Stratospheric six figure salary. Never home when we were married. Never home with his new wife, either. Kathy sits mesmerized by the late morning news.

"...what do you want me to do, Mom, fly down there? Remember what happened in that Toronto airport? And I can't drive either. You, drive up here? All right, try it then. I'd love to see the look on your face when you hit Pennsylvania...(*laughing*)..."

A sudden thump at the window. My heart races, and for a second I feel light headed. Kathy sits frozen, staring at the white blinded window, mouth open, listening to the whistling, squawking and chirping outside.

"It's nothing Mom…just something bumped against the window. What? Mom please don't say that. Do you really think…oh…okay, I'll do it when I hang up. Alright… I'll do it now then. Kathy say bye to Grandma."

"Bye Grandma Katherine. We'll see you soon. I love you, too."

"Alright then…I'm so glad you called, sweetie. (*laughter*) I love you too."

I finally click away three hours on the phone. Considering whether or not it is necessary to go through the house, pushing and pulling furniture in front of the windows. After all, they have been here for so many hours already…

At that moment, something crashes though the side window. The blinds shake and wobble violently. A shriek escapes my mouth, and I hardly feel my daughter grabbing my blouse. The fluttering behind the blinds falls to the floor, and we both cry death screams. The black bird beats huge, crippled wings, hobbling, flapping, squawking wildly, sending chills through our bodies.

"Kathy! *Kathy!*"

I don't know why I called her. The words came out on their own. But something inside the girl rips her from my side. She grabs the fireplace poker, and runs towards the thing scuffling on the floor. But I take it bravely from her and thrust it into the huge, black body. It makes one last, sickening squawk and seems to die instantly. But I keep stabbing.

We both stand lost, frozen in something more than fear. The blackbird lays motionless.

"Bring me a towel from the kitchen," voice quivering, bitterness forgotten.

Kathy obeys. I take the beige dish towel with the beautiful blue pattern, and drape it over the carcass.

"Raise the blinds for me."

Kathy raises the white blinds, and we both jump when something pushes its, long, black beak through the broken window pane. I cringe as I use the toweled carcass to push it back. The towel is bloody. I push the whole mess through the pane, realizing it is a perfect fit, leaving it stuck there.

"Was that a raven?" Kathy asks.

My thoughts trail into my mother's voice, what she had told me I'd better do. *She was right,* I think, as I look around the room, wondering what I can possibly move in front of the windows. There are no bookshelves to move. They are all built into the walls.

What if it happens to the whole flock

"Put those blinds down, Kathy."

The twelve year old's face anguishes, reflecting the youth of her age. Her ravened Jenny-braids are beautiful.

"When are they going away?"

"Soon. Maybe tonight."

The entertainment center is too heavy to move. The grandfather clock is too narrow. The front window is just too big to cover with anything.

Mattresses

"Come upstairs with me, sweetie."

Young Kathy quietly follows her mother. Watching full hips swivel as I take the stairs quickly.

"Go in your room and take down all the books and toys from your bookshelves. Hurry now."

Kathy's room is lined with those convenient, home assembled bookshelves. The kind everyone buys but no one admits to. While Kathy strips her bookshelves without questioning why, I strip off my expensive pearl necklace and throw it on the dresser. I pull my crème colored silk blouse out of my tight gray skirt, opening two buttons, pulling it off over my head. I unzip my skirt and let it hit the floor, sliding my pantyhose unceremoniously off afterwards. It is a short trip into my comfortable, faded jeans, and a new white t-shirt with a blue "Chappaqua Soccer League" logo. My Reeboks are slipped on quickly.

"Mom!"

Shock grabs me! Whipping me into a dead run down the hall.

"Kathy! What is it?"

When I get to her room, I see the biggest pair of white wings in New York at Kathy's window, flapping wildly, bumping against the panes in a half hearted attempt.

"Oh my God, what…"

I run to the window, fearfully disgusted, feeling the cold needles pricking my neck. I slam against the window. Yelling, screaming as though it had comprehension, for it to stop pecking and scratching its huge, curved beak against the glass. A strange, exotic creature, with bizarre coloring about its head and eyes. It seems startled by the noise I make, and it flies away.

"What the H… God that thing was huge."

"It looked like a vulture," Kathy says.

She glances at her mother's wardrobe change. My t-shirt and jeans reveal shapely athleticism. Pure hourglass beauty, I've been told. Pure hourglass ass, my mind tells me. Unflattering.

"You know what? They're not even trying to get in. Some of them just get a little curious every so often."

"What about that blackbird?"

"It must have been an accident. Birds bump into things all the time."

They'll kill us soon

"What do you want to do?"

"I was going to use shelf boards. But…stay here for a minute. I'll be right back."

I bounce down the stairs, ignoring how heavy and sore my bosoms feel. *Damn Katherine's curves*, I think, of my mother's heavy breasted body passed down. I hip switch across the big living room into the kitchen, retrieving a hammer and nails from the utility drawer. Refusing to look at the place on the carpet.

When I get back to Kathy's room, I take the top sheet from her bed, and stretch it tight across her window, nailing it into place.

"Is that good enough?" she asks.

"If another one breaks in, it won't be able to get past the sheet, and it'll fly back outside. We don't even need the bookshelves."

We gather a few sheets from the linen closet, and go downstairs first, raising the blinds, stretching the beautiful sky blue sheet with its full color floral patterns across it. We do the same to the other, then pull two of them across the huge bay window. I am the picture of domestic puttering, holding a few small nails in my mouth, tacking the sheet veils into place. I do my best to ignore the birds, which blanket the lawn like a poultry farm, or like hungry pigeons in a park.

But there are no chickens, and no pigeons. Only many strange looking devils, and several kinds of blackbirds of all sizes. I even think I may have seen some large white owls, but I don't look twice. It looks less like a flock, and more like a gathering. An overlapping of kinds. Many species, congregating together unawares. Or unconcerned.

"Mom?"

I stand tiptoe on the bay window ledge. Tacking the sheet tightly.

"What is it, Honey?"

"I heard you telling Grandma Katherine about what happened in Toronto."

"You mean the airplane?"

"How did birds make a plane crash?"

"I don't know."

got sucked into the engines and they blew up

Kathy sees my jeans while my arms are stretched up, knowing her father would have seen a bulls eye and would have whacked me good. Her other thought is of spectacular nighttime explosions, and a giant plane crashing in a ball of fire. Three hundred and nine souls departing.

"Dad's going to fly back, isn't he?"

"You don't have to worry about Daddy," I say, climbing down. Voluptuously. "Nobody's getting anywhere near these airports for a while."

"Why are they here in the first place? When are they leaving?"

Both questions I would like answered myself. But even the so-called experts, plastering the TV screens with their fifteen minutes, have no idea under the sun why the most massive migrations in human history have swept from the Arctic Circle, down over the mountains and lowlands of Canada, and have settled in every northern state from Washington to Maine. There are no answers to the question of why some long stretches of countryside are practically empty, while every major northern city is so overrun that life is positively fearful, and human activity is at a standstill.

There are no sufficient explanations. No valid reasons why species not even known for migration have joined this bizarre odyssey. They don't know why every theory is being challenged. Why every rule of bird behavior is being broken. Why flocks are breaking down, merging into a collective. Why water fowl are so far inland. Why increasing numbers are becoming more restless, more aggressive with each passing hour.

Truthfully, they know nothing.

I put the last nail in the sheet, stepping back to admire the curious handiwork. Our elegant living room is bathed in an eerie hue of tropical oceans. And the distant hope of clear, summer skies.

The sun climbs high above the Eastern seaboard, to shed gray light upon a dark future. Foreboding clouds have gathered already. They rob the sun of its warmth. Threatening to descend power on the population below.

The city is awake. Breathing the scent of filth and feathers. Listening to a quiet clamour of noise. Every so often, parts of the unearthly sound break up just enough, so that a sliver of birdsong can be distinguished.

Kathy and I are huddled together on the huge sectional, remembering the late breakfast eaten, watching the special news reports. An overwhelming sense of doom flows from the TV screen, though the smarmy news quartet struggles hard to offer reassurance, no longer cozy in million dollar contentment.

But already, the gravity of these events is being forgotten, as the cameras are peering at individuals, everyone playing 'name that species.' Suddenly, every false memory of youthful bird watching is being conceived and tossed carelessly about, served up on trays of smiling, slick phoniness and sickly sweet condescension. Some of the more unusual birds have been given nicknames.

The heat of approaching summer is held captive by a chilly Northern breeze. A whisper of winters past. And of those yet to come.

"It's getting darker already," Kathy says.

For the whole day, we have both been trying to ignore the incessant *cak cak* and whistling, *aawk aawk* and tweetering, screeching and untold scores of other clearly distinct calls, so many concentrated just outside that broken window.

"It might rain tonight. The birds will probably leave before it gets here."

Something had pulled out the toweled carcass long ago. That same something is pecking at the sheet. Deliberately.

"I think it'll hold." Kathy says. Her bravery has diminished.

"There just pecking at it a little. They're not trying to get in. See?"

But the pecking, the pushing against the sheet becomes more regular, until we see that a sharp, knife-long beak has pushed a hole through, and is pulling, as if trying to tear the fabric.

"Uh…Mom?"

"God," I breathe with a sigh. "Your Grandmother was right."

The beak disappears. The silhouette moves suddenly away, replaced by the shadows of many tiny birds hovering near the window. Before we can pass another thought, the shadows move from a single spot near the broken pane, until several of them flap and whir about, trapped between the sheet and the window.

"Come with me Kathy. Hurry!"

We run up the stairs to her room, grabbing an armful of small bookshelves from the bookcases. We hurry back down to the window, looking disgustedly as the sheet trembles from silent wings.

Hummingbirds…

"It's the flowers, Mom."

"What?"

"It's the flowers in the sheet."

"But they're not even real. How…"

It doesn't matter

I begin to nail the bookshelves across the window as fast as I can, being thankful that they are wide enough.

One shelf. Two. Three. Four. Five. Six. Then the pretty flowered blue linen is covered.

"Let's get that other window."

"These are the only ones we've got left," she says. "It's not enough. We need to get some furniture."

"We can't nail the whole bookshelves to the windows. These will have to do. Besides, the backs of those shelves are nothing but cardboard."

We should still do it, she thinks…*maybe even take them apart…*

I nail like a blonde carpenter, not listening to the voices on the television:

"*…reports of isolated attacks are coming in from all over the city. And we're being told that one two year old in Brooklyn has already been…it is, yes that's right…it has been confirmed that one two year old girl in Brooklyn has been killed just outside her family's home. We are getting calls now from all over the state that emergency personnel cannot be dispatched, because in many places every inch of road is covered for several miles in either direction…*

"*…it may be interesting to watch from inside, but people we ask you to please stay in your homes until they have all left whatever area you live in. The approaching storm may begin to clear them out as early as this evening. We're even getting a few reports of power outages in some communities. Emergency has not yet been declared, but they are discussing plans for fixing the problem… everything short of actually exterminating some of the millions of birds that have gathered across the entire northern part of the country…*"

Sudden, extremely loud popping noises split the air outside. It sounds like a war.

"Firecrackers," Kathy says. "Somebody's trying to scare 'em away."

My hand is pressed against my big bosom.

"They almost scared *me* away."

"Shouldn't we nail shelves against the other windows?"

Loud, Fourth of July noises crackle.

"Somebody's shooting a gun," she says.

Like throwing rocks at a swarm of bees

"The windows, Mom." Her voice is urgent.

"I know what we can do. We can—"

Suddenly, a loud crash invades our world. The living room echoes a thousand pieces of glass, unseen tragedy, and a million voices of doom. The blue fabric over the big, bay window bulges writhing, until it breaks from its pitiful hold, and scores of small and large blackbirds pour into the house like a tar river.

Through a fog of noise and confusion we stumble up the stairs, feeling phantom claws on our necks, invisible beaks on our heads. We run to my room, slamming the door hard, seeing our own terrified reflections in the full length door mirror.

In disbelief, we listen to the noise. An atonal symphony of lost melody.

Echoing.

The late afternoon mugginess grows thicker. The sun drifts behind the dense cloud cover, until it hovers unrevealed over the western gate. The thickness in the air is palpable across the city.

The noisy flocks have not fed to their contentment. And now they walk and hop among each other in dumbness, uncertain of what to do next, or where to go, their northern homelands having sent warnings into their blood to never return there. For now, these misty regions are their home. Their place of refuge, from whatever approaches from the icy north.

But every single one of the millions knows it cannot, and will not end here. They understand that this is an impermanent place.

A harsh temper seems to ripple through, like a wave of irritability from East to West. Some species, especially the smaller ones—sparrows, starlings, wrens, common blackbirds—have become aggressive. Flying into windows. Waiting at doors. Attacking and killing the unfortunate animals and pets who are still outside. Some zoo animals are grateful for their enclosed spaces, while others cannot be protected by iron bars and fences. Many large animals have already been dead long enough to be half eaten.

In more than one home around the city, around the country, invasions have caused heart attacks, fatal falls, and even the occasional slow death from the clawing alone. And as it is with the animals, every human carcass is being picked clean to the bone.

Thick clouds have formed on the Northern breezes, gathering with purpose. While the arctic wisps merge with this late southern spring, the atmosphere hangs heavy with promises of drenching, violence, and cataclysm.

Along the shores, the gulls still fly. Swerving. Rising. Flowing downward on currents of primal hunger. The beaches are covered, every inch with black legged egrets and kingfishers, pelicans, herons, loons, ducks, snow geese and the like, to wade among the shallow waves, which break and foam at their feet.

People have wisely barricaded themselves where they are. Some in radio and TV studios, some in high rise office and apartment buildings. These are privy to the sights of their beloved city, buried in birds of every conceivable type, the whole scene illuminated by the gray of approaching twilight. All of them praying. Wondering if either God or man will be their salvation.

Behind the storm clouds, the sun slips away in cosmic indifference.

A mother and daughter rest in nervousness. The two of them, glaring alternately at the mirrored door, and at the fading gray light of dusk. They draw small comfort from the posh, palatial palace of fine art and tasteful shear white draperies and colored blinds. Porcelain statues, crystal displays, a mirror or two. Big dressers and a huge closet full of fine clothing and private, perverted secrets unrevealed. The dim, pale light mocks them, flashing blue energy. Presaging a time of outer darkness.

The bedroom TV is gladly off, after so many hours of the clamour of non-solutions. *Why can't they just gas them, while everybody's inside?* The

Army could just gas every *dad-blamed* one of them, and we'll gladly clean it up afterwards.

I would give every penny of the two million net worth, every ounce of the golden prestige, to be safe on my mother's big, prairie farm, some 1500 miles south-west of here.

Lightning flashes dimly. Thunder rumbles heavily from the clouds.

They're killing us. They're killing us by being here

"I'm hungry."

"I am too, baby. They'll be gone soon. As soon as they leave, we'll get something to eat. Okay?"

I know Kathy can feel my desperation. My need for her to believe the lie.

We sit huddled close together on the floor, leaning cozily against the corner created by the wall and the dresser in front of the window. The big mirror is just large enough to cover it. But it cannot keep the lightning, and the gray dusk from creeping inside. My favorite yellow phone is downstairs.

The brightest flash of lightning. The house lights flicker.

"Mom..."

"It won't happen. Don't worry, it won't."

Another flash of lightning.

The lights flicker dangerously...

A brief silence of dark. Broken by the thunder. The room is lit by gray silhouette, with flashes of blue. Every so often the phone twitters, whistling from downstairs, joining the live sounds. The birds are louder than ever.

They'll peck the stupid useless phone...they'll kill

It's been a long time since a window has crashed. Maybe, it's because every first floor window in the house has already been broken.

"Why…Why are the lights out…"

"Shhh."

From the television, Kathy, me, and the rest of the world have been made to understand that there is no war to be fought. No coexisting to be done. As with a fleeting thunderstorm, or a lingering hurricane, the only option is to wait in prayer, until nature's ire has fallen away…

Convocations of eagles. Huge casts of falcons and colonies of gulls. The owl parliaments and the tiding of magpies. Unkindnesses of ravens and scourges of starlings. From lapwings' deceits to the exaltations of larks. One conglomeration so dense, so packed with life as to defy action short of battle, or hope short of desperation. It is as though the heavens have opened, and rained a maelstrom.

The largest migration the earth has ever known now looms—a series of massive ones that has merged, threatening to fill the skies from the Atlantic coast to the Pacific, in a jagged line as thick as North Dakota. Plunging whole states in the black of night, whole regions in the outer blackness of Hell. From Maine to the Pacific northwest, across to Japan. Through China and the Middle East, to southern England over London. Untold hundreds of millions. Billions feeding. Dying. Driven by instinct. Tormented by fear.

Now, two rest in Chappaqua. They are sheltered by privilege. Cushioned in their exclusive cages.

Waiting alone, in the upper room.

"We've got to do something."

"All we can do is wait. They won't be here forever."

"But we can't get to our food. It would be okay if we could get it. The food's no good if we can't eat it…"

I'm so hungry

A sharp flash of lightning makes her jump. Treble thunder sounds, cascading into a low, booming rumble.

"The storm will drive them away," I say, unable to stop my own voice from trembling. "They're getting louder, see? That probably means their leaving."

"But how did this happen?"

"It was something in the climate."

"Well what's making them attack people?" She looks up at me. "They're breaking our windows."

"They're just confused, Kathy. They're not attacking us. They don't even know we're in here and they don't care."

A light brushing, whirring, beating of wings against the door. A loud, furious tapping.

"Can birds really chop through wood?"

"I don't think so." I hug her a little.

"Woodpeckers…"

"There aren't any woodpeckers here."

We hear the gathering energy in the clouds, and the gathering outside the door and the window. Truth has drifted on the wind, on the wings of swans and sparrows, settling on the roof of our grand palace. The ground is covered for miles around them. The house inside is a blackbird pond.

"I'll bet we could open the door and walk right through them into the kitchen—"

"Kathy, *listen* to me." I sit up straight, taking her by the shoulders. "Under no circumstances are you to open that door. Did you *hear* me?"

A loud crash above our heads rips a scream from us both. There is a loud flapping, thumping, screeching against the wooden back of the mirror dresser. Outside is the chaos of bird noise. Thunder crackles. The room at once feels colder...

And security is banished in a ripple effect, which moves in a wave of lightning from one side of the world to the other. Uneasy hope vanishes, as the flocks hiss and trumpet eerie voices. Restlessness gives way to fury, as houses from Montreal to Mongolia are sieged, with every ordinary window being shattered to pieces. Madness grips every raptor and corvid, every songbird and scavenger, until the ground is cleared mightily, while the sides of houses and buildings are covered, and every little home is devoured in a thunderous frenzy.

These two bid farewell to memories, waving goodbye to prides of high living. We cower together against the wall, unable to hear our own screams over the sea of thunder and bird sound. Wings numbered to infinity, creating a loudness never before gleaned by man. Voices pitched in quantities so great, that no such noise was ever heard beneath thundering skies. A whirlwind. An epic retelling of man's history, with doomful promises of terror's future unfurled.

My daughter and me sit screaming, eyes wide open, clutching, clawing into one another. We tremble at the storm, while we perceive the terrible scratching, thumping, chipping of tiny hatchet beaks and razor claws into wood, watching the finely finished sides of our mirrored barricade being slowly eaten away.

Jonathan Lovejoy

Outer Darkness

From east to west, across a condemned landscape from the Atlantic to the Pacific, there ebbs and flows a series of mysterious reprieves. Whether underneath storms or clear skies, as untold thousands, unheard of millions of them ease their attacks on mankind's hopelessness. Taking to the skies in sudden and inexplicable masses of blind purpose and determination, in determined blindness of purpose, where they respond as if hearing *en masse*; clearing the ground as no manmade noise could cause. As if moved by something far beyond the hunger in their blood, something beyond any flood of rage or fear in their souls of determination and death.

And my daughter and I are among the millions of witnesses to this, as the unearthly clamour of noise outside our mirrored barricades begins to slowly subside. Until there is barely a trace or even a twitter of lonely birdsong to scratch our souls to jitter and pain. I sit huddled on the floor with my daughter's face buried in my bosom, feeling the weeping continue to flow from her in a river of trauma unleashed, while I stare at the sides of the mirrored dresser in awe and disbelief into my memory. This, the image of what appeared to be the beak and head of an enormous raven, twisting and squeezing its head into a tiny space chipped away.

I am suddenly aware of the rapid, heavy pounding of two hearts. The beating of my own in rhythm with my daughter's, and the sound of her fearful sobbing, and my heavy breathing that will not subside. Although I have sat still for the last few minutes of this eternity, of this echo in outer darkness, I feel as though I have just given my body in sacrifice to a sprint at the end of a two mile run.

As I listen to the sound of reprieve fading to a hush in the massive, soothing rumble of rolling thunder outside, I gently caress my daughter's ravened hair. Drying the tears from her face with the palm of my hand, daring not to shush a single breath of her remaining sobs away. I let the music of her crying bathe the both of us to tranquility, hearing even the storm itself acknowledge death's reprieve, with a flash of daylight bright, and a blast of apocalyptic might from the sky. And this calms to the booming, heavy roll of rumbling sound from one side of the earth to the other, as I continue to hold my quietly weeping daughter tight to my chest, until I can no longer feel the beating of her heart, and only the occasional sniff and whimpering of her voice are where epic screams and end of the world sobbing had been.

For the better part of this next half hour, we sit still in the corner created by this dresser in front of the corner window, so grateful that the armoire served its regal purpose in front of the other. As we recover from this premature burial, this entombment in otherworldly fear, I half expect to hear the nightmarish scraping, the brackish clawing of talons, the monstrous beating of wings trapped inside the armoire, where at least one of them was able to chop its way inside. But mercifully, the only sound we hear is the rising wind, and the unleashing of a torrential rainfall, a deluge, in pouring sheets of rain.

The deafening silence from inside our house is blessedly real. Where we hear not even as much as a single chirp from outside the bedroom door.

"It sounds like they're gone," I say, hardly able to believe it enough to inspire any sort of bravery. But what instinct for survival there is, I suppose, has its way enough to make me finally have to move a sore muscle or two, to pry us out of this frozen position on the floor.

In a soreness remarkable from head to toe, I am able to coax the two of us up from this corner of fear, as my daughter holds on tight to my arm as if we were walking a ledge along a high canyon wall in a stiff wind. But this is only the plush, ivory carpet of my bedroom palace, as we watch ourselves approach our reflections in the mirrored door, seeing our hopelessness reflected to infinity. This, caused by the mirrored dresser behind us, and the reflection of ourselves in it, mysteriously captured by the door mirror in front of us as we walk. I see the infinity of myself lift a feeble hand to the doorknob. Turning it. Foolishly, stupidly opening the door into the twilight darkened hall.

Migration

The smell of rage in bird feathers is strong in our nostrils, as we take each careful step into the smelly dark, able to hear the sound of the angry rainstorm from the broken bay window down below. And though the house smells like the inside of an avian nightmare, hardly even a feather is here to mark our steps in the dark, and not a single bird carcass is anywhere to be found. But the glass in every mirror, every picture, every ceramic and crystal vase lies in pieces, camouflaged somewhere in the twilight dark, done away with by the beating of a thousand wings, and the clawing of a thousand talons in twilight and fury.

Down the long, carpeted staircase we glide, where we can see the remains of our tropical sheet blowing in the cold north wind, waving surrender in futility in the storm.

The scene is one of utter devastation, illuminated by the many flashes of lightning from the clouds. In the gloom of the evening day, the room bears resemblance to a room attacked by an angry grizzly, with beak and claw marks barely visible to us both, up to the ceiling on every wall, with every knick knack knocked out of place by the maddening horde that had flown and pecked their way into the house, done by the insanity poured through the sheer numbers of beating wings that made their way into the house, looking for whatever it was they needed to satisfy their new craving from within.

A craving for human flesh, are the words that form on their own in my mind. Independent of my will, to rise up from my spirit inside. To meet this touch of arctic cold on my skin. To deliver a visible shudder in my body. This, I know my daughter sensed, causing her to grip my arm tighter as she looks around at the broken clocks and ripped house plant leaves—blinds torn to shreds, and sofa fabric cut by beaks and claws with ease.

"Mom... how..."

"I don't know, Kathy... I don't know."

On this current of cold grief and confusion, we drift across the carpet of feathers and filth remaining, Kathy flinching at the next flash of lightning, and its revelation of the scarred and blood stained walls; the two of us trying not to be afraid of the blue ocean linen cloth blowing almost majestically at us in the eerie, twilight dark, as we approach the window crashed open; standing at the edge of the storm's angry proclamation, feeling the mist of this cold warning drift through the open window onto our skin.

Julie Weinberg

Rides the Wind

9

*J*ulie Weinberg rides the wind. On the eve of eschatology.

Divorced. Mother of two. Wealthiest among them. The queen of those in Chappaqua, the ones who have left their husbands behind for the lust of the flesh. The lust of the eyes. And the pride of life.

Julie Weinberg rides the wind. On the eve of eschatology.

Mother of 21-year-old Jessica Weinberg. A junior in the Ivy League. On track already to the literary PhD. To set herself up to hide on the right track. The one that cruises through the forest of delusion, where the hopeless wander and drift in the snows of false hope. Among the trees of promises unfulfilled. Taking Dr. and Mrs. Weinberg's advice. *Stay in school.* Use your love of books to your advantage. Ride the easy track to heaven on earth.

Professor Julie Weinberg rides the wind. Along the timeline beyond her oldest daughter's departure. In the wake of a life of bitterness grown. A daughter who left their wealthy home in Chappaqua in the pain of bitterness. In the agony of deep memories come and gone. Memories of her smart, literary minded mother, who herself had been raised under the lash. Under the cane. A mother who had kept her oldest daughter in repression. Suppressed under the weight of corporal punishment. Punishments designed to cause more than physical pain. Punishments designed to break the spirit. To shed blood beyond what is skin deep. To burn the soul in black fire laced in blue.

Julie Weinberg rides the wind. On the eve of eschatology. Having considered her oldest daughter's punishments the privilege of her position. A private prerogative since she was seven. Since her youngest daughter was born. Feeling the orgasmic flow to her bowels when she told her fourteen year old daughter, *"bare your breasts."* Braving the pissing twinge in her groin. Even the shock to her nipples, that begged her to remove her own bra.

And in the heart of her soul's memory, this, she does. Leaving her skirt in place. Baring her own breasts in their long, flopping D minor key. Breasts pulled ad nauseam when she was a Jewish daughter under her mother's lash. Under her mother's cane.

In the heart of her soul's memory, she bares her breasts in league with those of her fourteen-year-old daughter. Telling her daughter to *"stand up straight, put your legs together."* This, because her eighth grade daughter brought her two C's on her report card. A C+ in algebra. A C in chemistry. Not knowing that Jessica Weinberg only wants to read her history. Her English. Her novels, and then be left alone to imagine.

In the heart of a house's dark memory. Somewhere in a wealthy corner of the world. A dark haired, sensual minded lover of literature, of what is hidden in *The Bell Jar*, and what its author was looking for in the stove that day. This Lupone-faced, flop breasted feminist stands her fourteen-year-old daughter up in her bubble bottomed jeans. Raising the wooden paddle of legend. Bringing it down in burning heat and noise to her daughter's bottom. *"Until you learn that B's and C's are not acceptable,"* she says. Subjugating the young girl's personality to oblivion. Crushing her esteem down to nothing.

In fear, a younger sister sits in her room. A seven year old terrified. Listening to her older sister's bottom be broken under the paddling wood. *"Now, slide your pants off,"* the lady professor says. *"And your underwear."* So that now, the young girl stands naked. Bottom already bruised in pre-trauma. Already in the proverbial frying pan before the fire.

This mother takes the black caning rod in hand. Laying it in repetition in *whip whop* sound across the fat of her eighth grade daughter's backside. Feeling the orgasmic wave return, when the first welt appears, accompanied by her daughter's wailing, weeping cry. Feeling as though she may piss herself from the feeling in her groin. Losing her composure in the rhythm. Flashing, lashing the cane in burning repetition, to criss cross a network of angry welts across her daughter's bottom and the backs of her young thighs. Striping the girl's white skin to blood. Playing the music of this overture to completion. To portend her daughter's present and future.

Julie Weinberg rides the wind. On the eve of eschatology. Moving forward in time. In the heart of a new memory. Memories of a lonely life in academia. An oldest daughter away at the Ivy League refuge. A literary like herself. An oldest daughter, with a twisted appreciation for her mother's discipline. Remembering the orgasmic wave when she was sixteen, when she slid her jeans to her thighs, and laid herself across her mother's knee.

In the heart of this memory come and gone. In the years of the oldest daughter's departure. There stands this woman's younger daughter. The sweetness which is Jenny Weinberg. Smarter than her older sister Jessica. Knowing already that she wants to be a doctor. Like her bygone father.

Julie Weinberg rides the wind. The winds of a conundrum. The winds of a tragic dilemma. Tragic for her youngest daughter. A daughter that has inherited a shape from she knows not where. A beauty for the ages passed down. To rival even the Indian looking doll named Kathy Van Scoy, daughter of her best friend. Daughter of Meredith Van Scoy.

Julie Weinberg makes her thirteen-year-old daughter understand that there are things that must be done in private. Things done in the name of a mother's prerogative. In the name of mother-daughter pleasure. Mother-daughter pain. On the eve of a migration. Before the flocks arrive on a cool north wind.

This woman feels the twitch in her groin, as she picks up the black leather curled serpentine. The sound of the buckle on her black leather belt. This, done in private. This, behind the walls of secret. Holding the belt in one hand, while she sits on the bed naked. Her daughter's tight, young bottom firmly in the other. Holding the girl close, as she sucks the girl's pubescent nipples deep into her mouth. Marveling at the untold apocalypses. In awe of what feelings are possible in the human body. Knowing that the feeling in her own breasts will send a pre-lightning strike to her groin. This, not allowing her to release her daughter's breast from the sucking. Feeling it happening. Able to only step aside, and let this train pass itself to where it will. Feeling the nerves in her own breasts twitch the nerves in her groin. Which twitches a muscle in her right leg. Sliding her leg back against the side of the bed against her will. Flooding her body with a cloud of unendurable ecstasy. Which threatens to haze her vision, and make the room go spinning around.

Julie Weinberg rides the wind. Having to release her daughter's nipple from the sucking so she can breathe. Holding on to her daughter tight. Knowing now that if it is the last thing she ever does, she will use this leather belt, to stripe the knowledge of good and evil into her younger daughter's bottom. Onto her back. Onto her breasts. On the front and backs of her thighs.

This, she does. To the music of her daughter's screams. To the rhythm of her sobbing and tears. Taking deep pleasure in the girl's bewilderment. In the girl's confusion. In the girl's epic loss of dignity. The loss of her hope for the future.

In the days before the flocks came. On the eve of the sign of His coming. The naked woman lays her welted, bleeding daughter in kindness on the bed. Laying on top of her thirteen year old daughter naked. Whispering reassurances in her ear. Kissing the remainder of the girl's tears away. Pressing her naked self to the daughter's naked self below. Amazed at the rise of the lightning strike in her breasts again. The rise of it at the center of her groin.

With hardly a motion gathered. With barely a hard squeezing of her hips onto her daughter. She stares her beautiful young daughter in the face. Locking her gaze into her teary, fearful young eyes. Not daring to move a muscle. Gauging how it is possible to give the body its own will upon which to act. Knowing that the slightest twitch. The tiniest move of her hips will start a chain reaction. Will begin this tragic domino effect.

Against her better judgment. Against her own will to lie still. Her hips squeeze downward of their own volition. To cause the spark in her breasts to strike her groin. To make her exclaim the words *oh...GOD*, in pitiful acknowledgement. In tragic realization. Learning the third part of the truth. Which is cataclysm.

Julie Weinberg can only roll her eyes back. Closing them involuntarily. Hearing the wail of a banshee, as if from the woodland lawn of her property forlorn. Taking a breath of life into her body. Hearing the cry of the motheress come into the room again. Feeling the plateau break from underneath her at last. Enduring an apocalyptic shaking. An Armageddon quaking in her body from head to toe. Grunting. Groaning. Bellowing deeply in the crashing of the wave.

Somewhere on the other side of life. Along the rainy, deserted streets of Chappaqua. In the wealthy home of privilege come and gone. Julie Weinberg kneels in the twilight dark. In the scent of bird filth and feathers left behind. Unable to do more than stare at the clawed, bloody remains of her younger daughter. Remembering her daughter's screams from down below. Remembering the sight of her disappearing in the sea of feathered things in every color. Remembering how the fear turned her away from the stairs, and chased her to her closet. Holding her inside, in the pitch black, until the cataclysmic noise of birdsong had come and gone. Until only the sound of rain and thunder remained.

Julie Weinberg remembers her walk through the twilight dark. To where the bloody remains of her youngest daughter lay at rest. She remembers the look of her daughter's face, where every inch of skin is clawed to blood. She remembers Jenny's eyes. The black spaces in her daughter's face, where Jenny's eyes had been.

Julie Weinberg rides the wind. On a decision that must be made. Of gunpowdered pistols, numbed wrists and a scalpel. Or her blessed pills, and a glass of wine.

Julie Weinberg rides the wind. On the eve of eschatology.

My Mother's Perversion

Our trip through the lonely, rainsoaked streets of Chappaqua fades into the past as we drive, rolling along so appropriately in black Mercedes luxury, which is our rolling chariot of hopelessness and despair. In the midnight pouring, we had gathered what few belongings, what few clothes and shoes we knew we couldn't do without, to leave our million dollar prison to its fate in the storm. South through New York state we drive, taking a breath of false hope that maybe, the storm dispersed whatever end of the world insanity it was that caused those millions of birds to gather and attack.

"I think they're gone, Mom," are the words I dread to hear from my daughter's mouth. As we roll into the Pennsylvania landscape in the rain and night, I begin to believe that maybe, she has not spoken our certain death in irony. Visions of running into a sudden wall of birds packed into the road haunt me like a dreadful premonition—our car unable to continue over the miles of them packed in, until the car is slowed by the force and weight of their sheer numbers gathered together in the darkness, the headlights illuminating the feathered nightmares being knocked aside and killed in futility by our stupid, rolling death chariot; smashing into the windshield hard enough to break it in five places, smashing into the headlights until even the both of them are snuffed out like a wet candle, our car finally stalling in the field of birds somewhere off the highway in the dark, Kathy and me in the blackness inside the car, screaming as every window is smashed into repeatedly...

I shake myself awake from this moving dream as I drive, seeing only miles of empty highway rolling west through Pennsylvania, drawing comfort from the brilliant flashes of lightning and booming thunder, and a landscape seemingly untouched by as much as a feather from the endless flocks of devastation there were. My daughter and me ride along in the spirit of this hopeful anticipation, this belief that maybe the world's nightmare has finally come and gone, and that this next sunrise will be one of hope and renewal.

I'm finally able to turn on the radio, to hear confirmation of what hopes we cling to. To hear them tell us once and for all that the birds are gone.

"...have gathered in southern Pennsylvania and the surrounding states, and every state due west of these, where the massive flocks appear to be amassing for another..."

I click this tragedy away as quickly as I can. Trying not to finish in my own mind what was being said. Trying not to hear the truth.

"They're still here, Mom. They said that they're..."

"I *heard* them, Kathy," I say. Sharply enough that guilt takes hold. Against my will and purpose. "I'm sorry," I say. Taking her hand. Raising it to my lips for reassurance. As to whether it is for her comfort or mine, this I do not know.

In keeping with the person my little Indian-haired beauty is becoming, my 13 year old Indian doll suppresses the rest of her childhood fears, being driven along in silence on our odyssey west to futility, to the open space of green grass, green tree groves and green leaf nothing which is my mother's big farm, the place where I was born and raised, where I learned early that the qualities of humanity run wide and deep. Churning beneath the surface of hypocrisy and cultured civility in lamentation, and pain that stretches from here to perpetuity.

Like so many others across this condemned, grieving landscape, I am a prisoner of my mother's unloving arms, doomed to return to my mother's loving arms. But fear is the world's greatest motivation, pushing past all the various lusts for dominance and control of the population, causing me to drive through this stormy, rainy night in grief and confusion, to live out the prophecy that has always been true that yes, the types of fear are indeed many, and uniquely distinguished. Among these is the Fear of Death; which drives me and my daughter forward through this rainy night, causing me to push through the barrier of dark memories, and wonder to where it is that my beloved mother could have gone.

And as we move forward in the storm, to leave Chappaqua behind in this part of the timeline, part of me is gripped by a desire unspeakable, to reconnect with the woman I call Katherine, the woman who gave me life, then took it from me so abundantly. This, after my father was inexplicably shot and killed by her when I was twelve, where she served not a single day in prison, because the bruises on my mother's body, the healed scars were so numerous and profound. These were the scars of my mother's perversion, where she allowed herself to be whipped and beaten in private by my grandmother, this, done behind my father's back in secret.

The mistake this poor man made was his lack of discretion. And the presence of a blonde waitress in my mother's suspicion, confirmed when she followed him to the tiny house where the bubble hipped, bubble breasted beauty lived. But one can only wonder—what is the farmer supposed to do, when his wife is as frigid to him as a cold, north wind? The crusted scars on my mother's back had served their purpose; along with the self inflicted bruises under her eye and the swollen lip, when the Sheriff was called that night by her, and she stood in front of them as though *not* playing the role of the pathetic spouse. Knowing that the dark eye and the bloody lip would serve their purpose to the female Sheriff and her lady deputy. And when the nurse at the emergency room took off my mother's shirt, the crusted welts and blood stained cloth was enough to send a ripple through the state of Oklahoma, that finally, an abusive son-of-a-bitch got what he deserved. I can remember the look on my half Indian mother's face when my fathers' coffin was lowered into the ground, as though she were burying the neighbor's dog after shooting it to death, because she was sick of it killing her big bantam roosters. As to whether or not I saw her bury this German Shepherd-Alaskan Husky hybrid in the forest grove behind our house, who's to say? As to whether or not I was seven when she shot the distant neighbor's dog, who's to say? I remember this look on her face when she put the dog in the forest grove near our house.

And then I was twelve, when the spirit came unto me. I was twelve, when the spirit of Katherine Hardwick hath come.

In the heart of this distant memory, as we drive through the wee hours of the darkened storm, the rainfall of my father's funeral day haunts me in melancholy and gray. I had told the truth to the authorities, who had asked me if I saw my daddy hit my mommy, and I said I heard mommy screaming and then I heard the gunshot. It was the proverbial shot heard 'round the world, so to speak, the shot that reverberated thirty years through time to the present day.

Through our rainsoaked journey, through the fall of night. In the heart of memory. In the rains of depravity gathered in latter day truth. I am the lonely. I am the twelve year old blonde little girl, being driven home by the Indian woman dressed in black, her veil of false mourning having been removed and tossed unceremoniously in the back seat. I am the lonely. The twelve year old blonde girl who heard her father's departure in a cannon of gunfire, that will haunt me in my dreams for an eternity of days and nights come calling. I am the lonely. Being driven home by the great breasted Indian beauty, who has hidden her shame, her private desperation in the loose, button down collar shirts of a farmer's wife, where the chord is played in the phantom key above G major, hung heavy and bulbous and free against her body. She does not bother with the bra cloth on the prairie green, in the outskirts of isolation, where I am destined to live in the shadows of what power she possesses. Where there is no one that can help me. And no one that could hear me scream.

I am twelve, when the spirit hath come to me. I am twelve, when the spirit of Katherine Hardwick hath come.

I am the lonely. The little blonde girl getting out of the charcoal gray truck in the summer lightning and rain. Following the squaw in her mourner's cloak of midnight cloth, under her umbrella now, walking slowly with her arm tightly around her daughter's waist, an inexplicable kiss pressed tightly to my temple, enigmatic beyond the context of a grieving widow comforting her daughter.

But even while this rainstorm gently rumbles its warning message to the two souls, strolling in a chasm of grief and loss far below; even in the storm's gentle acknowledgement of this kiss, I can feel the arrival of this place along the timeline; the arrival of this checkpoint along my pathetic journey, where the gloom of predestiny looms in clouds of melancholy and grieving.

I am afraid. I am the lonely. Walking through the rain with this murderess, whose back is laced with the scars of her own mother's deep perversion, and her buttocks and thighs striped with a variation on her mother's theme of depravity. With this woman, I walk through the door of our chamber of secrets, our own deathly hallows of the sacred and the unspeakable.

"Give mommy a kiss," this beautiful white Cherokee woman whispers on my lips, to send a flood of feeling in the shape of a bell or even a Hershey's Kiss, somewhere past my pubescent nipples down to my bowels and my groin. *"I want you to go upstairs and wait for me in Mommy's bedroom,"* she says, of which I can only say *"okay mommy."* So pitifully. So obediently. Walking in my navy dress up the stairs in so much grief and confusion. Walking in determined purpose through the waves of sound that cascade through the walls from the storm.

I go into my mother's bedroom in the spirit of hopeless longing. In desperation to know whether or not I will be kissed, or killed. Whether or not I will be caressed, or caned. Whether I will be lifted up, or lowered down into the caverns beneath the earth, by way of a slow and sadistic smothering, and a burial beneath the cold, wet ground of the forest grove across the prairie lawn.

After but a moment of this eternal waiting, I can hear the footsteps of my time, echoing strongly in clip-clop power up the wooden staircase, clumping quietly through the waves of the gentle apocalypse of rumbling from the clouds, each step getting closer, closer, and closer to the bedroom door.

I am the lonely. The little blonde farm widow's daughter, watching in breathless surrender as the woman of beauty opens the door, her gaze locking onto mine without compromise, without hesitation. Walking in grieving midnight cloth and black leg stockings, over to the lamp lighted bedroom mirrored dresser of dark burnished oak wood splendor.

"Take off your clothes," I hear her say, as though I barely saw her lips move, as though the words were formed from the mouth of a bound and determined goddess from the storm, who hath bestowed upon this house

the modern mother-daughter dynamic unrestrained. In tuck lipped obedience, I fumble at the buttons of my navy dress cloth, until I am able to slide it over my thin, white shoulders, down past the piece of plain, smooth white cloth that dares masquerade as a bra over my chest. Even so, I am a 12 year-old prodigy of the bosom, with these new and sensitive chords played in the key of false hope, the key of power and fungalooga displayed.

The woman in the mirror watches her daughter reach back, and remove the so-called bra cloth, to where the high, rounded cones point toward a macromastic future, in the happy key of C major nurtured and born.

I am twelve, when the spirit hath come to me. I am twelve, when the spirit of Katherine Hardwick hath come.

I stand in the middle of her bedroom. Watching the exotic, otherworldly features, her mouth having slipped open in slack jawed astonishment, staring at me from her reflection in the mirror, her eyes reading what message my slim and stacked little body may entail. As to the pubescent areola, the puffy nipples of my youth and calling, I see her gaze locked in as she begins to undo the zipper at the back of her black dress, sliding it off to reveal the rare presence of a bra strap as black as midnight, where the elongated, bulbous cleavage rises into dimly lit view.

I am unable to look away from the magnificence. The mountainous, monumental sight of macromastia on glorious display, lifted up just enough into the jubilee bra, cups in the phantom J-chord, the sheer size of which would have to be seen to be believed. I am unable to look away, as this mountain breasted woman—this farmer's widow in Indian braided beauty—I am unable to look away as she reaches back and unlatches the black cloth to slide it down and away. Letting them fall back to their natural state of bulbous length, and heavy hung roundness at the bottom of them against her sun touched skin.

The healing scars across her back and backside only serve to enhance what enticing allure this is, what otherworldly work of divine art this is, where the massive, dark areola display nipples in bottle top form already, poked outward in perpetual readiness, even before the onset of what greater size arousal may bring to them. I watch this long breasted goddess bend over, watching the bells toll for me in the storm, as she makes quick work of the black stockings pulled up to her thighs, and the underwear cloth pulled too small and tight over the widened hips of motherland legend. Her hips alone would be a thing of concern, were they not obscured in the shadows of her gargantuan sized bosom.

This curve waisted wonder of the natural world turns herself to me, so that we are mother and daughter in the latter day storm of grief and mourning. "Come," she says, in a tone laced with good natured impatience, as if I should already have been there by now.

With my mouth clamped shut, my eyes locked into her gaze, I walk stiffly, naively, so tragic and innocently over to this naked woman, taking her hand, both her hands, watching her look down at both her nipples, remarkable in that both of the big areolas have already shrunken like raisin skins, to push the nipples out to the size of grapes, with her watching as the nipples touch themselves to my own. And I am not able to keep myself from looking pitifully, stupidly up into her face, in time to see her expression wash over with an anguish that borders on a look of pain and suffering. And I watch her close her eyes, in deep concentration as her breathing charges forth in heaviness, a force of wind breathed from her soul and spirit, as she breathes through her body's desire to react tragically to the modest touch of her nipples to mine. They are hung low enough on her body that remarkably, she is able to press them directly to my own.

As to the feeling that flows bell shaped from my breasts to my groin… this, I do not know. I only know that the brush of my mother's breasts against mine tightens a tension at my groin that I have never felt before, to cause me to wish for I know not what, to relieve the pressing of pressure in pissing pleasure down below. Every gentle stroke of her nipple against mine raises me up higher, until my breathing can no longer be controlled, and I wonder why the feeling in my groin is about to cause me to have to scream…

And of this, I do in a girlish, high pitched shriek into the room, accompanied by my body's apocalyptic shaking, followed by my mother's lips pressed hard against mine, and her tongue pushed deep into my mouth. And this, she holds. Careful to swallow the spit of this innocence lost, to breathe the breath of naiveté destroyed, to absorb the twitching of purity corrupted with the mind of Eve passed down. Of this, she holds me there. Breathing deeply through her nose in this kiss. Listening to the heavy rumble of thunder subside; as the remnant of it subsides in the aftermath of my body's traumatic awakening.

With both hands holding my head, she gazes into my eyes in quiet, determined reverence and awe, telling me with epic, sober minded purpose and direction...

"Take hold of both my nipples," she says. And this, I do. *"Get a good hold of them. Now, pull them. Pull them hard."*

And I am compelled through fumbling, feeble strength to hold on to them with my little hands, trying to do what she asks, pulling on them so weakly, so inadequately, which only adds to the feeling that threatens to howl her voice into the depth of the storm.

"Step back a little," she says. *"Grab hold of them good. Mommy wants you to pull on them really hard. Pull on them like you mean it. Like you're trying to make it hurt. I want you to hurt Mommy's nipples..."*

And this, I do. To the best of my ability. Even gritting my teeth in a frustrated grimace of effort, pulling the great breasts out long and low, twisting them in a mighty pinch, which causes her to put her hand at the center of herself down below, her beautiful face twisted into the sensual suffering of pain passing through.

"Just hold them still for Mommy. Hold them still and pull on them as hard as you can..."

And this, I do. Ceasing the pinching, the twisting. Focused obediently on the mighty pulling. *"Pull 'em hard enough to make it hurt,"* she says, her hand resting perfectly still between her closed legs, her eyes half closed, staring at the twelve year old blonde girl, whose face is scrunched in angry determination, whose little white hands struggle to pull the great breasts like so much taffy, stretching them longer than they have ever been, until in the light of energy flashed from the clouds, the woman gruffly calls forth the name of God, and wails a long, lonely siren into the room as her body shakes, taking a breath, then wailing a longer, louder trumpet call of revelation into the storm, finally bending over as the tension breaks into her body, to grunt deeply the rest of her body's shaking and quaking into the air around me.

In the passing of this wave, in the oblivion of this energy come and gone, she stands up straight against me, hugging me tight while I hug her around her waist, feeling the raised scars on my mother's back. My body pressed hard against the mashed pillows pressed between us. Kissing the top of my mother's breasts. Caressing the healing scars on her back.

Loving her.

From the heart of this memory, I awaken. Phasing from the storm of this old reality, into the new one in which we ride. I touch my daughter's chin gently, rubbing my hand across her thigh from top to bottom. Infused with a spirit descended upon me from ages long gone. A spirit passed through the motherline.

At the onset of this predestiny born, I notice in the flash of river lightning across the bottom of the clouds, a new and powerful silhouette across the approaching overpass, which is the unmistakable gathering of winged, feathered creatures; extended across every foot of the overpass railing. Lit up in the storm just enough to reveal the power of their overwhelming numbers, stretched from one side of this dark, stormy creation to the other.

Jonathan Lovejoy

The Mind of Eve

Jonathan Lovejoy

Give the gray, vivid account in the morning light

As to the truth of this untold apocalypse—

And the bizarre nature of its latter day arrival.

The highland country of West Virginia is our sunrise over the bird kingdom, to show us the high hills and low mountain slopes covered in bird activity ad nauseam, to where the effect is more terrifying than tranquil, with every tree and acre of ground serving as part of this great bird sanctuary; where they flutter, flap and fly as if unconcerned about the goings on of mankind, showing little interest in the roads and the cars that pass in the looming gray. It is a sight that can hardly bear adequate description, except that the smaller part of *millions* of birds is the forest and field of West Virginia, where it seems that every species imaginable is out and about. Against this bird infinity, there is no war to be fought, except a war of waiting, as what we see is but a brief stretch of an apocalypse, that is spread from here west to the Pacific Ocean and beyond. There is but one reaction possible, which is absolute, uncompromising awe, at what possibilities there are when nature blooms and takes its course. Against this natural phenomenon, this anomaly unexplained, there is no urban sprawl, no manmade strips of farming countryside, no nothing under heaven, to deter this full flowering of predestiny to take place, as every human Army gathered on the face of the earth would have a snowball's chance in Hell of victory.

Through the rest of this bird kingdom we drive, my daughter and me, moving through Kentucky, down into Nashville, where the city is overrun by this bizarre notion, as we go west along Interstate 40 to Memphis, where thoughts of The King's preserved legacy do beg to wonder, as to what nightmarish visitation it has received in the looming gray. These long stretches of highway run through clear and dense patches of this end of the world migration, where it sometimes appears to be an endless ocean of them, which will gradually diminish over the miles and thin out to almost nothing.

Overhead, in the storm's brief rest and regathering, vultures slowly turn and glide their circles of death, mocking every passing car below with a gloomy prophecy, with promises of a future without hope for a reprieve. Along the countryside, it is as though they have been gathered and placed, guided to where they are on the four winds, winds of latter day grief and eschatology.

I give in to the craving to hear what the world is trying not to know, to listen to the fools' voices in the radio landscape, finding that I am unable to move past the song where Skeeter Davis asks the question, *"why do the birds go on singing?"* I listen to this divine prophecy, moving out of

Memphis into Arkansas, where the forests and fields along the highway begin to confirm what is being said, that we are moving south of the largest and thickest gathering.

We drive onward. Both of us in grieving to leave the north behind, and memories of our nightmare in Chappaqua buried in perpetuity. Past Little Rock we glide in our rolling chariot, so thankful that there are so few birds that it seems the whole world has returned to normal, as we ignore the signs to Hot Springs, moving west through Arkansas into Oklahoma Territory.

And it seems that I can feel the spirits that rule the powers of the air, pointing at our darkened silhouette as we drive, gliding us along our unseen course of what is predestined. Announcing this to us in the slow, steady return of every new raindrop fallen one by one on the windshield; until they are multiplied by the untold infinity of them, obscuring our path to tranquility and peace of mind. Simply put, we are both a bundle of nerves again, as the sky grows angry at our audacity. At our foolish insistence on an escape to nowhere.

In this new and pouring rainfall, which has reduced this daylight to an early twilight of gray all around us, I take my daughter's hand in mine as we enter the prairie farmlands west, moving past the signpost up ahead so appropriately written: 'Payne County.' In the pain of this memory reborn, we move along through the looming gray and summertime cold. Past the endless stretches of prairie grasslands and patches of forest groves so achingly familiar to me, but which I know are so painfully unfamiliar to my daughter, who gazes wide eyed through her rainy window, over the vast Oklahoma countryside in nervous apprehension, at the prospect of meeting and talking to this woman in person. This woman whose name she bears, who she has only known through a photograph taken before she was born, a single visit seven years ago, and as a distant, enigmatic voice over the telephone.

Past these grassy fields of enmity we drive, until the barrier of my grieving past is crossed again. Past the sign that shimmers through the rainy windshield, of a town named after what waters there are that run wide and deep in the human soul.

13

*T*he landscape of Stillwater, Oklahoma is rich and green. With vast, open spaces of prairie grassland, punctuated by the occasional leafy forest grove of trees. *Typical beauty is still beauty*, are the words that haunt me as I drive, as the trees and stretches of grassland become more painfully, more disturbingly familiar with each passing mile in this pouring rain. *Maybe it was all just a dream*, my mind has the audacity to think, as we roll to the turn down the long, dirt road, which extends past the summertime fields of green far off into the distance, where the two story farmhouse and barn sit in picturesque splendor and waiting.

It is a drive I have successfully avoided for seven years, swearing to myself over and over again that Katherine Hardwick's voice would be enough to suffice, that I never had to lay eyes on this Indian braided beauty again for the rest of my life. A woman with the fair skin of a white woman, though slightly darkened, and the brunette headed features of a Carolina Cherokee Indian in Oklahoma. Over a thousand and twenty five miles down east, where she was born and raised by her full blooded Indian mother under the lash, up until the woman died in her sleep at age 59. Until my mother was 42 years old, she learned the meaning of the word pain behind closed doors, and the heights and depth of what sweetness or suffering it may provide.

Already, the phantom itchings of my past tingle my back as I drive, tickling my spirit with an echo of a fear I have not felt for seven years. Along with a lust and desire more twisted and perverse than I could ever mention to another living soul. This cold touch and caress of this moves my hand in the company of a tremble to my daughter's hair, glancing over at her in the suppressed spirit of fungalooga that threatens, unable to hold in the pathetic words "are you excited?" to which she answers in tragic and hopeless naiveté, with a wide eyed, tuck lipped nod of her pretty little head.

And I can tell that as it is with myself, these cute little laughs and hopeful smiles of hers are every bit the mask she wears. To hide a soul touched somewhere deep inside by a fear unknowable. By the echoes of an apprehension unseen.

Down the long dirt road, we travel. Past these rainsoaked spirits of melancholia and grief, that whirl and swirl around us in the rain, in grieving to reach inside the car itself. To have their way with the feeble hearts of the mother and her daughter who roll onward in the foolishness of hope, and the naiveté of expectation.

Down the long dirt road, we travel. Trying not to feel the crossing over from day into night, from a yesterday where hope for the future was won. Past these melancholy spirits, we drive. My daughter's hand tucked safely into mine, so that I may protect her from this impending cold and darkness we feel, as we drive past the summer green fields of enmity. Past the corn which grows with its unwavering intrepidity, towards the two story white farmhouse in the nearby distance, where I know there waits for me a revisitation. A reacquaintance with a phantom from my past. One I had often tried so hard to forget, lest it latch on to me as a motherline curse, and pass itself on to my unsuspecting daughter. I have noticed so many times in the past, through the chiming of her shower, the song of the flushing, even the opening and closing of the bathroom and bedroom door, the spirits that haunt me from along the timeline have placed things in my mind that I dare not dwell upon. Not even now, as I hold her cold, smooth little hand so tight. A hand so delicate. A hand so fragile. A hand that could so easily succumb to a pressing squeeze...

From this wicked daydream, I awaken. Squeezing my daughter's hand with a firmness unbeknownst to her. Unbeknownst beyond the spirit of comfort on our strange and enigmatic odyssey.

Seven years is a long time, I say. Concerning how long it's been since we rolled the streets of this town, and the dusts of this long, dirt road. A road transformed to hard clay and mud, above which we are drawn forward in black Mercedes luxury. Half expecting to see the feathered manifestation of our fear, circling above the house in epic, black wingspan. But all we see as we approach are the big, white farmhouse, with its 2nd story windows of mysterious intent, and the porch that seems to wrap around from one corner to the other.

And much to the fearful fluttering of my heart's desire, I am entranced to nervousness unspoken. Gazing through the windshield wiper at the dark figure, seen blurry through the rainsoaked glass. Appearing on the front porch as we approach in the pouring rain.

*I*n pouring rain, in the grieving mist of the Oklahoma prairie green, we disembark our rolling chariot, the two of us underneath the single black umbrella, me feeling as busty and pear shaped as I have in many a year. Splashing tuck lipped across the wet ground to the high porch steps, my daughter tightly secured with my arm around her waist.

Standing high above us, as regal as a pioneer forest queen, is the ruin of my fancy. We take each step as weighted down in a dream, as if every ounce of strength is being drawn away by her presence, which is the tallish figure of a brunette woman over 50, who bears the youth of late 40's maturity, and the seasoned, sensuality of her age. Cloaked from cleavage to calves in midnight blue cloth, whose look bears the tone of ivory skin, touched deeply by the tint of her Native American blood, in hair the color of the raven's feathers, fallen about her shoulders, and surely halfway down the length of her back. In her eyes is the mind of Eve, and upon her lips rests whispers from the forest leaves east of Eden.

As she relaxes the full, ruby lips, to where the white bottom teeth are visible, my body tells me that I have never been so simultaneously afraid, and aroused in my entire life.

"Meredith," she says, as though her lips moved independently of the deep, sultry sound I just heard. And I open my mouth to speak, but finding the disrespect in her first name choked in the back of my throat.

"M...Momma..."

And this word I speak, for the first time in more than twenty years, since I turned sixteen in this house. Four years after Katherine Hardwick gave her spirit to me. I step forward, hugging this woman unashamed. Pressing my breasts to hers in mashing, to feel every bit of the massive roundness of them. Of their watermelon girth pressed like pillows up against my own.

And I back away from this hug, all yellow blonded, teary-eyed suburbanized soccer Mom, smiling in the shy, sly grin she understands. Refusing to release me from the power of her gaze, from the beauty of this Indian eyed stare. *A white woman that is an Indian*, are the words that form themselves to me as I look at her, sniffing, smiling in knowledge, wiping my eyes.

"Momma," I say again, with a deeper commitment and satisfaction. "Momma, this is her. That little voice you've been hearing on the phone all these years..."

And I watch this woman of impossible appeal, stand without a smile above her namesake, who looks up at her in this selfsame sober minded gaze, as if looking across a generation of years, to where the pain of one seeks to be passed down to another.

As I watch this Indian white woman, this Zeta Jones-Pocahontas momma hybrid, press her lips to her young likeness' forehead, then press the girl's little face to her cleavaged bosom, I am burdened by the truth that remains, that the types of fear are many…and uniquely distinguished.

My daughter is thirteen, when the spirit of Katherine Hardwick came. My daughter is thirteen, when the spirit of Katherine Hardwick hath come.

Jonathan Lovejoy

Jenny's Eyes

Somewhere in the Ivy League madness. By the hallowed halls of confused, cultured learning. Professor Julie Weinberg has left her wealthy, Chappaqua home behind, in the wake of an end of the world tragedy. As she walks the evening time dorm of privilege, finding one of the penthouse suites of college living, she is burdened by the memory of Jenny's eyes. Of the bloody, black spaces where eyes used to be.

Julie Weinberg arrives at the ninth floor of Ivy League luxury. The on campus tower of delusion. The mirage of collegiate struggle. Floors of financed, fancy living. Bought and paid for by wealth and means, pre-paid credit cards for living expenses notwithstanding. *You only need a thousand dollars a month,* Julie Weinberg has said, reloading the Bluebird card every 30 days without fail. Satisfied in the pretense of her daughter's pre paid, Prius poverty.

Julie knocks on the door of her daughter's private dorm room. Having to take a deep breath in preparation. For this meeting.

Jessica Weinberg opens the door to her dorm, immediately stepping into the hall, into the hug with her mother.

"I thought you were dead," she says. "Where's Jenny?"

In the non-answer unspoken, is the chiming of the whistle train. A refrain across the rain soaked cemetery landscape, whereby the body of a thirteen year old end of the world victim lies.

"I was upstairs when it happened," Julie says, being escorted into the small, luxurious space of her daughter's road to the Wealthen Stream. Target and Pier One Imports supply their call to Lazy Boy plush and leisure.

"I saw them cover her from head to toe," she says. "I knew they were gonna kill her, and I knew I couldn't do anything about it. So, I ran. I ran to my bedroom closet and slammed the door just in time. I heard them slamming against the door... it was a nightmare. That Alfred Hitchcock movie was *nothing* compared to this. I could feel... I don't know... *rage.* Just plain, God awful rage, and nothing else. I'm telling you, if God is real, Jessica, he is *angry."*

"That's the problem," Jessica says. "God's *not* real. And this proves it. It's just nature, that's all. Nature vs man. And once again, man is the loser. I mean, life on Earth is millions of years old. Who knows how many undiscovered phenomena like these bird attacks, these migrations... who knows what kind of weirdness nature is capable of. Things that happen in multi-millennial cycles that we've just never experienced before. All we can really do here is…hunker down and wait it out. Because any attempt to fight or stop this is a lost cause."

Julie stares at the news channel's brunette mannequin doll, the talking head mouthing words in closed caption on the 50-inch flat screen, with pictures of an airplane exploding above an airport runway and careening to the ground in a fireball in the rain.

"Oh my *God,*" Julie says. "When did *this* happen?"

"This afternoon…" her daughter says. "An airport in Denver. I can't believe you didn't know. It killed 300 people.

"Was it the *birds?*"

"Of course it was," she says. "Planes all over the world are starting to come down. Mostly at night when they can't see them. And always when they're landing or taking off for some reason. A whole flock will just appear out of nowhere. The engines blow up like they were time bombed. They keep landing and taking off on these runways covered with *thousands* of these birds like stubborn fools. How many more planes are coming down before they get the picture?"

In this opportunity seized, unbeknownst to them—the older, women's studies scholar takes her daughter's hand, then places it nonchalantly on her daughter's thigh, a thigh naked in her daughter's blue denim shorts, below a gray sweatshirt in four letter announcement of this academic path of ivy. The blue letters of her gray Yale sweatshirt are royal.

Julie looks away from the disaster flaming across the TV screen. Gazing at her daughter's brunette hair at shoulder length, hair the lightest shade of brunette that is possible (and can still be called brunette), Pressing her lips hard to her daughter's cheek. Inhaling the scent of the candy kiss. Taking her daughter's arm. Laying her head on her daughter's shoulder.

"You want something to drink?" Jessica says, practically yanking her arm away, hopping up to her feet in cheerleader enthusiasm (though she was never one herself), switching the abundant bottom into the tiny space of a pre-suburban kitchen. The mother returns a second non-answer to a second epic question, this one concerning the diversion away from Perversion's wine.

Julie stands up in deep knowing. A look of intellect touched with a nonexistent smile.

"I felt that, you know."

"Felt what?" Jessica says. Popping the blue Pepsi can noisily open. The cola bubbles sizzle loudly in the ice glass as she pours.

"You pulled away."

"Hmm?" Her daughter says. Peering wide eyed over her burning cold drink.

"You pulled... *away.*"

Jessica sighs after the cold burn, lowering her icy drink to the counter. "I'm just thinking about Jenny," she says. "I feel like I hardly even knew her. How come you're not hysterical, Mom? She was your daughter. She was my sister."

"You don't have to tell me that. I watched her be covered with those damned things. I listened to her die. I watched them lower her into the ground. So, if you've got some high brow, Ivy League ideas about judging me you can just..."

"Shh," she whispers. Touching her hand to her mother's lips. Leaning in. Replacing the palm of her hand at her mother's lips.

With a kiss.

Jonathan Lovejoy

My Mother's Orgasms

16

My mother's orgasms come in stages. And this has been true for as long as I remember, that she is probably as powerfully orgasmic as any woman in the world. It is an apocalyptic secret that I share with this beautiful woman, this half Indian exotic, who I remember was always the talk of everywhere we went when I was a girl. Katherine Hardwick is a long breasted, wide hipped woman of deep, sensual means behind closed doors, with every ounce of her sexual energy stored up and dispensed toward me, from when I was twelve years old, throughout my teenage years and into my adulthood.

It is a triumphant or tragic secret for so many women and their mothers in the shadows. So many mothers and their daughters, to where the craving they develop is unendurable, and the private satisfaction of it is cataclysmic in nature. I know that for myself and Katherine Hardwick, it is something like a drug, with a craving so unbearable, and a payoff so monumental as to be absolutely irresistible when we are together. But it is a secret that I have sworn to keep, and to keep it away from the generation that my beautiful daughter is in.

And so, in late night secret, the two of us have taken to my mother's bedroom behind a locked door and a dimmed lamp, where I can again marvel at what this woman is capable of behind the walls of secret, in the freedom of what churns beneath cultured civility.

Her orgasmic power is so complete, that she need only stand pressed up against me from behind if she wishes. Not moving barely a muscle at length, before the first stage of devastation will begin. And in her private bedroom this very night, nearby the starlight of earth's departure, I stand naked, blonde haired and ivory white skinned in front of her, my hands held behind my back while she squeezes these F cupped pillows of mine, sent down the line from the ones that swing beyond G major from her chest like two great bells of warning. She is fascinated, over and over again, she says, at how firm and rounded mine manage to stay, though they are so much bigger than she remembers. I watch her as she stands close against me, not needing to watch me in the mirror this time, though we are in front of it as always, so that I may see first hand the beauty and prowess of this older woman on display.

My breasts appear so big and spongy, so white, so enormous in contrast to her sun darkened, feminine hands, as she squeezes them both with one hand back and forth, always ending by pulling firmly on the nipple, not for my pleasure but for her own. I am able to watch her, staring in something like bewildered anguish, and anguished bewilderment while she squeezes, as her beautiful mouth hangs open now without closing, so she can breathe through this deep state of arousal she is already in. For her, I know, this hard squeezing she does is as the power of a kiss. And when she finally lowers her lovely head to my nipple to give suck, this has the power of a hand at her groin.

And I stand with my hands behind my back, lit up inside that this secret happens right under my daughter's sleeping nose, and in the shadows cast by the end-of-the-world flocks sleeping somewhere near and far away from our perversion.

These are the shadows of fear. Cast over the grieving souls of latter day humanity, where mankind is evil, and latter day womankind is wayward and corrupt. I am lit up in the shadows of secret, as I watch my beautiful mother pull on a single one of my big breasts with her mouth, her brow wrinkled deeply from the stress of pleasure. And her cheeks are sunken in, in desperate sucking motion. I watch. I *feel* this woman's body tension grow to what alarming level it is capable of, as I marvel her extraordinarily curved shape in the mirror. Where there is the perfect balance between the gargantuan breasts, the soft, cinched in waist and full, fleshy hips in hourglassed, teardrop shaped perfection. Hips that have twitched once already from the itch of the witch's crown impending, as the first stage of her devastation begins. This, the arrival of a deep, heavy breathing that does not subside, but only grows until it manifests a whimper, which always amazes me in its genuine fearfulness of anticipation, as if she is truly afraid of what must happen to her body.

She gives suck to me as though her life now depends on it, with her head bobbing up and down in this full fellatio of the nipple, sending her to the beginning of stage two, which is the sudden, convulsive jerk of her lower body. Starting a chain reaction that gives her the Amazonian quake, shaking her in jackhammer glory from head to toe in total silence, followed by a mighty shriek that she has never been able to contain, as she grabs onto me and braces herself for the second wave of quaking every bit as powerful as the first, where the shrieking returns, this time trembled by the shaking that passes through her body.

And from this second earthquake, she holds on again for dear life, as the rest of the tension in her body breaks all at once. Sending a lesser wave of trembling through this third stage, where her voice lowers into deep, powerful grunting, as the rest of the energy makes its way through her body. Throughout these stages of her Armageddon Orgasm, I hold her up in support as she holds on to me for dear life in the dimly lit dark, as her body carries her smoothly to the fourth stage of apocalypse, which is the long, deep breathing that returns her to her senses. This, she must do with her tongue in my mouth, and her hand at the center of my impending destruction down below.

Of this, as our mouths are clamped tight together, she rubs deeply and with skill, to throw fuel on the fires that burn the color of royal blue and pitch, until my mind flashes to the face of my sleeping daughter, which blasts the first wave of trembling through my own body, and the gruff, Amazonian mating call, muffled by my mother's mouth clamped tightly over my own.

The rains over the nighttime prairie green fall in grieving, pitched in some unknown and melancholy key, so that a melody drifts in lamentation from one end of the earth to the other. Somewhere in the world of sleep and dreaming, the rains of this real world journey are drowned out by the noise of screaming, and the sound of exploded gunpowder in my ears. I wake up in the dark, drowned by the unfamiliarity of wherever it is in the world that I am, until I realize that yes, I'm actually in the house of my youth, and this strange bed I'm in is in my mother's bedroom.

I sit bolt upright in the bed, with nary a stitch of clothing on under the white linen pulled up over my breasts, which feel so heavy and conspicuous to me all of a sudden, as if I have hardly noticed until now just how disproportionately big they really are.

"What is it?" she says. Sitting up beside me in the dark. The concern in her sultry voice is genuine.

"Nothing," I say, running my hand back through my blonde hair, a shoulder length mane, wildly unkempt in the aftermath of trauma.

Katherine lies back toward her pillow, coaxing me back down beside her, to relax my head nearby the flesh pillows, with my arm draped across her middle, and my leg crossed tightly over her own.

"You never told me how beautiful she was."

And in the chiming of these words, is the warning I have felt in premonition already, which actually flutters my heart with enough apprehension to make me raise my head, and gaze directly at her in the dimly lit dark.

"No," I say. Shaking my head. And she does not bother in pretense, as if she doesn't know from whence I speak.

"I never said *that*," she says. "I truly meant that she's a very beautiful young girl. Her face is incredible. And she is so sweet."

"And *innocent,*" I say. Still gazing in defiance.

"You were innocent too," she says. "And so was I."

"But just because it happened to us doesn't mean it has to happen to her. I don't want this in her life, Momma."

"And just what is…*this?* A mother and a daughter's private secret?"

"A mother and a daughter's *perverted* secret," I say, accompanied by the deep, rumbling acknowledgement from the nighttime clouds of grieving.

"If it's so perverted, then why are you here?"

"Because... Kathy and I endured a nightmare worse than anything you can possibly imagine. It's a miracle that either one of us is still alive. I don't know if I'll ever be able to go back."

"Millions," she says. "They said the death toll could be in the millions. There's never been anything like it in the history of the world, they say. Nobody knows when or how it's going to end. They could all just suddenly break up and spread out again. Or..."

"Or what?" I say, laying back down beside her.

"Or they could keep going."

Outside, the rain falls harder on the roof above us, being taken up into the rising wind, and swirled angrily into the sides of the house, and across the nighttime prairie green.

"If you want to know the truth," she says, "I don't know how you've lasted this long. Considering how beautiful she is. She's *sexy.*"

"Momma..."

"Well? It's the truth. She's a sexy little girl."

"My God," I say. Sighing in fearful reticence. In fearful defeat. "What an apocalyptic thing to say. Can you imagine saying something like that in public?"

"I don't know. Women can get away with it if it's said just the right way. As if they're indicting the little thing for being overly sexualized, like so many little girls really are. Or they'll say *she's a cutie, isn't she*? And what they really mean is, *Oh, she's a cuntie, isn't she?*"

And though I try not to let it happen, the sinister part of me erupts a quick, convulsive little laugh of pure understanding.

"Tell me you haven't thought about it," she says, staring me deeply in the eyes as she lays on her back. "Tell me you haven't thought about laying on your back," she says, pulling me on top of her under the sheet. The feel of her breasts against my own tingles my body to ruin. "Lying on your back, with her little groin pressed against yours... with your legs *wide* open..."

As the storm gives its judgmental account in rumbling, I feel her hands buried in the cushion of my naked bottom, squeezing it for all its worth, holding her legs back into position, to where I can feel the connection of generations passed down, breasts to breasts, groin to groin, causing me to have to close my eyes in frustrated acknowledgement, slightly afraid to look her in the eye at this moment, lest she discern the truth that she herself has planted in me.

"One look at her," she says, her voice deep and breathy on my lips, "one look... and I knew. I knew that if you hadn't done it already, you had thought about it," she says, pushing her middle finger past the barrier into my rectum, to ignite the fires that burn as black as pitch tinted royal blue. And this causes me to have to open my eyes and stare at her in anguished frustration, in frustrated anguish, as the twinge of feeling flows in conduit to both breasts and back, to cause my hips to move against her on their own.

"Yes," she says, staring me directly, deeply into my eyes. "You want to *fuck* her. You want to fuck your own daughter, don't you?"

"I...I can't."

"But you *want* to, don't you... I want you to *admit* it to me, that you want to lay on top of her and hold her down, and smother her with your tits until she can't breathe..."

And my mind sparks the fires of my devastation, feeding me the image of my daughter naked underneath me, struggling with her little head covered between my breasts, unable to draw a breath, pushing, kicking, trying to cry out for mercy...

The sound of her pitiful, muffled voice in the theater of my mind, the feel of my mother's breasts mashed against my own work in tandem, ignited by the fires pushed into my backside, until I have to slam a slow, steady and hard rhythm into her groin, waiting for the energies to meet at the center of my body.

And suddenly, unexpectedly, the fire is lit on this renewed thrust with the prowess of a match struck properly, to flare up an explosion in my womb that spreads, passing through my body and into my voice, causing me to breathe a siren howl onto my mother's waiting lips, through the walls of nighttime secret, and out into the storm of bereaving.

Katherine Hardwick Rides the Wind

atherine Hardwick rides the wind. On the eve of eschatology.

Half breed. Daughter of a long breasted, Cherokee bride. A woman named Pia, married to a horse rancher named Joe Hardwick. A man who did not live to see his little Katherine's 13th birthday.

Katherine Hardwick rides the wind. On the eve of eschatology.

A twelve year old Indian white girl. A little white Indian beauty. At the rainsoaked gravesite of the millionaire horse farmer. A flimsy little support for the grieving Indian woman. A woman of stature. Native American features touched by beauty, with hair the color of midnight silk in the rain. Standing at the gravesite of the rich and beautiful horse farmer. In the company of the little half breed. A little white Indian beauty her husband named Katherine.

Katherine Hardwick rides the wind. The winds of grief and bereavement, flowed from the spirit of the woman who gave her life, and took it from her so abundantly. Feeling the cold breeze of resentment having begun to flow freely from the heart of despair.

Beyond the grieving waters of her father's funeral. In the rains of latter day disillusionment. The Indian mother Pia Hardwick takes her daughter by the hand at their sprawling, 152 acre Oklahoma prairie green. Suffering the last days of "those stupid horses," she always says. Taking the daughter by the hand, escorting her into the two story white house. The little half breed.

Katherine Hardwick rides the wind. On the eve of eschatology.

The Indian mother pulls her white Indian daughter along. Navigating the corridors of spirits that weave in and out of their reality. Good and evil spirits, angels and demons that move on human behavior. Guiding all human decisions through the flow of time. Creating Fate and Destiny by human choices made. Controlling every consequence come and gone. Influencing every dark and light outcome. Adding to, subtracting from every series of steps planned and taken. Opening, closing every door down the halls of life and living. Opening those to happiness for some. For others, the darkened entranceway to the gray world. The entranceway to melancholia.

The Indian bride takes her daughter by the hand. In neither love nor hatred. In nonchalant defeat, the Indian widow takes her new little bastard by the hand, the insignificant child of rain, escorting her past the spirits of melancholy decision, into the bedroom where the loving white man is no more. Into the shadows of the upper room.

Pia Hardwick escorts her quiet natured, somber little brunette girl into the room. A little girl whose face is rarely touched by a smile. A little girl whose love for her father ran wide and deep. His little Prairie Doll, he called her.

Pia takes the prairie doll through the door to the Indian Queen's chamber. Through the door of plush domesticity bought and paid for. Closing the door behind them.

Katherine Hardwick is twelve, when the spirit came to her. Katherine Hardwick is twelve, when the spirit of Pia Hardwick is come.

In the predestined words from the motherline spoken. The white Indian girl begins to undo the buttons of her dress. Hardly able to take her eyes away from her mother in fear. Not knowing what form this punishment is going to take. Not knowing at all within herself *why* this time. What wrong look. What wrong tone of voice. What wrong step in the rain across the prairie lawn. What wrong breath she breathed. What phantom disobedience was the cause of this tragedy.

Before long, quick work is made of the twelve year old's dress and underwear. The mother sighs within herself, as the rush of heat twinges her groin. As she gazes the girl's overdeveloped and prodigious young breasts. Firm, rounded melodies in the melancholy key. A song pitched in D minor naiveté.

The daughter's bulbous young nipples tingle in the cool of the daytime dark. Memory twitches and tingles upon her breasts, from the many punishments given. From the perversions done in the name of discipline. The twisting. The pinching. The bitings. The canings. To where the truth is told of which it is written, *"Discipline, thy name is pain."*

"Come here," the mother says. A voice trembled in cold grief repressed. Calling the naked young girl to her mother. "Take off my clothes, the mother says. Feeling the wave flow through her own breasts from the sound. Feeling the pissing twinge in her groin.

Katherine Hardwick rides the wind. Undoing the black buttons on the front of her mother's grieving dress. Hands fumbling. Trembling at each button. As her Indian mother watches patiently. Judgingly. Unable to fathom what pleasures are possible from the passive precondition. From the merest suggestion of the inevitable.

At long last, slow, steady work is made of her mother's clothing. Ending with the girl's fingers at her mother's underwear. Pulling the tight, black fabric down and away from the widened hips. From the hips spread out to infinity. Of her gigantic, macromastian breasts hung down, of their allegiance to the curved waist, and the hourglassed hips. Of her mother's modesty in front exposed, she does not know. She only knows that the new feeling tingled in her breasts hath flowed to her place of chastity down below.

"Put your mouth to my nipples," she says, her voice still trembled in sorrow. Standing perfectly still, her hands back on her hips. Watching her daughter's clumsy decision unfold, as to which of the G major bells to ring.

The naked girl takes one of her naked mother's breasts into both hands. Proceeding to lightly pull a nipple into her mouth. As to the powerful twitching at her mother's curved waist, she does not know.

"Suck it deep into your mouth," the mother says. "Like you're trying to get milk from it."

This, she does. As to the look of shock and anguish on her mother's face, she does not know.

The mother readjusts her stance. Holding her head back. Eyes closed. Mouth open in unspoken awe of what she feels.

As to the sudden, violent twitch of her mother's body; as to the shuddering, thunderous quake of her hips and thighs, she does not know. She only stands there. In the aftermath of her mother's trauma. Holding the woman around her waist in support. Listening to the woman's deep, heavy breathing, in the wake of a single, maniacal shriek into the room.

She stands there. Hugging her mother around the waist. Listening to her breathe. Feeling her spirit recover.

The mother pulls gently away. Away from her little Indian Prairie Doll. Switching a busty, big hipped body, boldly to a drawer in her dresser. Removing the brown leather serpentine. The brown leather belt of legend.

The girl looks up at her mother, mouth trembling, half open. Eyes pleading. Shaking her head once 'no.'

"Take this," the mother says. To shock the girl's expression into bewilderment. "I want you to whip me," she says. "I want you to whip Momma's bottom with it as hard as you can. Like you're trying to make blood come." This, from that same voice twinged in melancholia. That voice haunted by the spirits of gray.

The mother hands the folded belt to her daughter. Turning her back to her. Facing the mirror of her dresser. That she may watch her own tragic descent. Facing the mirror. Her wide, naked buttocks facing her daughter.

"Hit me," she says. "Beat my skin to blood."

In confusion, the daughter raises her hand. The brown belt looped in classic whipping form. Bringing the first lash down upon her mother's skin. Causing a flinch of expectation. A twitch of anticipation cut in two.

"Harder," she says. Not flinching this time. Tolerating her naked daughter's fearful, confused effort. Afraid to hit her mother. Afraid not to.

"Harder," she snaps, no tolerance left for mediocrity. "Unless you want me to *show* you what I mean."

Oh, what tragic motivation, Unholy Fear!

She watches the young girl's fearful uncertainty lose ground to angry assurance. Feeling the difference down deep beneath her skin. In disbelief at the power of imagery. The picture of her big breasted little twelve year old. Breasts now wiggling mightily with every swing. Teeth clinched with the effort. Her little twelve year old face twisted in anguish touched by fear. Fear tinted by a rage to succeed. By a desperation to avoid a whipping.

The little girl whips onward. Driven forward by a lust for pain. A lust for blood. Striping each new welt with another one. Cutting her mother's white skin to blood. Unable to lose focus now. To see her mother's face in the mirror. To see her mother's expression washed over with amazement. To see her holding her own nipple tight. Not knowing that what pain there was in these welts has been replaced. Where every hit sends a signal to her groin. Rising the built up energy inside of it to a mountainous high.

At the edge of the daughter's exhaustion, at the brief trickle of blood. The striking of the belt strikes a fire in her mother's body. Where the bolt of lightning strikes from her buttocks to her groin. Beginning a long, steady quivering of them. A quivering that shivers a low, melancholy moan from deep within her voice. A long, ghostly exclamation of energy flow. Energy flowed from the shaking inside. From the quaking of her hips and thighs. Every new welt. Every bloody lash of the belt. Sending the waves up her spine, to flash both of her nipples in grieving.

Little Katherine Hardwick rides the wind. At the quaking of Armageddon. In the modern mother-daughter dynamic unleashed.

Katherine Hardwick rides the wind. On the eve of eschatology.

Little Pocahontas

19

*I*n the spirit of what strange domesticity, what bizarre tranquility we can find as a family, the three of us enjoy our country morning time together. Filling the house with the sights and sounds of breakfast being cooked and eaten. And Katherine and me, *Mother* and me, (or Momma, as she seems to require now), Momma and me have spent the morning so fascinated, so delighted and entertained by our daughter and granddaughter, our little Indian girl, who truly is the physical, the spiritual reincarnation of her grandmother. And it appears that she does not notice our sudden and newfound worship as anything special or different, just that Mom and Grandma Katherine are a part of whatever happiness there is left for her to have in this world.

Momma and I both listen with so much desperate attention to every little thing she says, as though she were an actress on stage, and we had paid good money to watch and listen to her perform. Every bite of bacon she takes is cuter than the last, I think to myself, watching her smile though every little white-toothed bite of the perfect bacon, where Oscar Mayer hath dared to achieve. And I notice that she loves the bacon strips the most, ignoring the grits and eggs for the most part, with hardly even a bite of the waffles and buttery maple syrup. *Is this how she's always eaten*, I hear my mind ask, unable to reference the fullness of her eating habits in my memory. *She's a meat eater,* I hear my mind say, knowing now why maybe she has achieved such classic slim and stacked form even at 13, where it seems that what fat she has is packed into her adult sized bra. In the D minor key already, they are, though she is barely out of the seventh grade, waiting with the rest of the world to see if any other grade at all will be possible anytime soon without terror.

At the breakfast table, I watch mother descend from the heights of her somber, enigmatic maturity, to focus on her granddaughter's every word, smiling with her, laughing, giggling at every silly little story from the heart of my daughter's memories, from her desperation to leap backward past the incident in Chappaqua, to when she was just a normal seventh grade girl with friends, hopes and dreams, even mentioning her best friend Jenny Weinberg, whom she says she hasn't talked to since just before the birds came. *Some of the birds we saw were so beautiful,* she says, as if the worst part of what we saw never happened. And I watch my mother give Kathy her full and focused attention, not caring at all about how strange and phony she looks to me, as she smiles and *oohs* and *aahs* at everything Kathy says, even mentioning that after breakfast, they should get the umbrella and go feed the big flock of chickens that mother still has.

No, they haven't acted strange at all, she says, *they haven't done anything different than they usually do, accept eat and lay eggs...*

Then mother picks up a piece of scrambled egg on her fork and pops it in her beautiful mouth with a smile, causing her granddaughter to laugh and giggle as if she is being tickled to death. Then, Katherine picks up another piece of the buttery, perfectly seasoned eggs and leans over to Kathy, putting the fork at her mouth, watching her open and close her lips around the fork in mild hunger satisfied, though Kathy acts as if they are the best damned eggs she has ever tasted. *The little faker doesn't even really like scrambled eggs,* my mind forces me to hear, as I watch my mother do it again, then saying with a nerve that she knows only I can hear...

Let me taste yours.

Kathy then enthusiastically stabs her pile of cold eggs (which she hasn't touched, by the way, until now) and holds the fork a playful mile away from my mother, forcing her to lean so far over that she has to grab my daughter's hand, wrapping her big lips around the fork as if it were ice cream instead of eggs, performing such a hilariously sensual *mmm mmm good* wrinkle of the brow and shake of the head, which causes my daughter to laugh again. And I am forced to suddenly confront the truth, that these two are connected across this generational gap, and it is suddenly as if I have faded somewhere into their background.

She never acts this way with me, is the forked tongued serpent slithered into my brain, a double sided accusation unspoken, with one side pointed at my silly acting little Pocahontas bird, who hasn't smiled and laughed this much at one time in the 13 years I have known her. The other side is pointed at my mother's fungalooga, her sudden and blatantly false joy and giddy happiness, which I *know* she is using as little more than a tool, a set up for something she wants to accomplish that I don't dare allow myself to think about.

Just look at that face, she says so skillfully, holding Kathy's face up by the chin. *Give your grandma Katherine a kiss*, she says, closing her eyes briefly as her granddaughter kisses her lightly on the cheek.

Mm mm, she says, shaking her head 'no.' *I mean a country kiss.*

What's a country kiss?

Like this…

I watch my mother lean forward in her most apocalyptic delight and dream answered, pressing both lips in full against my daughter's. Moaning, shaking her head back and forth at least three seconds, before she releases this big, bold kiss in a loud, near comic smack, staring at my daughter who is clearly disarmed and embarrassed by something she has *never* done with another human being.

Country kiss, her grandmother says. Touching her own lips with her finger, her beautiful, sensual face leaned down at her granddaughter in waiting.

Kathy leans forward without much of a smile that I see, pressing her lips naively, warmly, fully against my mother's lips, with my mother holding her chin, moaning another long, deep moan of satisfaction.

And in the haze of this slow motion dream, I watch a fifth second tick off the clock of history, before my daughter knows to finally pull away in naïve uncertainty, looking up at her beautiful grandmother for absolution, to be rescued from the devastation of a wrong move here, of a second too soon, or too long left in the forest east of Eden.

Jonathan Lovejoy

The Pope Insanity

I wanted to beat the Hell out of her...

As she drives through the rainy gray mist back to her mansion home in Chappaqua, that new American wasteland, that wilderness of lost hopes, and dreams shattered to oblivion—as she drives back to her beloved, million dollar palace already restored—dreaming of every window repaired, every broken piece of glass and ceramic replaced, every dirty, bloody beak and claw mark smoothed and glossed over—as she drives back to the Wealthen Stream of Chappaqua, she comes to terms with her own latter day burning, with the fires that burn in dark and alabaster blue. Remembering how badly she had to resist the urges boring into her when she was but a girl of fifteen, when she held her nine year old sister down underneath her in the basement until she cried. The feeling that ran from her groin up to her brain and back again, that made her believe she had pissed her jeans soaking wet, though it had only been a single gush that dampened the front of her underwear. The more her little sister had struggled, the more she had tried to scream through her hand that had been over her little sister's mouth—the more her sister struggled, the mightier the feeling in her groin had been, until she felt a slow explosion happen, spreading a warm length out between her legs and up into her beating heart. And Julie had held her little sister there in secret, feeding on her fear and desperation to get to their mother and tell, so that Julie could get a whipping for what she had done.

This moment had been an awakening in Julie's life. Ground zero for a wave stretched 30 years into her future, culminating in what had to happen to little Jenny, *before* the birds came. A feeling resurrected from the grave of her youngest (Jenny), before even the memory of her perversion has grown cold—a feeling that had haunted her ad nauseam through the years, until she had to take it out on Jessica, before she escaped to Yale.

As to whether or not her actions called forth her dark destiny, she chooses not to know. She only knows that there are fires that burn in her that need to be fed, spaces in her soul that must be filled with the energy of purpose. Energy that she wonders if her daughter felt just last night, after the sharing of their cola kiss.

Julie Weinberg remembers back beyond her daughter Jessica's time last night, to when one of her Women's Studies undergraduates made the mistake of asking for mercy in grading. Made the mistake of being just *assy* enough, to cause Professor Weinberg to have to invite her to her office in the after hours. And it was the big, rounded backside of this 21 year old Michelle Pope that found its way into the theater of Julie's mind, when she achieved her first climb up the hill, with her daughter laid on her back naked in their early evening bed, legs open in missionary, barely even aroused herself physically, but laying there in fervent support of her mother's sickness, not knowing what end-of-the- world truth was burning her mother's brain as she laid on top of her daughter.

This, the truth of what was done, what was said, what was seen in the professor's office in Shattalon Hall. This hippy young blonde was made to strip every inch of her clothing off to the floor, which she gladly did, in exchange for the promise of an A at the end of the Fall semester. In the heart of this double memory, Julie remembers the deep grind on top of her daughter last night, how she had to take her daughter's head in both hands to anchor herself against the wave that approaches, as she thinks about the young Pope girl standing naked in her office, facing her desk, legs together, with her hands up and clasped behind her head.

Julie remembers the fumbling of her own hands at her skirt, raising the front of it up, not having to lower her own underwear in this achievement. Knowing that she is among the privileged few in the history of mankind. Knowing that this is a calling, a dark destiny that must be obeyed. As she grinds atop her daughter in their early evening bed, she remembers the unlucky Pope Girl, standing naked and so pear-hipped in the office, perfect breasts so high and firm, played upon the happy C major chord, her hands now down and gripped upon the desk, as her female professor's naked breasts are pressed against her back in her unbuttoned blouse, feeling the female professor's hand tight around her throat. Amazed at the strength of the woman's smooth, quiet, pressing rhythm, and the size and hardness of her arousal underneath her underwear cloth.

The Pope girl has to wince in pain, from the grip of the lady professor's teeth at her ear. Feeling the tension tighten every muscle in the woman's body, until she feels that tension break, and hears it in the professor's deep, Amazonian moan in her ear, and the shaking of her entire body against her.

In the heart of this double memory, Julie Weinberg must grab tightly her daughter's hair with both her hands, to use her body as an instrument of orgasm, having to open her mouth and call the name of God when the lightning strikes, to grunt an animal wailing gruffly into her daughter's ear, as she remembers the pear-hipped beauty of the naked Pope girl in her office, and the Armageddon Quake that she did gloriously achieve.

She lays atop her daughter in pure dominance, wishing to pull the girl's hair to a greater agony, while the pain of this energy flows like a raging river through her entire body. As Julie drives on, feeling her heart register a greater rhythm, she remembers the depth and power of the kisses she must smother, the kisses designed to take her daughter's breath, to take her daughter's autonomy in post apocalypse. To remind her that even in these hallowed halls of Ivy, there is no escape from what Destiny there is apt to be given. *You will be fucked,* are the words that pop into her brain, as she puts her hand over her daughter's mouth, so that she must struggle to breathe through her nose, to try and find her way back to sanity.

Of the Pope insanity, Julie Weinberg still contemplates as she drives, remembering without guilt, without remorse as she low graded the girl's term paper out of pure revenge, because the girl refused a session in her office.

But you said you would give me an 'A' if I did those things, the Pope girl had said, as the tears ran down her face from the sting of a C minus impending.

As bad as that paper was, just be glad I'm not giving you a D+, she had said. *Good day, Ms. Pope.*

And the girl had only sniffed and mouthed the words *"fucking bitch"* too low to be heard, as she walked out of the office in total humiliation.

Julie Weinberg drives on. Understanding now that there is a fire that must be fed. There is a space of grieving in her soul that must be filled. That even in the hallowed Ivy halls, her oldest daughter cannot hide, from the burning of blue and black fire.

Pamlico Sound

21

The stubborn highways of mankind's discontent ebb and flow with traffic still, from shores of Virginia Beach westward, as far south as Pamlico Sound and Cape Hatteras. The roads and rivers wind through the sea of chattering birdsong, stretching vicariously through West Virginia, Kentucky and Tennessee, through Illinois and Missouri into Arkansas, on into Colorado, Utah and Nevada, until half the state of California is covered in this endtime fascination, where it seems the 3000 mile wide swath of birds has settled in for whatever long haul this is, leaving the world to wonder when this migration would continue.

Those in the midst of this new bird sanctuary hide and creep along in perpetual nervousness and apprehension touched by fear, knowing that around the world, hundreds of millions have already died in the last wave of bird attacks, until there is call for an international emergency to be declared. Television cameras can hardly do justice to what is the most massive bird migration of all time, where four footed animals of every kind run and cower in terror, lest they be swarmed, subdued, and eaten alive by this end-of-the-world cataclysm.

Nervous onlookers roll the streets near Pamlico Sound, on the edges of the Atlantic. Complacent that this infinity of gulls and blackbirds are just casual observers, mere visitors to this part of the timeline, and will soon gather themselves up into the four winds, and be carried somewhere out to sea. These locals nearby the foot of the lighthouse at Cape Hatteras roll on in stubborn resolve, unconvinced that the birds are a sign of anything, and this migration will come and go without further incident, and fade like an echo into history.

This is the complacent coo and laughter of the blonde, Carolina mother on the streets of Elizabeth City. Somewhere North of the lighthouse at Hatteras. Somewhere north of where the vultures perch and congregate near the diamond shoals, on the beaches nearby the light that shines over the Atlantic.

These Elizabeth City streets glide the calm and complacent blonde mother along, who rubs the knee of her little eleven year old Rebecca doll, who smiles at her mother in full understanding of secrets untold, leaning over to her mother at the traffic light, pressing a big and friendly kiss to her mother's lips in childlike simplicity, and adult sensibility. These two giggle and hold hands at the precipice, on the edge   of whatever life has in store, on the edge of the modern mother-daughter dynamic unrestrained.

And this southern, suburban soccer mom leans over to her little Rebecca doll, whispering something in her daughter's ear so shocking as to be unmentionable, causing the girl to tuck her lips in a smile of embarrassment, gazing through the misty windshield view. And the mother raises up again, glancing at the red light shimmering through the windshield, *shocked* by the sudden crash against the window, blurring the shimmering light into a pattern dispersed by a circle of shattered glass, Evoking a shriek from both the mother and her daughter in the rainstorm, a shriek multiplied by the shattered glass circles that appear in every window of their silver Sonata, until at last, a circle opens the barrier between worlds, allowing the head of a gull to push its way through the windshield, as the Rebecca girl's window is shattered, into a shower of a thousand pieces of glass crystal at their feet.

22

"*Residents of Elizabeth City, North Carolina endured today what is the first new bird attack in this massive migration, killing thousands of people in just this town alone, with no reported attacks anywhere else across the country today. Officials and experts are fearful that this could be a sign, a warning that future bird attacks are impending, some believing it's simply a matter of time before millions more are killed. People in cars all over the North Carolina town were violently attacked through rolled up windows shattered with ease, some devoured in their cars by the swarming flocks of mostly seagulls and blackbirds. It is being reported that as many as seven thousand people around Elizabeth City were killed in this lengthy attack, more than a third of the city's entire population. I'm Cora Leeds, the Associated Press.*"

23

I find my way through the maze of words
On this trip toward the crashing sounding sea
As I gaze across this infinity of birds—
From here to the shores of eternity

The Tiding of the Blue Sword

$\mathcal{S}$ometimes, there are issues in the air. Things that have weight and substance, that make the air itself harder to breathe. These are issues. Things unspoken, sometimes to the cause of unspeakability, so that the heavy weight of them can only be endured, as we navigate through the powerful tension they cause. These are the avoided looks in the eye, the avoided words spoken on the subject, until the unbreakable tension becomes unbearable.

From this drowning inside our country house, even while the world outside endures a cold, drowning summer rain—from this tension, I feel the need to escape if only briefly, so that I can breathe normally again.

"After what just happened in Elizabeth City, I need to get out of here."

"Where in the world are you going in all this rain? Why don't you just settle down? Relax and watch TV. Play on that laptop or something."

"Playing on that laptop' is exactly why my nerves are in a shambles. You weren't in Chappaqua when those damned things showed up at my house. They broke through so-called shatter proof glass and poured into our living room. If it hadn't been for that sheet—I think it confused them for a minute. Otherwise…"

"Otherwise what?" Mother says with cold mischief, breaking two eggs into the cake batter. The melted stick of butter and the condensed milk follow soon after.

"Or else…"

In the whir and whine of the cake mixer's attack, my mind drifts to the reality of that day. "Or else, we wouldn't be here. You act like you don't believe me."

"Just trying to picture it, that's all. It's hard to imagine. They're just birds."

"Unless there's a thousand of them," I say. "Then, they're just certain death. It's like… like some predatory instinct takes over the whole flock. A spirit of pure rage. A hunger. You know that if they get to you…"

And these words are choked off by the sudden appearance of my daughter in the kitchen, which actually startles me to an almost flinch.

"If *who* gets to you," she says, in genuine naiveté.

"Nothing," I say. Holding my chest. "It's just my nerves. I was telling your grandmother that all this craziness is starting to get to me."

"You mean the birds? I just saw on the news that they—"

"I think… we've heard enough bird news for now. I was just telling your grandmother that I need to get out of here for a while before it all gets to me.

I'm taking a day trip in this rain to the nearest mall. I want you to come with me."

"Do I have to?" she asks, wrinkling her pretty little mouth. Her Pocahontas face and silken black jenny-braids are beautiful.

"Since when do *you* not want to go spend money with *me* at the mall?" I want to stand up, and actually confront this oddity with courage.

"I want to stay with Granma Katherine," she says, whining a bit, grabbing my mother by the arm with both hands, leaning her pretty little head against her. My mother's look of unspoken satisfaction as she mixes her cake is epic.

"Well... are you sure Grandma Katherine wants to be bothered?"

"What's that supposed to mean?" Mother says, smiling her false shock in my direction.

"I only meant that maybe you need some time to catch your breath from us, that's all."

"I'm breathing just fine," she says. "If you need some fresh air, go right ahead. Kathy can stay here alone with me as long as she wants."

And this is the rise of the unbreatheable. The rise of the unspoken. The tension in the air, unspeakable, that gathers itself around us in a drowning wave, until every word, every glance, is laced with the energy of the subject forbidden. I watch in something close to *fear,* as the two of them smile and giggle delightedly at one another, tickled in the throes of grandmother-granddaughter secrets impending.

$\mathcal{S}$omewhere on the Oklahoma landscape. In the misty region of the Prairie Green. A grandmother feels the tiding of the blue sword. The burning of blue and black fire. And this, to the exclusion of all other fires that burn.

Somewhere in the drowning mist. In the farmhouse overlooking the prairie green. The beautiful older woman, in the seasoned, mature twilight of her 50's, knows that this time alone with her 13-year-old granddaughter is epic and divinely ordered. A gift bestowed to her from across the miles. Across the years of waiting. After the girl's mother has left the farm. To reluctantly leave the two of them alone with Predestiny. After the frivolity of cake batter has come and gone.

In the assurance of the mother's temporary departure. The exotic, half Indian woman sits on the black stool by the kitchen counter, drawn by the formation of something beyond her groin and womb. Drawn by something reached down deeper, into the darkest recesses of her human spirit, of her soul touched by spirits from along the timeline. A touching that calls her to pull the young girl close to her to say…

From the moment I saw you, I knew. I knew there were things that we could share between us. Things that only you and me were meant to know. Things that only you and me could understand. Things that you and me could never tell another living soul. Things that not even your mother would understand. I think you know exactly what I mean. Don't you?

By the soft caress of a grandmother's voice that is low. Almost whispery. The girl is unable to nod her head just yet. Staring into her granddaughter's beautiful eyes.

I want you to kiss me, the grandmother says. And this, she does. Leaning forward to her granddaughter's beautiful lips. Lips full with desire. With instinct. With craving.

As to the feeling this kiss sends to the girl's lower body, she does not know. She only knows that it is a feeling which gathers itself in magic, as if to lift her up by grabbing her insides with a pleasure unbearable. An ecstasy unendurable. And in the wake of this, there is this kiss that lingers. Releasing this kiss. Hearing the beautiful older woman say…

Kiss Grandma Katherine like you mean it…

And this, she does. Egged onward by this feeling gripping her inside. Unaware of the powerful and tragic quiver at the waist of her exotic grandmother hidden in dress cloth. Hidden in cozy, country fabric.

And in the fires of this kiss that burns, the cuteness of innocence, the sweetness of naiveté is done away with by the tiding of the blue sword, by the ingestion of forbidden fruit. And the fruit of this kiss is the sweetest of all time to the palate; is the nourishment of the ages for both their bodies in flame. And the woman is amazed in the power of this kiss, that the tiding of it gives rise to the danger down below, so that she understands that it must end at this moment, lest her body ignite prematurely.

Did you like that kiss? she says. The girl nods her head 'yes.' Staring boldly. Wide eyed at her grandmother. *Do you want to come upstairs with Grandma?*

And to this, the girl nods her head again. In her feeble attempt to understand her body's new craving. Her body's new desire.

The beautiful older woman takes the young teenage girl's hand, guiding her through the sound of rain from the prairie. Guiding her. Gently pulling her along through the ghostly halls of waiting. Finally, into the queen's chambers, through the doors of the upper room.

With nary a word, in the daytime dark unrestrained, the grandmother removes her granddaughter's clothing. Standing before her in towering, Amazonian strength unspoken. Watching the girl's eyes calm to a state of knowing. A place of understanding.

In the wake of this, she undoes the buttons of her country dress. Sliding the cloth away from the white underwear cloth uncovered. Reaching back, unlatching the bra cloth, to allow the mountainous flesh to fall free, to hang free in a melody played far above and beyond G major, to the phantom key of H to Double H to J, to sing the Hallelujah chorus to the condemned in Jubilee.

Then the busen busted beauty leans over, to slide the underwear cloth down and to the floor. Feeling the weight of them hang and pull against her. Standing up straight in Vesuvian power once again.

Take Grandma's breasts in your hands, she says. *Lift them up. Squeeze them.*

And this, the girl does. Finding that the mere touch of them calls her again to the feeling in her groin.

The woman watches her granddaughter. Feeling her fumble clumsily at her breasts. Kneading the gigantic things like so much bread dough. Lifting them up in her little white hands. Letting them fall back to hanging perfection. Grabbing them at the nipple in the handfuls of flesh, wobbling them mightily back and forth. Causing her grandmother's face to anguish over in grieving.

Lift this one with both hands, she says. *I want you to suck the nipple. Suck it deep into your mouth. Suck it like you're drinking milk from it.*

And upon this beginning. At the very origin of this suckling, the woman feels the instantaneous warning in her groin, stronger than any other time in her years of suffering instinct, unable to tell the girl to stop, gathering herself to endure the lightning strike impending. And she watches the young girl's lips in nursing, studying the girl's cheeks dimpled in sucking form, suddenly feeling the lightning strike from her nipple to her groin, lurching her forward in a massive convulsion, becoming a quiver in every inch of her widened hips squeezed in, holding on to her granddaughter as the powerful shriek bursts forth like a fountain into the upper room.

$\mathcal{I}$n the aftermath of lightning flashed. In the rolling thunder of the upper room. The grandmother stands in the middle of the floor, breathing. Holding on to her granddaughter to prevent a deadly swoon. In awe of what inherent knowledge has infused the little girl, to cause her to kiss and lick the woman's neck in such profound and new understanding, a rare and special lust across the face of the earth, scattered pervasively across the landscape of the human population in secret.

This girl returns to her grandmother's lips. Holding the kiss, perceiving the woman's heartbeat, the rise and fall of the great bosom uncovered. The woman pushes herself to a brief recovery, to escort her little accomplice

and rounded against her grandmother's body. Then the girl returns to her determined, bouncy rhythm, bringing forth the bed's unique voice, the signature sound of every bed in creation, the sound that lives in each one individually, bouncing up and down on the woman without mercy, staring down at her face anguished over in anticipation, knowing that now, the fires in this woman have been reignited, and that she must bounce her into whatever second trauma she has left to endure.

In this, the grandmother holds on to the granddaughter's waist, preparing herself for the inevitable, catching sight of the young girl's bouncing breasts one last time in lucidity, as the next slam down into her body crashes past the surface, to push a spark into both breasts, to infuse the grandmother with fear of what power this is, as the double flash of energy connects to her groin, to cause her entire body to tense in live wire on its own, making her hold her head far back, gritting her teeth in effort, as the girl's bouncing pushes wave after wave of explosive energy from her groin to her breasts and back again, until the woman must pull in a breath, and howl a second and more violent shriek into the room.

And she knows to not disturb the girl's enthusiastic bouncing, so that she may endure this unique orgasm, the Armageddon Orgasm, that flows from the top of her head to the soles of her feet.

$\mathscr{T}$he grandmother lays there. Breathing through the devastation. Through the second part of the truth. In awe of the girl's natural instinct. Her ability to navigate these unfamiliar waters with familiarity. With inherent knowledge and skill.

The grandmother lays there. Absorbing the energy of the girl's kisses on her skin. Feeling the cushioned needle pricks of nerve twitching, brought about by the girl's lips at her waist, by the girl's lips at her thighs. By the rubbing of the girl's big, erect nipples against her groin, causing her to have to open her eyes and look down, watching her granddaughter rub her full, firm young breasts up her waist and down, feeling the sensation contrast, the dynamic between the girl's silken hair hanging down, and the soft rubbing of her breasts against her skin. This rhythm of ecstasy, punctuated by the soft, gentle kissing back up from her naval to her big bosoms, where her areolas begin to shrink again, at the onset of her finale, the revelation of truth in the latter day.

The grandmother lays there. Enduring the ecstasy of kisses. The luxury of silken hair caressed. The rapture of firm breast flesh pressed and rubbed against her. The woman's body responds with a shudder. A twitch that signals for her to act, when the girl's breast brushes her proper place. When the girl's breast brushes her improper place.

Stay down there, honey, she is compelled to say, lest the girl naively brush this cushion of energy back up her body, and away from the point of contact. From the third part of the truth.

The woman reaches down. To the center of herself. Opening herself to oblivion. Exposing the core of energy aroused. The bud of a flower grown to significance. To an end-of-the-world proportion.

Put your nipple right there, she says. Feeling the spark of it flash bright through her body. Through her soul.

She lays there. Quietly enduring the girl's fumbling clumsiness. Her attempt at accommodation. Feeling the girl's nipple in its own arousal, rubbing firmly against her arousal raised. Feeling the heat of this energy grow. Taking hold of her own nipple with her other hand. Looking down at her beautiful granddaughter, rubbing her darkened nipple against her down below. Seeing herself grown to the greatest arousal achieved. Seeing it raised up in a monumental proportion.

The granddaughter lays there. Her entire body tense with renewal. The stress of this new arousal in full. Watching her granddaughter's understanding begin to grow. Feeling the benefit transferred to the rubbing. To the firm and fast new rhythm achieved. The prowess of a rubbing to start a fire. And suddenly, beyond her control, the woman's mouth opens wider on its own, to allow the flow of energy out though her voice, as a pitiful, wailing moan starts low, as in the early onset of a weeping, as the flow of pissing touches her feeling down below, which springs like a blast wave through her groin down both legs, to where she glimpses a fountain squirting of a crystalline stream, shooting up from her groin onto her granddaughter's breast, as the pissing moan spreads from her groin up the length of her back, quivering her body to a violent and fervent shaking, lurching her upward when the feeling hits both breasts in full, causing her to grab on to her granddaughter, as her body pushes her groin up into the girl's breasts in a hopeless searching for an anchor, to protect her from this last and greatest fall from the heights of ecstasy, into a shuddering, thundering abyss of rolling cataclysm down below.

he heights of orgasmic oblivion hold Katherine Hardwick on her back. A prisoner of its memory in the wake of total devastation. Although it had tormented her from the day her daughter and granddaughter arrived, this had gone so far above and beyond the call of duty, so far into the essence of orgasmic bliss as to have been unendurable. The last orgasm held her in a state of trembling, even after she returned to sanity, as her granddaughter had climbed on top of her face to face, gazing directly into her expression as her grandmother wrapped her legs up and around, her lying still with her eyes closed, while the trembling waves went passing through.

Katherine had always been a prisoner of the violent orgasmic mind, but never in a triplicate so powerful and so uniquely devastating. In the first, she remembers that she had not gotten off as much as she had *shot* off, and lurched forward into her granddaughter as though she had been whacked with an invisible paddling board. Even from the first orgasm alone, the room had very nearly begun to spin around, until it felt as though she might have to swoon and follow a twirling path to the floor. But through this devastation, she survived a near fainting, to make it to the bed, where the Andante to this end of the world concerto of the forbidden was to be played, where the sight and feel of the girl hopping up and down on her groin had sent her body to even another place it had never been. And this had flowed into a finale for the ages, a power even greater than the first two, which had sent the feeling down both legs in electric heat, where it had felt as though a space had opened up underneath her leading to a cosmic fall, where she had no control over whatever pissing stream it was that shot out of her onto her granddaughter.

Katherine Hardwick lays there. Still coming back down from these Olympian heights, feeling her granddaughter's own heart beating as she lays still, relishing the feel of her frail little hands and fingers, gently twirling and twisting her nipple.

"Do you think Mommy would get mad if she knew?"

"I know she would," Katherine says. "She wouldn't understand. You have to swear that you'll never tell another living soul what we've done. Do you swear?"

And in a pause fearful enough to flash pain through her body, the grandmother stops breathing, to wait for either life or death to appear.

"I swear," her granddaughter says, but with reluctance.

And defeat.

Jonathan Lovejoy

The Modern Mother - Daughter Dynamic

29

The tragedy of the modern mother-daughter dynamic haunts me into bewilderment as I walk through the big mall in Oklahoma City, an hour's drive away from the prairie green back in Stillwater. It seems that I have a sudden radar I never gave heed to before, perhaps because I just didn't want to deal with the truth of what I know. Is it because of how I was raised on that Oklahoma farm, that every other mother and daughter I see, allows me the knowledge of whether or not they are fucking behind closed doors?

And this bothers me about as much as even those damned birds, flocked somewhere just north of here, deciding when and who to kill next. Between the phenomena that burdens me from the skies, and the one that lurks in disguise all around me, incognito to seemingly everyone but me—because of all this, I know that the so-called end of the world is as close as the next sunrise and sunset over oblivion. Nearby the hidden sunset over east of Eden, I wander through this busy mall to escape the tragedy of my mother's life again, as if I am somehow above this new desire that grips me, wandering in judgment over these busty and hippy middle aged mothers in their dresses and jeans, walking with the younger girls and women brought into the world as their daughters, some of them being more obvious than others, but none of them hiding themselves completely from me.

The revelation of this secret is eschatology (whatever that means) are the words that actually find themselves somewhere into my brain, as I drift and smile past the sexy and sophisticated among them, considering myself as much a part of their money and beauty clubs as they are. And I notice that it is the so-called sexiness or prettiness of them, the mother, the daughter, or *both* that is the warning sign, that is the telltale warning to me that somewhere along the way, something has happened between them.

It may often begin with the innocence of a compliment. Or with the naughtiness of a whack on the bottom at the kitchen counter. Or even the forbidden squeeze of a pair of bra-clad bosoms in front of the mirror in the bathroom. And I know for sure that this is a girl thing, a woman's thing, so far beyond the man's pathetic, penile understanding, that causes these deeply heterosexual, these perfectly straight women to be drawn to the sexiness of their daughters, sometimes to the rise of resentment from the mother in the form of hidden jealously. Psycho-sexual energies misplaced and displaced all over the daughter's life, where sometimes the daughter is aggravated into acting out because of their mother's constant interference with their lives. *Why won't you just leave me the fuck alone,* the daughter will say in anger, as the mother pushes her way into the daughter's bathroom time to tell her again that her phone privileges are suspended, in the latest punishment to avoid a spanking for being late for curfew.

At least one of these mothers and daughters I see burdens me with this very thing, as I find myself in the irresistible aisles of JC Penney again, where the modern, middle class mother-daughter dynamic goes to live and die. I wonder if this woman, this averaged height, light skinned, wide hipped honey thinks she's hiding it from me, as she follows her slightly irritated but emotionally dead daughter around the store, on her heels like a lady cop on an impending teenage girl drug bust, hardly allowing the tall, yellow skinned Jordin Sparks clone to take a step or a breath in peace, monitoring everything the girl even thinks about buying as if it's a potential crime committed.

And this girl I notice, is twice the beauty that her pretty mother is, inheriting all of the mother's sensuality about her features, but combined with a beauty pageant level look about the eyes and mouth. And it is fascinating to watch this tall, beautiful girl—with her freakishly wide blue jean hips and double D cupped breast under her sweater—it's amazing to watch a girl this tall and shapely in obvious emotional subjugation to this shorter, plainer, *ass*ier woman who is her mother. I could care less about the male dynamic in their lives, whether he is there or no, whether he is rich or no, whether he is white or no—for what I know is happening between these two has absolutely nothing to do with him.

It is a series of lengthy, hard spankings that has occurred from the mother to the daughter, as well as the belt and the hairbrush, but all under the pretense, and in the name of discipline, where this heavy hipped woman enjoys the lecturing of her daughter to tears, ending with this girl in her tight grip in the bathroom or in the mother's bedroom, or in the kitchen, or in the mother's room-sized closet with the door closed, where the most brutal and uncompromising has occurred.

And in these busy, crowded aisles of the JC Penney heaven, I find myself nearly wincing at the truth of what I know has happened between this brainy, beautiful band girl and her mother in private, where the walls of this perverted discipline are at last broken down in the mother's closet, after the spot of blood was spanked onto the daughter's hips in claustrophobic screaming. With the daughter's bra still in place, with her gigantic hips exposed, I see the brown hairbrush of legend, brought down over and over again onto her sixteen year old's naked hips, stopping to rest between sessions, standing close beside the girl who grips one of the closet shelves in desperation, gazing at her mother's golden pumps at the teary eye level. This, the yellow skinned beauty does, while her underwear clad mother punishes her "sassy little bitch" of a daughter, who had the nerve to say *"why don't you just leave me the fuck alone,"* when she asked her daughter to get off the phone.

After this band geek beauty has screamed herself hoarse in the closet, after the spot of blood hath appeared from the hairbrush ad nauseam, this mother takes the bra from around her daughter's breasts, dropping it unceremoniously to the closet floor. Unable now to stop the energy of this train having begun to move, energy crashed down upon her from the River of Time, flowed from somewhere in the distant past, to her and her daughter's privileged present.

She raises her bra up, to mash her bulbous, low hanging blobs bulging against her daughter's back, sliding her own underwear down low on her hips, hearing the daughter's inward breath drawn coldly through her clenched teeth in a painful grimace, as the underwear cloth scrapes past the bruises on her naked hips. The mother presses her curvy, bottom heavy self hard against her young daughter's hips, at the place where the mother's arousal has grown to at least two inches out the front of her. Gripping her daughter's breasts in full, as commanded by the feel of her own breasts against her daughter's back, balanced by the dreadful pushing of her lower self in deep squeezing, pressing against her daughter's backside.

Who doth thou hast this hidden from, accursed woman! As you mash yourself against your daughter's teenage insolence, against what is left of her innocence, to ease the burning of the black fires inside tinted blue! The mother ignores the pre-shudder of her body, when she feels her lower self aroused outward, tucked between her daughter's buttocks, to simulate in the mother's soul the depth of their future coalesced into a dreadful present, where the mother's hips take on a hard, slow, pounding rhythm on their own, where no greater speed can be possible, and no softer pounding can be obtained. The closet shelf rattles with the daughter's thighs slammed against them, as the mother's mind and body both abandon her to insanity, where sixteen years of repressed energy explodes into her body.

In the confines of the closet, there is a pitiful howling, a hidden cry of the condemned, a siren high pitched into the daughter's ears, then lowered to gruff, low pitched animal grunting, as the blast wave passes from the mother's trembling hips and groin to the rest of her body and soul. With nary a kiss, with nary a whisper of tender feeling. *Don't you never cuss me again,* she says breathlessly. *You hear me bitch? I'm your momma. AND your daddy*...and this, in the current of panting, of heavy breathing, and in the return of the mother's grieving sanity.

This, I am burdened by, as I wander helplessly over to them, pathetically saying *"she's either a cheerleader or a pageant queen, which is it?"*

Gauging the mother's resentful, *"she's too lazy for either one of those, believe me—they ask her to be a cheerleader every year and she won't do it. Likes playing that French horn too much I guess. She's in the band..."*

And before long, I am pulled away from this corner of the modern mother-daughter dynamic uncovered, to drift away from the desperate conversation in whispers, where I endure the apocalyptic shock, of hearing a woman tell me with her lips of what manner of bruising, and bloody belt whippings this straight 'A' daughter's teenage insolence must bring.

Jonathan Lovejoy

The Nature of

Orgasms

30

*A*s the wind and rain drench the nighttime Oklahoma Prairie, I am cursed as one possessed, to use my own mother's body as a door under the power of a battering ram, in late night lust unbridled, slamming into the back of her without mercy in slow, hard rhythm. My mind alive with images burning from the mother and daughter at the mall, knowing what I know partially from what she told me, and from the spirits that burden me with revelation.

"You wouldn't believe the mouth on her," her sexy pretty, sassy-assed momma told me in secret, *"the smart mouth on her...she's not as sweet as everybody thinks she is... sometimes I have to take my belt and try my best to*

stripe the blood out of her... I'm not kidding, I have stripped her BUTT naked and took her father's belt and tried to beat the blood out of her smart ass..."

And this is the image that haunts me even now, phased over from seemingly half a day in the past, with the mother in my mind, naked breasts swinging long with every swing of the belt, hips jiggling from the effort, bringing the belt down hard over her naked teenage daughter's naked skin. The image of the daughter's own jiggling, flopping breasts bounce and swing in chaotic tandem with her mother's in my mind and spirit, coupled with the chaos of angry yelling and fearful screaming, all of it driving my hips forward into my mother on all fours in front of me during this perpetual storm, shocked when suddenly I hear my mother's breathing give way against her will, her head lowered, where I suddenly hear a violent, high pitched siren in the dark—a sound born of its own volition, causing me to feel a lightning strike directly to my groin, shuddering me from the inside out, drawing a bovine bellowing noise out of me that I cannot stop, nor can I stop pounding into her until the wave of explosive energy passes through.

And even as I try to see again in the vaguely lit, late night bedroom, I contemplate with fascination the nature of orgasms, and how this one was brought on by merely the sound of her voice in forced ecstasy. I just literally fucked my mother. And part of me is deeply empowered by it. In the aftermath of this trauma, I press myself hard up against her, pulling her up to her knees, memorizing every inch of the powerful breasts hung in the phantom key of J, moving down quickly to her waist, then to the center of her body's devastation, rubbing the front of her without mercy to hear her version of this same gruff, bovine call from deep within. The shuddering, the shaking of her body, her hands anchored back against my thighs—the spasms return me quickly to this odd plateau, as she is too ingeniously stubborn to beg me for mercy.

I intend to win this battle for her surrender, rubbing her with new energy, staring at her with wicked intent, watching her focus all her energies to a magnificent battle of wills, with a monumental shaking and grunting for the ages. And I suddenly realize it is a battle I have lost, as the pain *receiving* part of her is even more astute, reminding me that if she had to, she would grunt and bellow for the rest of the night to obtain this victory.

I release her from this torture, though not in mercy as much as surrender, pulling her frustratedly by the hair, staring at her beautiful, Indian face with determination, turning her face to mine, taking in her tongue as far as it will go, then rubbing her again just enough to hear, to feel the muffled grunting in my mouth.

And to what epic, Amazonian desire this is, I cannot know—only that the taste of her tongue in my mouth sends a wave of pleasure somewhere beyond the palate, to touch me deeper than what the body can know or understand. The taste of my mother's tongue is nourishment to my spirit. The feel of her suffering is energy for my soul.

The two of us rest still, in the aftermath of this trauma, listening to the gentle rumbling of the sky's confirmation from outside our window.

31

The spirit of mother-daughter perversion looms heavy over our resolve. To cast a roving shadow over every corner of our grief and mourning. In the morning after our night's engagement in the storm, I stand at the window of my mother's bedroom, allowing myself to be pulled deeply into the sorrow of the grieving earth, and the gloomy, oppressive mood of this perpetual storm.

"The end is coming," the beautiful, sultry voice says softly in my ear from behind, startling me a little, as if she had drifted up behind me from out of another reality. "I've felt it for a long time. The birds. The birds are just a just a warning. Like flashing red lights at a night train crossing."

The truth of her small town, country analogy is acknowledged by the low, gentle rumbling from the clouds, to presage a hidden voice of doom and eschatology.

"I have something to tell you," she says. Pressing herself against the back of me in motherline possession, her humongous breasts mashed in full against my naked back. By sensation alone, the fullness of her macromastia is on full display.

"I allowed it to happen," she says. "And there was nothing I could do about it."

Sometimes, the substance of spoken words appear as adrift, like a ghostly echo in the wind.

"Let what happen?"

"My granddaughter," she says.

And from this phantom, this apparition of words suddenly appears in my brain, in my body, as the third part of the truth uncovered.

"What... what do you mean?" I say, turning to look at her, feeling my own features twist in bewilderment and fear.

"You *know* what I mean," she says. Unable to speak the tragedy of our lives, brought forth in the deep, booming rumble of the storm.

"Momma no," I say. Shaking my head slowly. "Tell me it didn't happen..."

"The opportunity presented itself to me," she says, turning me around, grabbing me by the shoulder. "And I had to take it."

"You didn't have to do anything," I say, unable to manufacture anger over the confusion and terror. "You did it because you *wanted* to."

"I did it because I *had* to," she says. Pinning my arms, locking her hands behind my back. The near masculine strength in her upper body is epic.

"I didn't want this for her," I say whining, "tell me you didn't do it to her, Momma. Tell me you didn't do it to her..."

"Honey, I wish I could tell you that," she says, suddenly gripping the sides of my face, the strength in her hands deeply apparent. "But the truth of who we are cannot be denied. We can't change what's meant to be..."

The audacity of these words serves the fire inside, allowing me to express the fullness of this rage impending.

"You did it to her because you're *sick,*" I say, trying to pry her hands from my head, succeeding only in making her pin my arms to my sides again. "You're sick and you're *twisted!*"

And upon this last syllable, I manage the scream I've been trying to start, like the clicking of a spark at the head of a blowtorch, finally blasting this end of the world shriek into the room around us, as she holds on to me in full strength like a lady wrestler, watching me shake my head back and forth in madness. After a brief moment, as the wave of violent revelation passes through, she takes hold of both my arms behind my back, locking my wrists together with one hand. Covering my mouth with the other.

"I didn't choose to make this happen," she says, unaware of the single tear streaming down her face. "This happened on its own. Its why you brought her here." And this brings another wave of violent screaming from me, but this time, muffled in the pressing of her strong hand over my mouth.

"That's right," she says, her voice deep and sultry. "Accept it. Let it pass through your body. I know it hurts, Meredith, but this is who we are. This is who she is. Deep down, you know you brought her here because of it. And I'm sorry. But not because I did it to her. I'm sorry because you never had the nerve, because you never had the guts to do it to her yourself."

And this brings one last attempt, one last wave of muffled violence. A quieter, more helpless struggle against my mother's uncompromising strength and power.

"You brought her here because you knew it was time," she says, removing her hand from my mouth, holding both my arms tightly again. Even in rage and sorrow, the feel of her breasts pressed up against mine is epic.

"I brought her here to get away from those birds," I say pitifully, barely able to see through the pain and mist of tears formed.

"Oh no," she says, shaking her head 'no,' pressing her gaze in deep knowing. "You know that migration had already passed. You could have stayed in New York but you chose to come here. You chose to come here because you were drawn here. You were drawn here by a calling. A calling that you feel burning in your blood. Baby, come here…"

She releases her grip on my arms, pulling them around her waist, hugging me tight around my shoulders, this epic breast pressing notwithstanding.

"Hold on to me, baby. Hold on to me while the spirit enters your body. Hold on to me while it happens…"

What deep and depraved power is this I feel! The power of the motherline curse, the curse of the motheress, which caresses me now against my will! To pass the truth gently from somewhere in my womb, up to my breasts mashed against hers, until I have to whine my pitiful, hopeless pleading to the storm for mercy!

"Tonight," she says. Her voice low and whispery. "You'll go to her. Tonight."

Yes. The types of fear are indeed many.

And uniquely distinguished.

Part Two

Jonathan Lovejoy

The Color of Life

32

Along the veldt of the African plain. In the grasslands of latter day grieving. Eyes of cold, predatory instinct. Blinking from the pride of great cats. King and queen of this wild, animal kingdom. Rulers of this part of creation, gazing the heard of creation animals wandering by. Animals in the manner of horses, painted in black and white striped display. A roving, roaming canvas of divine creativity. To counteract the foolishness of natural selection. The depressive nonsense of evolution. These creation animals move casually nearby the herd of predators, exchanging their wary, worried glances across the nearby distance. One, in apprehension of the chase. In mild, distant worry of a bloody possibility. From the golden predator, these eyes are wary of opportunity passing. Their means of survival moving onward. Having already engorged themselves on the brown, leathery carcass of another. Leaving the blood and bones for the scavengers to pick clean.

These well fed predators look on. Gazing contentedly in the complacency of conquest. In the pride of their lives gathered up in survival. Done with prowess, and apocalyptic skill.

These golden predators look on. Comfortable in their place at the top of the food chain. At the mountain peak of nature's violence passed down. To burden all others with apprehension. With fear.

From among this well of tranquility, chaos ensues. A sudden roaring, maniacal twitching, rapid clawing at the air. Chaos born from the sudden swooping of winged, feathered devastation. A single bird of prey, monumental in stature. Massive in wingspan. Wings flapping wildly, talons unfurled. Claws of lightning instinct, evil, fiery intent. Clamping hard into the back of the youngest predator. Of the least fortunate among them. Lifting the condemned thing from the safety of numbers. From the security of family come and gone.

This bird of prey flaps its great wings mightily, escaping in a blur of noise, and the sacrifice of a feather or two. Lifting above the roaring, growling pride. Rising above their hopeless anger. Taking up the youngest predator among them. Feeling the tingle of hunger in its own blood. Energy given by the pathetic screaming of prey. The hopeless squirming of a condemned little hunter.

The great bird carries its prey aloft. Circling a small distance upward. Swerving, turning back toward the lone tree from whence it came. The tree of knowledge. Where the pride had been watched. Where their sleepy, well fed complacency had been observed in hunger. In natural instinct.

Tragedy drifts the condemned into the top of the nearby tree. Where it is held down in struggling. In growling, yowling fear and anger. Where the curved, golden beak is opened, and brought down upon the fur of the young predator's neck. Fur now stained the color of life.

The color of death.

Little Indian Girl

33

The storm itself seems tragically aware of what fear and pain I feel, as these Oklahoma winds do rise and fall, in whirling, violent warning of future choices made. Though I have hardly spoken to, touched, or even been anywhere near my daughter all day, I have been unable to resist these heavy spirits of solemn change, and the growth of tragic inevitability in my heart and mind. It is a sensibility that I fight tooth and nail, with the inner strength and clawing of a raptor, focusing my perverted self even during our lonely dinner, on my time with my mother impending. Trying as hard as I can to ignore the spirit of her words tormenting me, telling me that whether I like it or not, I am going to my daughter's room, and obey the calling that she has risen in my blood.

My greatest regret in life now is that I left New York to come here, not realizing that I was bringing a fresh young lamb to a hungry she tiger on the prairie. All day, I have been looking at them both in profound disbelief, but struggling to keep it to myself, so as not to alert my poor little Indian girl to what I know. And as I think of what it is that my mother has done, what poison she has injected, infected into my daughter's life, the lightning strikes in this raging storm over the prairie green, and the cascading thunder screams in the voice of pain and eschatology.

This is twister weather, she says in audacity, causing me to turn from the bay window, the prairie window, and look her dead in the eye at long last, amazed that her façade is fully in place around her granddaughter. All through dinner and beyond, Mother acted as through somehow we were *normal*, and not prisoners of mother-daughter perversion passed through the generations. Once, I even had to stop myself from shaking my head in pure judgment, remembering that I am half of the perverted pair that is the two of us, and I am definitely no better than she. Even though I have never touched my daughter that way, how can I claim some kind of moral superiority over her, knowing that from this morning to now, I have been tormented in like manner as she?

For this reason, I have tried to avoid eye contact with Kathy all day, staring at her in the periphery, with her thinking that I am focused on the television, or whatever foolishness I find on my laptop in front of me. And sometimes I wonder, how many other women have I looked at on the streets, in the churches, in the stores, or in the schools when I was a girl, that have been tormented by these same tragic depravities as I.

As another country paradise has turned to twilight. As the evening rolls onward, to where the stars are no longer allowed to give their light, I have tucked my daughter into her bedroom under cloak of innocence, not letting on at all that I know what she and her beautiful grandmother did. As this part of rain world moves past the eleven o'clock hour, I already know that my twisted, perverted self has a deeper desire for my mother's tragic whispering than I have since I've been here; to be held down by her this time, with her strong arms wrapped around mine, pinning them to my sides and behind my back, as she punishes me with a pounding unlike anything she has done before, to drive my punishment home until I am sore from the taking.

My heart beats the rhythm of this impossible craving, as I slide out of the bed in my country, cotton nightgown, gliding down the cold, hardwood hall toward my mother's bedroom. I touch the silver knob in reticence, shocked when I turn it and nothing happens. And though I work hard to pretend it isn't so, I have to process the fact that yes... my mother's bedroom door is locked.

"Momma," I say, tapping on the door. "It's me Momma. You can open up."

But the only sound I hear is the rumbling of truth and resistance from the clouds, in the nighttime echo of my impending tragedy.

"Momma? Please open the door. Please? I need to see you."

And for some reason, I cannot resist the requisite shaking of the locked doorknob, as if I could ever gain entrance without a key or a sharp hatchet.

"Momma... you *punish* me if you want. Whatever you want to do to me is okay. If I've been disobedient... just punish me for it. I can't do it to her Momma. I can't. Don't make me *please...*"

And this last syllable cracks in misery, in the pain welled up into my throat, threatening to cause a nighttime haze through watery vision.

"Momma? Momma have mercy."

And I close my eyes on this pathetic begging, this pitiful pleading, not understanding that the sickness I have, the cure for it comes with a price. I turn in shame to the mocking spirits that stare, moving in time to the rhythm of the rolling thunder, until I am standing still and quiet, in fear and grieving to touch this unlocked door knob, and open the door to my daughter's bedroom.

34

ith nary a whisper of a knocking, I open the door to predestiny, walking slowly, stealthily, across the big, country bedroom of my daughter's nighttime dreaming, sensing what tranquility there is she hath achieved in this prairie green, somewhere in the plains of our Oklahoma arrival. *I love Grandma Katherine's house,* she says every day, *I could stay here forever.* And oh, even now I know, that this is not the chirping of innocence I hear! It is that talk from behind the veil of knowledge, where there is no longer the curtain of the unseen, where the truth is no longer hidden from eyes of naiveté!

In this tragic knowledge of the forbidden, I am pulled along the flow of time and history, in our little space of unknown tragedy, moving in something close to fear, to the edge of my sleeping daughter's bed. I stand over the beauty of this sleeping form, marveling at the extraordinary features, exotic appeal passed down from my mother to my daughter, to sandwich me between two pressings of irresistible beauty. At the behest of a single tear, I ease the busty, small waisted hippiness of myself down onto the bed beside her, sitting bolt upright, looking down upon this sleeping Indian beauty, knowing in my heart as to the only way such a creature should be brought back to life again.

Mesmerized by the sight of every strand of her silken black hair brushed long over her shoulders and underneath her, laid from her pillow down the entire length of her back, I lower my head toward the most beautiful little girl I have ever seen, pressing my lips in full to hers, and not releasing this kiss at all, but breathing the breath from her nostrils into mine, to capture the beginning of her essence, to breathe what remains of her life down into my greedy soul. As my womb already twinges the echoes of the forbidden—as the pissing twinge rises in pre-lightning down below—I hold this pressing down on her lips in authority. Breathing in deeply as she begins to move. Raising up in time to meet her resurrection gaze. Giving her time to come to terms with this inevitability. To process the soul of fear I have awakened in her body.

With nary a word spoken, she gathers her senses in this nighttime storm, staring up at me in inherent knowledge, in an instinct born and bred in her thirteen-year-old body, in her thirteen-year-old gaze, that her purpose in this night storm is to be obedient, to accommodate, to be the beckon call, to serve whatever motherline curse this is, to become whatever manner of motheress she is destined to be.

I sniff the rest of this melancholy tear away. Lowering my head back to her mouth. This time, my body enraptured by the feel of this kiss returned, but done with an inherent skill, shocking to the touch of my lips, then to the touch of her lips at the tip of my tongue. In this, I am suddenly a prisoner, as I *have* to let this happen, to let my tongue slide the rest of the way into my daughter's mouth, to serve the pissing part of my perversion, which threatens to cause me to flood the sheets at the spot where I sit.

I control to the best of my ability what lightning threatens to strike, feeling the echoes of it coming from my soul in waves, flashing through my womb to my groin, to make me wonder how one might survive the fullness of such a thing. I greedily pull her tongue deep up into my own mouth, to try and ease the suffering in my body that I feel, but to no easy avail whatsoever. Somehow, I know that when the tension in my body breaks, it will be in the company of a flood, a gush of energy formed in water somewhere inside my body.

In fumbling, in trembling strength I know she can perceive in the faint glow of this nighttime dark, I rub my hands down her shoulders, then across the front of this white cotton nightgown she wears in the latter day storm, undoing the first button in agony, the second button in suffering, and the third button in pain. In the pain of this third button of hers undone, I slide my trembling hands inside, to squeeze these pubescent breasts so firm, to stroke, to pinch this nipple so erect, so large, so fully grown in her own epic pain and desire.

From this alone, the girl closes her eyes in a deeply anguished expression, as I move the gown away from the breast I feel and squeeze, to lower my suffering lips, to touch them to my daughter's breasts in grief and mourning. Feeling the wave of pleasure flow through my soul and womb again, to cause me to deliver the Virgin's Intercourse to my daughter's breast, without mercy, bobbing my head up and down, up and down upon the nipple pulled deep into my mouth, until I know that to take another suck into my mouth could mean the death of us both in this storm.

I can only sit her up, and begin to help her pull this nightgown off over her head, pressing my lips to hers again when her breasts are exposed, sliding my hands down the front of her underwear, amazed at the swollen softness and wetness of what I feel. But I am obedient to these spirits of Perversion, to obey their call to restraint, causing me to finally slide out of my gown, enduring the touch of her frail little hand at my nipple already, to cause a visible shudder in my body.

I push the girl back to the bed, still sitting up beside her, my head lowered to one more hungry kiss of her lips, at last sliding onto the bed closer to her, underwear still in place down below, sliding myself up to where she can nurse one of my nipples in full. I raise up on one arm, watching her take my nipple into her mouth, sucking it as though there is milk to be had, as though there is nourishment for her body for Christ's sake.

In the flow of a weeping moan, I know that I must pull it away, lest the power explode into my body prematurely, to rob me of what full punishment the spirits have in store. I slide my underwear down and away, watching her do the same, unable to take my eyes from the center of her young desire, beginning my hopeless journey towards it in full, ice cream licking of her waist at the naval, feeling her entire body tense up under my tongue, working my way down to where the scent of innocence beckons, where the remainder of chastity threatens to be broken. Without mercy, I slide my tongue to this Virgin desire knobbed in full arousal, sucking it into my mouth, feeling her body go tight, listening to her breathing give way, feeling her hands gripped tightly in my hair.

motion doth entail, to move my hips in grinding and slamming into her on their own. And I feel her grip tighten as she holds me, trying to grip the skin of my back, clawing, scratching, as if to anchor herself against an arousal she cannot easily endure…

And as the Amazonian plateau approaches in my body, I hear my daughter's breathing at last escape her control, where the words *Mommy please, Mommy please help me,* are spoken aloud followed by a loud, shrill shriek, and then a loud second one, and then a third one screamed to the Heavens in the nighttime storm.

These little girl screams, colored by the knowledge of forbidden womanhood reach into me unbeknownst, to strike as a bolt of lightning from the clouds, to where I must grunt loudly *"Oh…GOD"* in total fear, as the striking energy has the effect of a bomb exploded, sending a blast wave from my groin up to both my breasts, causing me to have to slam myself hard in non-stop pounding, as if to push the wave through to completion, while the power of it sounds an Amazonian yell into my daughter's ear that lingers, growing louder as I slam this message home, until I have no more breath to yell with, as my body sets me up for a *double orgasm,* where the second energy wave hits with the same power as the first, this time spreading from my breasts back to my groin, where I have to draw another breath so that I can make the Call of the Motheress, the wailing siren of Armageddon, as the second wave passes trembling and shaking through my body from head to toe.

Jonathan Lovejoy

At the Foot of the Eastern Mountain

$\mathcal{F}$rom the sandy shores of Pamlico Sound. Up through to Virginia Beach, west across the southern forests and fields, over the windy slopes of the Blue Ridge Mountains. A complacent determination has settled in upon this bird kingdom. On these new rulers of latter day creation. Those that dare be out and about, those who cruise to Sunday morning services do so in calm awareness, in the acceptance of their fate, that what winds have blown these creatures in, will gather them up again at will, to carry them somewhere beyond their hopeless horizon.

The Sunday morning worshippers cruise the streets of their Virginia town, somewhere at the foot of the eastern mountain chain. Church going locals, so *White And So Pretty*, families of middle and upper class privilege in their Escalades and BMW's, in Lexus and Mercedes luxury notwithstanding. Rolling chariots of privilege, nearby the Great Appalachian Forest, and the morning mist of Blue Ridge tranquility.

These locals disembark their rolling chariots without fear. Without respect toward the possibilities fluttering the length and breadth of the cropfields, and the branches of every forest tree thereabout. In every yard, upon every rooftop, lined across the top of every abandoned set of neighborhood swings and trampoline foolishness. Suburban paradise commandeered for a time.

These unwary onlookers walk in Laodicean comfort. Strolling in smiles unhidden. Walking through the parking lot surrounding the southern mega-church in tinted glass and finely minted brick splendor. Barely able to see beyond the power of their own prosperity. Unable to focus on the hawks that soar majestically in the winds high over the towering steeple. Unable to acknowledge the spirits in these high places. Unable to care.

The Sunday crowd drifts through the fine glass doors in end-of-the-world audacity. In the stubbornness of privilege. Greeting one another in the heady, high-mindedness of upscale community. Suppressing the lust of the flesh. Diverting their lust of the eyes. Laughing, grinning, hugging feverishly in the pride of life. Purveyors of latter day heartlessness and love waxed cold. Church committee outreach men and women. Ladies on the board of charity. Those who take the eviction notices and utility disconnect notices in disinterest. In mild contempt. In resentment unspoken. Those who reluctantly give their time in food bank donation and dispensation, who package the old cans of unwanted beans and unsalted peas in bitterness restrained. Handing the heavy, archaic paper grocery bags to the poverty mothers in condescension. A week's worth of groceries in perspective long gone. Church wives called and set high in latter day hierarchy, in endtime church government. Responsible for the distribution of monies for rent, for lights. Even for the car payment to a lucky soul or two. Deciding in the interview who will be blessed in the door among them. Deciding early on, who they would like to see punished by a refusal. Gazing in judgment at the single mother, divorced, who sought no alimony or child support from her husband. The single mother with two children, whose job barely pays enough for survival. The mother whose rent was already due last month, who has been served an eviction notice in yellow paper. Who sits at the table surrounded by an old deacon and three middle aged matrons. All gazing at the pretty young mother in a swirling of emotion. Lust not being the least among them. But this, the lust to see the young mother broken, to hear of her tragedy impending. To hear of what happens when a sheriff is called to an eviction. To hear of her trip with her nine year old and thirteen year old daughters to a homeless shelter. Devising in their minds how best to pull the young woman over their figurative knee. To punish her raw for her life's choices made. To discipline her for being an accursed woman. For not being smart enough. Talented enough. Blessed of God enough to have a better life. To feel the spirits of sadism caress the church bosoms bound in repression, when the poverty mother most begin the flow of tears. The voice in useless cracking. The quiet tears in pointless sniffing.

The women of the church hierarchy. Watching the young, pretty poverty mother suffer without compassion. Watching her blue eyes redden without pity. These women of charity drift among the Sunday morning church crowd. Smiling. Hugging. With no memory of the one hundred and fifty dollar check held in tight fisted reluctance, to be dispensed only if the mother can come up with the other 450 dollars herself in three weeks. A hundred and fifty dollars, and a list of other churches and agencies to call or visit. Shocking the poverty mother into disbelief.

"Then, lets just pay my light bill instead," the poverty mother says. But this, in hopeless futility.

"Do you have your payment agreement with the power company?"

"Just the bill," she says. *"But I can call them on the phone."*

"We need the agreement letter," they say.

"Then, why don't I just go home and email it or fax it to you?"

"Its almost three o'clock," they say. *"We only meet once a week. On Tuesdays."*

"Can't somebody just get it later today or tomorrow?"

"We're sorry," they say. *"We can't help you. When you get the rest of your rent money, come back."*

These are the latter day charity queens. Doctors' wives. Professors' wives. Lawyers' wives. Chosen to oversee the boundaries of endtime charity. To set the limits of what love is in the church budget to give. These complacent locals. At the foot of the Blue Ridge Mountains. They rest easy in their Sunday morning ritual. To remind God that they have worked in his name. To demand from him Salvation without belief. To expect Redemption without repentance. To put in their time on the Sunday morning church clock from eleven to one. To pay the Laodicean cost of Christianity. These worship and honor God with their lips, though their hearts are far from him. Hearts in love for the things of this world. A conscience seared by a hot iron.

These are the charity queens. In secrets hidden and unspeakable. In this Sunday morning farce, giving no thought to the migration, nor the arrival of the Sunday morning rain and thunder from the clouds. Scattered among the hopeless husbands. The sad sons. The depressed, dominated daughters. They clap and clamour for the music band on stage. The Christian university trained amateurs, disguising mediocrity in noise and effort.

The charity wives clap and clamour for the pitiful, Broadway staged voice that sings the same as they all talk; in WASP prettiness and prestige. Worked into a frenzy of themselves as queens of the Appalachian land. Ready to receive the word of prosperity in worldly glamour from the pastor's beautiful wife. In envy of her blonde hair and blue eyed, Hollywood face and style. Knowing that they are truly blessed among women.

"These birds are not doom and gloom," she says. *"They are the beauty of our Lord and Savior in bloom…"*

And upon this, is crashed a violence unheard in the modern day. A chaos of noise untold. As the tallest stained glass window in this part of the world is done away with in a screaming, screeching clamour of unearthly sound. A noise risen up above the quiet shock of the parishioners down below, and the first scream of terror from the pretty faced, aspiring Broadway singing girl off stage, an alarm to signal the arrival of chaos and terror. Through the stain glassed window crashed open, pours in a sea of white gull things, with nary another color among them; sharp, yellow beaks and claws tearing at the faces and hair of the pastor's wife, to where her screams are amplified a hundred fold over the microphone clamped to her pretty pink lapel, covering her as she tries hopelessly to run, causing her to fall hard on the stage as the wings and feathers flap down from the noisy influx from the storm, clawing her face, tearing and ripping her blouse and skirt, scratching and clawing her legs exposed, cutting every inch of her white skin to blood. The charity queens turn away from the truth they see, in hopes to escape, to flee the wrath to come.

Migration

This screaming charity queen is helpless in every choice made; to run down the crowded aisle toward the closed double doors, or stop and try to fight the clawing, flapping things pecking at her son's face, pecking at her fifteen year old daughter's eyes. This heavy hipped, blue skirted, blue heel pump charity queen cannot see beyond the pain of her own eyes being pecked and scratched, to see the young woman fall from the balcony while holding her baby, her husband leaning far over the balcony in stupid futility, losing his balance when a beak is thrust into his eye from a bird in flight underneath, tumbling hard from the high, second floor balcony to a broken back on one of the seats below. His wife lies in this selfsame repose, her back broken, arms open, child being eaten alive while still screaming, the mother's dead eyes open in unseeing observation, as the snow white flock touches in slicing agony every one of the two thousand churchgoers with a spark of pain and terror, leaving fifteen hundred of them screaming for their lives being taken, as the rest scramble for what cover there is to be found in offices, bathrooms, closets and the like, while a few of them scramble bloody through the lobby and out into the driving rainstorm to their cars, where one of the charity queens sits in sobbing, breathless disbelief of her fate, with the clawing, screaming death of her fifteen year old daughter burned deep into her memory forever.

Jonathan Lovejoy

The Lesbian Mother

36

$\mathcal{L}$ightning strikes somewhere beyond the gray, rainsoaked horizon, reminding Julie Weinberg of nature's wrath impending. She drives on in big, burgundy SUV luxury, content to ride the Wealthen Stream from Chappaqua, to the campus where she has walked the halls in academic superiority these many years. Long, brunette hair pulled back and pinned up, glasses in place. Big curves loosely bound in cleavage showing blouses, unafraid to let the top button of the forest green fabric lay open.

Julie rides on. Unfearful of the news from the latest bird attack; some big church down in Virginia on Sunday. *New York and all the northern states are beyond it,* she tells herself, though she feels that somehow every place in the world touched by this migration will never be the same again. As if they have been warned. Alerted to what end of the world possibilities lie ahead.

But Julie rides on. Protected by the spirits that govern the flow of privilege, by those that create the boundaries of prosperity. The secret that she shares with her Ivy League daughter, the sacrifice of her youngest, the unneeded million dollar support from her bygone husband, they all pave the yellow brick road she travels upon, streets paved in the gold of this life, and the jewels that are scattered in the fields therein abouts.

Julie drives from her privileged home in Chappaqua, to her teaching campus an hour away. Lulled into complacency by her daughters' lives come and gone. Feeling as though she has earned this latest phonecall that came to her in the storm of yesterday morning.

"Hello, Julie."

"Yeah, Maggie, what's up?"

"Something big happening over here. Can you come in tomorrow? It's too important to discuss over the phone."

"Maggie, what is this b.s.? Why have I got to drive all the way to campus?"

"You're concerned with tenure here someday, aren't you?"

"Yeah?"

"Then I'll see you tomorrow morning. Ten o'clock?"

Tenure. What light through yonder window breaks! It is the east, and Lady Tenure is the sun! It is the academic lottery ticket. The literary light at the end of the tunnel. It is the reality beyond the years of desert mirages, the gateway to the promised land. And she knows that few in the halls of her pitiful little school have deserved it more, her acclaimed literary novel *The Lesbian Mother* notwithstanding. A book hailed for its *"groundbreaking glimpse at the behind closed doors reality of the modern mother-daughter dynamic,"* having taken every small literary award known to man. And to woman.

Julie Weinberg knows, has always known, that the road to tenure is paved with award winning publication, the road to greatness with tenure itself. Helped along by the exotic, Jew Girl face and strong nose, big lips and deep, dark eyes blinking hypnotically from behind the glasses she hides so bravely behind. A real life Diana Prince. Shorter. Hippier. Bustier than.

The road to local greatness is paved in gold bricked lust. And *that* created by the three B's of feminine irresistibility. Beauty. Breasts. Buttocks. With the fourth B, brains thrown in for good measure.

Julie Weinberg rides the cushion of luxury. Comfortable. Complacent. Confident. Understanding that many are called, and few are chosen. In the parking lot of East Lincoln College, Julie opens the door to burgundy SUV comfort. Stepping a tenured leg out into the rainstorm. Giddy with the rising of hope for the future, as a tickling at the center of her spirit. Fluttering her heart with the echoes of gratitude for life. A feeling of privilege unobtainable. A feeling that cannot be achieved. A feeling that must be predestined and bestowed by the mercy of Fate.

Julie Weinberg walks slowly. Cruising the pleasure of this ride through the end of struggle. Walking alone, across the summertime space of East Lincoln College. Protected underneath her umbrella from the droplets of this cold, summer rain. Unflinching underneath the distant flash of lightning, and the roar of rolling thunder. Down the finely crafted hallways. She glides. Enamored by the sound her shoes make in echo. Having pity for what few young souls that sit outside the classrooms and professor's offices, waiting in desperation. Locking her gaze to the face of the pretty young blonde, who dares sit in confidence of her beauty. Stepping firm in authority of who she is. Professor Weinberg. Refusing a proper greeting to the thin young chippie. Managing only a smile laced with resentment. With contempt.

Julie glides in regal repose. Long past the pretty blonde who sits in false hope. Finding the office of the dean of undergraduates. The large, luxurious academic space. The office of Magdalene St. John.

A bold, forceful knocking at the door. Done in the unspoken apprehension, that from either side of it, there is always so much to fear, from a fateful knocking at the door. At the far end of this knocking, at the twilight of fearful waiting, the door to her future is opened in statuesque, middle aged brunette prettiness not unlike her own. A beautiful woman, Maggie St. John. Black hair cropped short, lips painted deep red in feminine power. Eyebrows arched in former pageant queen perfection.

"Julie," she says, in shocked, enigmatic tone. As if surprised to see her.

Julie glides past the door to this hopeful future. Unaware of what lies beneath. Unaware of what looms over every new horizon.

In the office of Magdalene St. John, there sits a revelation. A shapely ghost from academic days past. A girl named Michelle Pope. Her lucky peach. The forbidden fruit of her years of hard labour. A ghost of Julie's forbidden past. Resurrected. Without a word. Nor an attempt at a fungalooga smile.

Julie Weinberg sits in the office of Maggie St. John. Staring at the secret from her past. Staring at the third part of the truth.

Which is cataclysm.

37

Excerpt from *The Lesbian Mother*, by Julie Weinberg:

Mt. St. Helens

I've felt it ever since I was a little girl. And I have kept it buried under pressure. But what happens when forces gather, when energy pressed down builds up, and is given no cause to vent? What happens when those forces reach critical mass, and the chain reaction that governs devastation must begin? It is a geyser, I suppose, or even a volcano, as testified by the tranquility exploded away at Mt. St. Helens.

And I already know that this is the beginning of the end of my so-called marriage, though the poor fool has done nothing to deserve what he is going to get. But the sound of his voice, the feel of his big, rough hands, the ugliness of his gray face shaven to death, the stink of his onion breath, the furry scratch of his hairy chest grown back in—the sight and sound of his masculinity makes me sick to my stomach...

38

Excerpt No. 2 from *The Lesbian Mother,* by Julie Weinberg:

The Curling Iron

I don't care whether or not my husband deserved my cruelty. I antagonized the poor son-of-a-bitch into rages he couldn't resist, until he was stupid enough to grab me by the arms and shove me against the refrigerator. But the bruise on my arm, the curling iron burn I accidently put on my own breast were enough to do the trick. It made the divorce so much easier. It made my alimony so much easier to get. I guess I was entitled to it anyway. For pushing his two daughters screaming into this condemned world. But I don't have to lay beside him anymore, and touch myself in the night when he snores, and fantasize about laying on top of that big breasted babysitter I hadn't seen in years, until I had to get my hands out of my underwear to keep myself from shaking like an epileptic.

And the spirit of this kind of thing has haunted me to sleep almost every night of my life, from since before I knew what a grown woman even looked like naked. So by the time I was married, who I was inside had matured into itself, until my husband learned what it meant to have blue balls, and he learned what it meant to have a frigid wife…

39

Excerpt No. 3 from *The Lesbian Mother,* by Julie Weinberg:

Lust for a Woman

And the thing that pisses me off the most, I think, is the hypocrisy. The determined, direct assault on the truth that they wear like a red dress in a white room, with the way they hug and kiss, the way they stare at each other's breasts and butts like horny teenage boys, the way they hide their lust in compliments like "oh, she's so pretty," and "her figure is so cute," when what they really want to say is "I want to strap on a cock and then put my dick up her ass..."

I know this, because it happens when I take my daughters shopping, and I am forced to endure the sea of teenage girls and their mothers walking through the mall unawares, walking in and out of the stores in beauty and big assed sensuality repressed and bound up—yes, even as a divorced woman, even as a mother of two daughters myself, I have felt the burning of this lust, which I can't really call perverted, because it is more natural to me than my husband's ridiculous cock ever was...

And now that my marriage is at least a year into my past, I am finally allowing myself to channel this power toward my sixteen year old daughter's life, antagonizing her with too many rules and regulations for her to handle, in grieving for her to explode at me in violence and profanity, so that I can strip her of every stitch of her clothing, and spank a blister onto the center of her white backside.

And this, I imagine for her and myself, because I want to bare her breasts, and see them swing low while she lays across my lap, then wrap my legs around hers, and spank her until it lights a fire inside my body...

And the way I feel has nothing to do with the cause of feminism, nor the history of women's rights anywhere in the world. The way I feel is simply what my body has burned into my spirit, or vice versa, which I know now that every time I walk down the street to my best friend's house, a divorced Asian woman hiding in the same pretense as I am—every time I visit her, I know that either in the kitchen, the couch in the living room, or in her pathetic little suburban garden out back, I know that I am going to cut her off mid sentence, by pressing my lips hard onto hers, until she understands that no man's lust for a woman can compete with that of another woman, the way that even the most violent tornado in history cannot compete with that of a category four hurricane...

40

Excerpt No. 4 from *The Lesbian Mother,* by Julie Weinberg:

Asian Eyes

My Asian friend is cursed with an hourglass figure that she despises. Which is ironic at best, being that the curse is seen as a blessing by every other human being except her. And this, I know, is because of the way she was raised, by a woman who barely spoke a word of English, who beat the Hell out of her at least once every few days her whole childhood, making her believe that "Fat Breasted Bitch" was her other name. I have spent this whole day with Priscilla, grooming myself to take this walk through the garden gate, to finally see what is in this secret garden I have been tormented in my soul so much about since I was little.

I have already decided that I can stand it no more. I can't bear the pretending, the sight of her breasts in the key of Beethoven, where Für Elise is in E minor desperation and tranquility. It happened when we got home to her house today from another day of wasting money at the mall, while I was content to leave my 17 and 15 year old daughters neglected all day. They don't really know where I am, and I don't really care. Neither one of them are sweet. Bitches, the two of them.

And maybe that's why I have been Priscilla's best friend these seven years. Because this Asian beauty's personality belies the look she bears. She bears the look of a suburban beauty bitch, with her husband's cock in one hand and his credit card in the other. But he was the stupid bastard who cheated on and left this exotic creature all by her lonesome, leaving her for a snow white volleyball blonde, all legs, arms and yellow ponytail bouncing. I don't know if Priscilla knows it or not, but in my heart I've been married to her since her stupid husband left her four years ago.

And this is the day when my love for her has finally crossed roads with pure lust, and have met in cataclysm in the pit of my stomach, down to my groin and somewhere past my womb into my soul and spirit. This happened today, when I caught the first time glimpse of this Jasmine Choi faced woman in her bra and underwear, leaned over the edge of her bed checking her bank balance on her laptop, her tiny underwear cloth hardly covering the smooth white hips, with two of the longest breasts I have ever seen, hung down like two giant bells from the bottom of her bra. A bra she had just changed into for house comfort, no doubt, and had not yet tucked the swinging torpedoes away.

Torpedoes, I'm obliged to call them. Because that is the effect they had on both my mind and my body when I saw them. I had stood there for the better part of a quarter of a minute, daring her to notice me, which she did not. Then I watched her stand up straight, tucking her breasts in and straightening her bra, where I was treated to the unusually long and inwardly curved torso, and hips widened to what I can only call infinity.

From this, I obey the spark that has skipped my heart aflutter, and I leave Priscilla to her privacy, walking back down the hall and down stairs to get into the rest of "The Good Mother" marathon we've been missing all day. And when she finally bounces down the stairs in her Asian eyed, silken black haired, ivory skinned perfection, smiling a glimpse at me in greater audacity than she realizes—as she turns the corner in small waisted, wide hipped blue jean splendor, E-cup breasts hopping and jiggling and wiggling under the tightest white t shirt she has ever worn (or maybe I just never noticed it before), as she walks toward her hunger kitchen, to gather up the slice of our supermarket sheet cake, I understand that this is the day the Lord hath made, for me to either shit or get off the pot. And this is the day he hath made for me, that makes me have to close my eyes while I sit on the sofa and wait for her, and take a deep breath to chase away the spirit of fear.

She offers me a slice of the white cake with white icing—truly the best kind of cake that exists, though the complexity-starved humanity refuses to let it be so. She walks over to our Lifetime sofa in epic simplicity, sitting down beside me in white T-shirt and dark blue jean repose, cake safely in hand, a huge corner slice cut and dug into. I watch her dig into the heavenly white, watching the sweet confection move in something like slow motion from the cake plate up to her full, ruby lips, her mouth opening and closing down onto the cake-heavy fork, sliding it clean out from her closed lips, closing her Asian eyes, wrinkling her Asian brow, grunting her Asian voice from her mother's homeland in no shame, as if she has just squatted in front of me on the toilet after a long held suppository. And I can see that there is nary a fake breath in it, knowing myself how impossibly good this cake is at the end of a day's hunger.

I make no secret that I intend to watch her eat half of this cake at least, smiling at her, trying to make her uncomfortable, making her understand that I am on the edge of saying 'damn this fucking movie,' and doing something to her she is prepared to neither resist nor understand. 'You fat breasted, Asian cunt' I want to say to her, followed by an evil slap of her cake munching face, to display my anger at her for ruining my life without knowing it, and fixing it so that from here to my grave, I know I'll never be normal again.

I lean back in comfort on the plush sofa, giving her a small enough reprieve for her to finish her cake, making sure I stare boldly at her when it happens, when she scoops the icing rich corner onto the fork and raises it in slow motion again to her mouth. 'Enjoy your last meal, baby...' these are the words sparked into my brain from somewhere, from somewhere outside my own will, from somewhere outside of 3D space, where phantoms of predestiny grieve and moan.

I allow her no time to breathe this last breath of freedom, as she turns back around from placing her cake plate on the dark wood end table, with its giant crystal lamp so carefully chosen. As she turns back to what is left of her day on this side of sanity, I meet her with a kiss pressed full to her cake sweetened lips, my eyes opened just long enough to see her eyes blared open in apocalyptic shock, that this is what Predestiny chose, to cause her last bite of tranquility to be choked in the back of her throat.

And this lip pressing is something just this side of a kiss, as I back up just enough to let her swallow what sweet confection that remains, and take a cake sweetened breath of shock through her lips parted. Whether or not the bewilderment on her face is laced with anger, I don't know, nor do I care. I only know that her attempt to speak must be cut off, done away with by my lips pressed against hers again, this time with my hand clamped around the back of her head, so that she cannot escape without descending into violence.

'Struggle then, sweetie,' are the words that find their way into my mind, as I slide closer to this

condemned woman, pushing my lips into hers with controlled fury, until my tongue finds its way past her lips, to tingle my body with the sweetened taste of hers coaxed out of hiding. And this rare and unique sensation upon my tongue, I know is a gift from God, which rings my ears from the trauma, and lights my breasts on fire. Whether or not she feels my body twitch, this, I do not know. I only know that her pleasure is not my concern at this moment, and the taste of her impending is as the taste of the cake confection she just devoured in hunger.

And I see the bewilderment in her face suddenly become touched by fear, as I push her down flat on her back, putting her legs up to lay her stretched out on the sofa. Sitting beside her, locking her in to this breast raping, to this predestined Nun's Intercourse that must happen. I stare at her breasts in the tight white shirt, to savor the moment, remembering the flash of her curvy hipped, long breasted privacy undisturbed upstairs, sliding her t-shirt out of her jeans without undoing them, fired on by the look of confused terror in her eyes. Rolling the tight, white T shirt up past the plain white bra, where her elongated cleavage mocks me to no end, to throw another splash of fuel on these fires of blue and black flame that burn.

Is it my mother, who made this of me when I was a girl? Is it the feel of my mother's lips at my breasts when I was nine, that ignited these fires within?

I move past her barrier of unbelief, her refusal to process that this is real and that I am committed, sliding my hand up to one side of the massive cleavage, pulling her breast up, up and over the top of her bra fabric, spilling the mountainous mound of magnificence free and clear, where the dark'ned areola is already shrunken to tell-tale arousal, to where the nipple is grown twice as big and as sensitive as what I know it would normally be.

But I wait. Allowing the water to build in my mouth. To swallow the sound of my hunger for her to hear. And in this moment I have felt since I was a little girl, I am helpless to control a muscle, as I lower my head to her breast, wrapping my lips around her nipple in starvation, sucking the nipple deep into my mouth, where nearly all of the areola is devoured, raising my head up without touching her breast yet with my hand, pulling her breast up as high as I can without losing my grip, so as not to lose a moment's power in the feeding, in the nursing of my soul's acclaim.

Migration

Upon her breast, I give suck, pressing her down on her back, leaning over in dominance, my eyes closed now, opening them again to grab hold of her breast with my hand, so that I can slide the sucking up and down, up and down, with nary a single pulling away, so that my jaws ache from the strain of this sucking. And my mind begins to haze into incoherence, as I feel both my breasts begin to twinge as never before, to wrinkle my brow in the trauma, my cheeks sunken deeply in this nursing pull upon her nipple, until what I have feared begins at my groin, to where I am made aware of the gushing into my pants, the soaking of my former life to oblivion, as the feeling at my womb flows upward to those at both my breasts together.

I am unable to release the sucking even once, holding on to anchor my body against the trauma at ground zero, which explodes a blast wave into my spirit somewhere beyond orgasm, reverberating from the center of my flesh outward, to bring a low, ghostly moan up through my nose, trembled by the shaking that begins to quiver my body from the top of my head to the soles of my feet.

And this trembling, this apocalyptic shaking trauma in my body has its Vesuvian effect on her, causing her to speak the name of Salvation and Redemption with authority, followed by a high pitched earsplitting siren, announcing the death of the both of us, and the precursor to the endtime trump of God, sounded over the landscape of every condemned soul, across the face of twilight and humanity...

41

Excerpt No. 5 from *The Lesbian Mother,* by Julie Weinberg:

The Well of Tears

Of the trouble my seventeen year old daughter is in, she does not know. Echoes of 'The Good Mother' marathon still burn the theater of my mind, especially the newest Munchausen by proxy entry, where the blonde beauty nurse sends sweet, suburban sickness and death to her daughter.

She told me to 'fuck off.' This, she screamed at me last night, as I provoked and antagonized her over her texting and phone calls, and the high cost of it on the monthly bill. We can afford it, to be sure, as my own mother's fortune flows freely from the top of the perverted tree. It is her poor father who is out in the cold, struggling in second rate, lower white collar mediocrity in some corporate office somewhere, with nothing of the seven figure splendor he enjoyed with me.

And of his middle class mediocrity, I speak, as I press this bubble hipped beauty of mine the next morning, the Saturday morning, up against the pre-breakfast counter when she is still in her morning gym pants and tight sports bra in their tragic D minor key.

"Leave me alone, I said I was sorry!" she yells at me. Attempting to push past me into the safety of the spacious kitchen, the safety of her fifteen year old sister's view. Of the feeling her younger sister braves while watching us, this, she does not know.

"Do you want to spend your senior year living with your father?"

No answer.

"Do not make me ask you again..."

"I said... NO!" she yells. Unafraid to stare at me at this close range. Unable to traverse the

barrier raised by money and privilege, and even the pressure of her mother, and her mother's beautiful Asian friend.

"Then go upstairs and wait for your punishment. Now."

"I can't... unless... you... MOVE!"

This, she yells fearlessly at me again. And so, so reluctantly, I move aside from my place in front of this dirty blonded Brittany, watching her switch these 17 year-old bubble hips past her 15 year-old sister Karen, who is beautiful enough to be a deadly threat in her future. Past the younger bitch Karen I walk, enduring from her "Mom, why don't' you just leave her alone?"

And upon this opportunity, I spin. Whirling around like a mannequin on a theme park pedestal, bringing my hand across her face in the hardest slap ever delivered woman to woman. From this stumbling to the side, the girl emerges, holding her face, already in teary eyed confusion, running past me up the stairs to her bedroom. Slamming the door in rage and defeat.

And just as I had felt when my friend Priscilla blew the endtime trump to our suburban paradise, I feel these selfsame spirits aching me at my groin, to whisper power and possibility to my mind, gliding me up the stairs to my finely décored Queen's Chamber, to my exquisitely decorated upper room, to gather from my closet the punishment phallus of legend. 'Strip your clothes,' I hear a voice say to me, causing me to slip out of my robe, long t shirt and sweat pants underneath, to expose the fullness of this motherline nudity to myself.

Of this long, thin member predestiny hath wrought, I engage up my legs and about my hips, pulling the straps tight, amazed again, as I always am, at the level of feeling it imparts to my groin. I have to resist the urge to stand at the mirror, and stroke it as if I were trying to start a fire, while staring at my D cups too high and rounded for my own taste, staring at the firm, cone shaped things in fascination as I plateau, unable to look away from them as my vision hazes...

I turn from the cone shaped things I wish were as low and bulbous as my Asian doll's, walking in full, broad hipped nudity across the hall to the master bathroom.

"You may as well unlock this door," I say. "Cause you already know I can get in..."

This, she does. With an angry little unclicking of the lock. I open the door in full breasted nudity, enjoying the look of disbelief clouded by disillusionment on her face. Closing the door calmly behind me.

"I said I was SORRY," she says again.

"No," I say. "Your exact words to me were 'fuck off.' Well, you know what? I intend to."

"Mom, what are you..."

"Shut...your mouth. And strip your clothes."

I watch her strip bare, doing so in red faced frustration, as if she knows she is being watched by the grieving spirits that stare.

"Put your hands on that counter," I say. Calmly gathering a handful of soft soap, rubbing it from the top of my perversion to the bottom. Enjoying the look of despair that colors her expression.

"This, you'll remember," I say. Holding the tip of it at her rectum. "The next time you get the urge to tell me to...FUCK OFF."

And upon this, I push past the barrier. Loving every ounce of strength she pushes with. Squeezes with. Tenses her body up with to try and stop it from going inside. But as though it is a part of myself, I feel it push past the barrier, evidenced by my daughter's howling, angry scream into the bathroom. And I need give no thrust, as I gently, smoothly slide the phallus deep inside her bottom, amazed at the force of her loud yelling, as the barrier of her angry resistance threatens to fall.

"Momma I'm sorry. I swear to God I won't say it again I swear to God..."

And upon this, I look down to see the last inch that begs to be crossed, and I give my daughter this thrust of a mother's will. To dominate. To disillusion. To destroy.

I stand there. Listening to her loud sobbing. Unable to keep it from phasing past the façade of this discipline. To cause the ignition in my groin behind this member strapped on, until I know that I must obey the voice inside that says 'grab your daughter's breasts...'

And this, I do in obedience as she sobs pitifully, this seventeen year old bubble hipped beauty, who intersperses her sobbing with such a loud cry of pain as I can easily bear. But it is not the noise of it I resist, but the feeling the noise brings into my body down below, until I can only shake my head 'no' and lower it in defeat, as the trembling starts at my hips, spreading to both my legs as I moan deeply, enduring the wave of quivering that moves from my hips all the way up to where my hands lay clamped at both breasts in full.

In the aftermath of this trauma, we stand there. Both a prisoner of the Well of Tears, and the endless flow of them from the reservoir of sorrow from the mind of Eve passed down. East of the Garden of Antiquity. West of the fields of Armageddon.

42

Excerpt No. 6 from *The Lesbian Mother,* by Julie Weinberg:

The Face of an Angel

My mother kept it bound up in church dignity. The biggest fucking hypocrite in town. I know for a fact that the word 'Frigidaire' had to be tattooed somewhere on her back, because except for what conceived me and my little sister, I *am certain she never let my father anywhere NEAR that burning bush of hers. We read about these bitches, we see them in the rare movie that's worth watching, and we think that it's not real. But my pencil can't stop writing this because I am a living testimony to the fact. My churchgoing mother was a fucking pervert, who did everything she did to me in the name of some kind of twisted discipline, and never justified a single one of her many orgasms with anything other than a kiss on the cheek or the forehead. And each and every one of them was preceded by some kind of intense pain in my body.*

But that's not the real reason this is my last journal entry. It's not the only reason that I can't stay. I thought that I had found a way to deal with the pain. To deal with it by passing it along to my daughters. But fate has a way of hiding the truth, until destiny is revealed. The truth is that while I thought I was saving a life, I was actually taking it. But I might as well remember the first time it happened, before I go. Maybe, I can find a way to forgive her if I do.

All I was doing was playing a game with my little sister. A game my best friend's older sister called 'soft serve' when she showed me. Nothing that a nine year old girl would even understand as sexual.

Migration

My mother caught my seven year old sister and me in the bathroom playing this game. I simply filled my mouth with vanilla ice cream, and pushed the half melted product out through puckered lips. Like a human soft serve machine. And as predestiny would have it, my mother comes into the bathroom, not when I was using the sink to catch the soft ice cream. No. My mother opens the bathroom door that late afternoon in summer when I was nine, and catches me pushing the soft ice cream out, with my seven year old sister holding her hands behind her back, with her tongue stuck way out, to catch the ice cream in her mouth as it falls.

When I think of it now, I wonder of what psychosexual origins there were, when my friend's twelve year old sister did it to me. I can remember catching the vanilla ice cream on my tongue, feeling a spark flash through my tongue and down to my bowels and groin. And when my friend's sister touched her tongue to mine, and then fellatioed my tongue 'like a popsicle,' she said. I can remember feeling like I wanted to piss my pants. And I didn't know why. All I know is that my heart fluttered from it, and the twelve year old girl's eyes were closed, and she had the face of an angel when she did it.

And this is the memory I had that day, when I let the ice cream fall into my little sister Anna's mouth. Not understanding that the feeling in my body was an awakening, where the flames that burn in alabaster blue doth begin.

My mother walks in on this little prepubescent tragedy, even before I had unleashed the 'popsicle' on Anna, even before I truly understood the nature of arousal, its causes and effects.

"You nasty little strumpet," she says. Pulling me by one of the long, brunette braids, slapping my little sister across the mouth and telling her to go to her room.

"Who taught you this?"

"Kelly's sister Robin did it to us. It's just a little ice cream game, Mom."

"Then why were you doin' it in the bathroom?"

"I don't know...I was using...I mean, I was..."

The next moment is that fearful calm. The calm of uneasy acceptance I've heard about, when the abuser settles down in her spirit, and accepts the inevitable.

My ear feels as though it may be pulled off as she escorts me to her bedroom. Locking the door behind us.

"Take off all your clothes," she says. Not even looking at me as she unzips her southern flower

made dress. Sliding it down from her slip. Then her slip from the bra and panty hose. Then the panty hose from the big, white cotton underwear. As to what feeling I feel in my soul, when she removes her bra, this, I do not know. As to what feeling that torments me as I watch her bend over, sliding her underwear away... this, I do not know.

The glow of the setting sun imbues our world with amber, as the earth turns toward the evening day. Mother stands before me in full hipped nudity, a sight I have never seen nor yet imagined on her, but understanding that the extreme girth of her backside, the cinched, fleshy curve of her waist, and the bulbous, bell shaped hang of her breasts is something I will never forget. I remember every dimple, every scar, the thighs that spread the width of her hips from extraordinary to extreme. Without being the slightest bit overweight, she is truly one of the assiest women on God's earth, I assume. Every hip lover's dream incarnate, hidden underneath the loose church dresses in summer, and the long coats in winter. With no one believing or understanding how such a thing could be possible on a woman of normal size. I watch this ass queen, Our Lady of the Hips walk naked over to me, holding the pantyhose stockings, turning me around roughly, tying them behind my naked back.

She sits heavily on the edge of the bed, her sitting hips spread out to goddess width and beauty. She pulls me close to her, sliding forward so that her breasts are mashed against my stomach as I stand in front her.

"You were playing a nasty game in the bathroom with your sister, weren't you?"

And I know that lies or excuses are only fuel for what fires that burn. And so, in keeping with what predestiny hath wrought, I tuck my pathetic lips, and nod my pathetic head.

The beauty of my mother's face is hidden. Hidden in no makeup, hidden by the years of self delusion and denial. There is no smile. No room for a wink and a nod to this. No strength to allow this to happen without the pretense of punishment to protect her sanity. Hypocrisy is my mother's life. Pretense is the air she breathes.

"This is so you'll remember," she says. "Not to play nasty little games with your sister."

And upon this, I feel the flat of her tongue in spit, rubbed across the front of both my breasts, which are only two nipples raised in prepubescent tragedy. As to the feeling that floods my heart and soul, as to the color of the new fire that burns—this I do not know. I only know that every ice cream licking of her tongue across my flattened breasts raises me to a higher height.

And suddenly, what pleasure I feel is touched by pain, as she pulls one of my nipples in her mouth. And she sucks it with extreme force and power, so that it feels as though I am being stung by an angry wasp, a sting which does not stop, until I am unable to stop myself from squealing in pain. This, she does to both my breasts without ceasing, pulling the mouthful of flesh there is into her mouth, sucking until they are raw, red and bruised from the effort.

And with my hands still tied, she wraps her bare legs around me tighter, keeping her mouth clamped in deep sucking to my tiny breasts, until I feel a tremble in her body, a tremble that grows into a quiver, a wave of quaking that does not cease, followed by a strong, animalistic bellowing from deep inside her, muffled by her lips still locked to my breasts in punishment form.

If people knew that this happened to me, would they have mercy for me then? Would the courts take my seventeen year old and my fifteen year old daughters away, if they knew what I had been born and raised in? Yes, I was going to do it. I was going to use their minds, their bodies as an emotional dumping ground, to corrupt their young spirits with the darkness I inherited. The darkness I knew from when I was nine. Would the world have mercy for me then? Would they forgive me, for what my 15 year old daughter recorded on her cell phone, of me standing at the locked bathroom door naked, with a strap-on phallus hung down? Would the world forgive me then, for what they saw on my daughter's endtime answer, as to why mankind is doomed? Can they forgive me, for the sounds they heard on the video, of my seventeen year old daughter screaming for mercy behind a locked bathroom door?

I feel an angel tap me on the shoulder, and I know now that I must go. But this is not the blood and chaos of gunpowder through my head. This is the peaceful poison of pills crushed to powder, and the tranquility of a sweet and blood red glass of wine.

Julie Weinberg, PhD
Women's Studies, Psychology
Yale University

Manifest Destiny

This storm of latter day discontent blows over the Oklahoma prairie, to drown me in a rolling sea of melancholy and regret. Any hopes I may have had at happiness, any thoughts and delusions of normalcy have dissolved in these neverending torrents of wind and rain, until I have no choice but to stop running from and fighting this gloomy, oppressive mood. In my full length waterproof rain cloak the color of the black fires tinted blue in my condemned soul, I sit on the porch in reclining repose, blonde hair in contrast to the black cloak I wear to protect me from the gusts of wind and mist formed against me.

I wonder what words there are to describe in depth what it is I feel, and what earthly implications there are for what I have done. I remember that no matter how many times I would have had it to do over again, I would still have done it, whether or not there were variations on the theme. This, the theme of child abuse, of mother-daughter molestation, the sound of which causes me to close my eyes and take a deep breath in this Oklahoma storm. I feel as though a barrier has been crossed, as if a forbidden borderline has been breached, that fills me with the pain of cold worry, and the burning heat of frustration and regret.

And these swirl inside me to create the perfect storm of apprehension in my spirit, that rises and falls with the storm that blows over the prairie green. And I endure at this very moment, the rise of this feeling in both my body and soul, marked by a river of lightning in the distance, and a crackling of thunder from earth to the floor of heaven. And this is suddenly accompanied by the distant sense of another presence nearby, causing me to turn suddenly toward the screen door, which I did not hear creak open in the aftershock of rolling thunder, to give credence to the theory that yes, a person can *definitely* have the feeling that she is being watched.

With the so-called storm door held open just a bit, just enough so I can see, my mother stands still in her country flower made dress, her face colored every bit the half Indian she is, gazing at me in the satisfaction of knowing, and the sinister pride of her epic, end of the world goal accomplished. In a cold, misty gust of wind blown at us from the prairie, neither of us can back down from this enigmatic stare, until I am burdened by this bewilderment, in a forced surrender from the dominating control I see.

And soon, this spell of bondage and domination is broken by the sound of my daughter's voice, calling *"Grandma Katherine,"* back to their apocalyptic movie on television. I study the unflinching, uncompromising look in her eyes, watching the somber, determined look on her features soften, followed by a pleasantness gathered and pushed forth...

"I'm coming, baby..."

Afterwards, I see the look on her face evolve into the self pleased, satisfaction of easy victory, the knowledge of manifest destiny at the end of the age, and the promise of forbidden fruit preordained. I watch this beautiful woman glide away as though adrift, holding her gaze to me until she is completely out of sight.

What was that all about, accompanies my sigh and rolling eyes in my mind, as I return to my view of windblown grassland, and the forest groves blowing wildly in the storm. *Sinister,* is the word sparked into my brain from the next bolt of lightning in the distance. And I am not exactly sure in what way, beyond the perversion she has passed down from her own mother to me, and down to my little Pocahontas doll. I know that in her own way, she loves us both—especially her granddaughter, whom I know she feels the burden of her behind-closed-doors calling for.

What warnings are there that flash and rumble in the storm, that go beyond what I am willing to believe or understand? Why can't I just take my daughter by the hand, and steal her safely away in the night? To drive us back northward through the looming bird kingdom, beyond their gateway to eschatology? Part of me wishes that my daughter and I had never come here, that we were safe back in the halls of privilege in Chappaqua, where the blue cloth linen still blows in futility in the northern wind and rain. I no longer have the strength to care about that house, nor the ridiculous job in a law firm that goes with it, understanding that for any earthly paradise, there is a price that must be paid.

I can rest my weary soul here on my mother's farm for as long as I need to do so, but at what cost? Is it one that I have already dearly paid, having given the flesh of innocence to her to be burned in blue and black fire? Am I so tragically out of sorts, so world weary in my soul, that I am truly a prisoner of her perverted desires, letting her do what she did to my daughter, then letting her make me do it just the same?

It is a feeling that I know I'll never forget for the rest of my life. A so-called double orgasm, that seemed to come from somewhere beyond my mind and body. As if to assure me that yes, it is a private, perverted life's calling that I was destined to meet, and could not have avoided if I had tried. How many years would have gone by anyway, before I was hugging her naked in the bathroom, or kissing her deeply in the shower? Or are these just hopeless echoes of the perversions that I have been privy too in real world confession, by the lustful mothers I know in Chappaqua?

These are the secrets of the privileged mothers and daughters I know. Twenty one-year-old, college juniors home from their private school havens, deep kissing their own mothers behind the locked door of a bathroom, with the shower running on full blast to mask the noise of the mother's quiet, desperate moaning. I can't pretend that I was never haunted by this, though I never believed in my heart that it would ever happen.

As I continue to listen to the booming thunder, and the infinity of rainfall from the clouds, I am assured that yes, the tragedy of human existence is Fate. What is the mind of Eve, passed down to the three of us east of Eden?

My mind is burdened by the weight of generations. By the North Carolina Cherokee woman who was my grandmother, who dispensed the rod and lash of pain to my mother without pretense, simply because it was something she needed to do, until my mother was broken down to nothing by the age of sixteen, where she would be grabbed out of bed in the middle of the night and beaten by her Indian mother in the nude, screaming to her mother *why, Momma, why?* And this beating in the wee hours would continue until the Indian woman was satisfied, until revenge from her tumultuous childhood had been elicited, until the beatings she received from her mother, her aunts and older sisters had been avenged on my mother's accursed flesh.

But whippings had been my grandmother Pia's stock and trade since my mother was two years old. So by the time my mother was thirteen, she was already a veteran of these belt whippings, which had progressed to the two of them in the nude, where Pia's J-cupped Olympians flopped and swung for my thirteen year old mother to see. And these whippings were dispensed in controlled rage, in stored energy from her Cherokee upbringing, until my mother's body began to bear light scars and dark lines where welts and abrasions had healed.

And yet, it seemed that my mother's stubbornness, her refusal to break persisted until she was sixteen years old, when grandmother Pia decided that it was time for a progression to the next level. This, when my sixteen year old mother had somehow believed that she was stronger than my giant breasted grandmother, and took it upon herself to try and fight her before another belt whipping.

I flinch from the power of lightning energy in the clouds, as Pia Rose Hardwick flashes the theater of my mind, and the day she made my mother understand truly, that to be born is to be cursed.

And to live is to suffer.

The Fires of Sadism

This is the pain of Pia Rose Hardwick, as it burdens the heart and mind. Mother of Katherine Rose, my mother, over the horizon of her sixteenth year. Katherine Rose, who would grow up to become the elegantly beautiful Katherine Hardwick, destined like her mother, to be the wife of a rich horse rancher. A rich horse rancher turned adulterer. I see the pain of Pia and her daughter Katherine, when the threat of another powerful belt whipping ensues. This, after the departure of Pia's husband Joe Hardwick by way of the grave. By way of an unbroken horse, and a broken rib pushed into his lung. A fortune eaten away by debt. Leaving the Indian Pia and her daughter to writhe in the pain of poverty and loss.

In the agony of this life's defeat, I see this mother and daughter when their expression of pain must come to a head, and break through the bonds of restraint. This, the sixteen year old Katherine. The busty, half Indian Carolina girl who thinks she is done. Who thinks she has graduated from her mother's constant belt whippings. Who thinks she can somehow be free. These two light up the theater of my mind, over the field of thunder and rain.

In this expression of pain unleashed, I see the daughter who would become my mother. Daughter of Storm in the Ocean. I see the daughter grab her mother's belt, and try to wrench it from her mother's hand. Unsuccessfully doing so, until the two naked women are on the floor of the daughter's bedroom in the classic behind closed doors fight, where the mother has released all of her life's pain upon the hopeless sixteen year old, holding her down on her back, even through the pain of a breast bitten down upon. The mother holds her position on top of her insolent, violently aggressive daughter, who has had her ears rung by the taste of blood, and the feel of it in her mouth and at the tickling edge of her throat.

The mother uses all of her Indian-momma strength to hold and pummel her daughter's audacity, punching the naked girl in the head and in the ribs, unable to cause the girl to release the painful bite. And so, in keeping with the agony of what must be, she buries her teeth into the daughter's shoulder, until the girl is forced to shriek and let go this brutal bite.

From this new advantage, the mother straddles her daughter heavily, breathing deeply in the midst of this trauma, the spot of blood marking her daughter's audacity at the top of her breasts, taking hold of her daughter's hair, pinning it to the floor…

Holding her daughter's hair to the floor, the mother slams her fists repeatedly to her daughter's face, until Katherine must struggle to get her arms up to protect herself from what further bruises and blood there must be.

But the heavy breasted mother holds her position, pinning herself on top of the girl, pressing her J-cupped Vesuvians hard to the side of the girl's face, making it harder for her to breathe than it already is from the struggle.

And now, Pia says, *it's gon' be worse than it was before. I'm gon' tie you up in the barn, and I'm gon' beat you to an inch of your life…*

After another long several minutes, after many deep, long breaths taken in recovery. The mother stands naked to her feet. Pulling the long haired, 16 year old beauty jiggling up to her feet. Not bothering to make eye contact with the double G cupped breast prodigy, whose beauty far exceeds even the mother's own. In bitterness and motherline resentment born and bred, the woman takes the girl by the hair and by the ear, escorting the angry, teary eyed loser out onto the afternoon porch, both of them as naked as the day they were born.

The Carolina woods bear witness to tragedy. To the modern mother-daughter dynamic hidden from the outside world. The summer breeze blows this warning through the hidden trees, somewhere in the heart of the Appalachians, where the two of them are free to live whatever it is fate hath decreed for them. This is the crossing over. The point of reckoning along the timeline, where the mind of Eve hath settled at its place at the end of the age, in the minds of this mother and her daughter.

Pia Hardwick escorts her busty, jiggling daughter across the hidden, grassy lawn to the small storage barn, where there is just enough space for them to exact the beginning of sorrows. And there is a length of old, dirty rope so conveniently wrought nearby, as though it had been placed there, as though waiting for when the doorway to this future should be opened.

The strong, Amazonian mother ties her daughter by the neck to the post at the center of the shed, then ties her hands tightly behind her back.

I didn't do anything, she says. *I don't deserve this. I only yelled at you because you were hitting me.*

You deserve what I SAY you deserve. And as long as you're my daughter, you will have the BLOOD striped out of you when I say you will...

And upon this, the daughter watches her breasty, full hipped mother turn and walk quickly, forcefully out of the shed, hurrying in her full glory back to her house, where the simplicity of the black leather belt, and two very large safety pins wait to be gathered.

This angry woman walks in the nude back from her bedroom, down the hallway, through the livingroom and out the front door, unable to hear what warning breeze blows the summer leaves through the forests of this western Carolina tranquility. Pondering by what spirit tickles and tingles her body down and far away below.

$\mathcal{U}$pon the breathless thrill of this ultimate conquest, of her daughter's hope and reason, the Indian mother glides the current of this feeling bestowed. Understanding that this day between them is a long time in the making, and every beating, every punishment has been a prelude, a precursor to what has been preordained, to the punishment that must happen between them today.

In the spirit of what was passed down from generations. By the power vested in her by the blood drawn from her days and years. The Indian poverty mother walks in the preordained footsteps laid, across the grassy lawn to the tiny storage shed, no bigger than the space of the small bedroom in their home. She opens the door to this predestiny, feeling the twinge flash straight to her groin when she sees the flop breasted young girl tied up by the neck, with tears streaming down her face in hopeless defeat. What spirits of Sadism there are to be risen, these come to life in the mother's heavy breasts exposed, to burden her expression with the somber nature of this calling, where she can already imagine the sound of these new screams unfettered, drifting into the southern forest countryside nearby.

She lays the belt, and the two safety pins carefully on the tool table nearby, shocked to a pissing twinge in her groin when she hears her daughter begin the quiet wailing, and the pleading, begging moans of apology, choked by her new struggle against the rope around her neck. The sound of this tragic wailing, the pre-weeping cry made by her insolent daughter strikes a fire inside, burning between her legs as she bends over, tying another small length of rope around the jiggle of her daughter's thighs. Standing up straight and tall. With no pretense toward tenderness or compassion.

In the spirit of the inevitable. In the tragedy of human existence. She takes a clinical, nonchalant hold of both her daughter's breasts, and twists them in the fires of sadism, in the burning heat where mercy is consumed, and where the ashes of compassion are formed and left to die in the cold.

Pia Rose Hardwick twists her daughter's breasts in a grimace of strength unleashed, as though trying to literally twist them off, to see what manner of pain can be brought forth at just the first level of three part agony unleashed. And already, she sees in her daughter's face, in her eyes a level of surrender and pleading, a level of fear and resistance beyond what the 'normal whippings' have brought. These have been the belt whippings of legend. The classic branding of the flesh to welts and bleeding with the hard leather belt, with the upper arm or the wrist grabbed, and the belt brought down upon the daughter's thighs and buttocks in pain and jiggling, in the company of screams of rage and resistance more than pain, and battle cries of defiance born from a soul of bitterness and contempt.

In the company of this new, screaming rage born, Pia Hardwick releases her daughter's nipples in the requisite hard, biting pull. Turning in the wake of this satisfaction to gather the black leather serpentine laid in waiting.

"Momma, I said I was SORRY!" Katherine says. The big, strong legged half Indian beauty yells in disrespect, as her mother takes up the hard leather belt, holding the end of it out unfolded, bringing it down in a flash on her daughter's breast above the nipple, then bringing it down hard on the nipple itself, to see her daughter react with a new and powerful energy, the energy of a thousand wasps stung at the front of her breasts, and flashed as a bolt of pure pain to the rest of her body.

On these flashes of heat, on the strings of burning red fire laid bare, the daughter learns a new meaning for the word pain, and the reference of it as the given name to behind closed doors discipline. The mother whips her daughter's breasts in steady rhythm, undeterred by the striping of her daughter's white skin to blood. Bringing the belt down in horse whipped fashion on this key played in G major, on this overture to their future played in secret. The last bloody welt is created on the first one, until the mother can only stand by in exhaustion, but not in admiration, of her daughter's breasts striped in angry red welts, and the pain of a trickle of blood that hath appeared in burning blue and black fire.

Pia stands there. Holding the belt nearby the buckle, the rest of it hung long and leisurely to the floor, studying the look of pain and tears in her daughter's face, and the look of defeat brought by fire and exhaustion. She turns to the table, tossing the black leather belt unceremoniously on top, her own body racked with a new pain. This, the pain of a plateau unconquered, the buildup of a lifetime of repressed lust unreleased. In the fires that burn the color of nighttime tinted blue, her hands move down to the first of the double passion that must be, to begin the third leg of her daughter's journey to oblivion.

In a power come from she knows not where. In an energy born from somewhere in time. The mother's hands move to the first big safety pin. This, to the music of her daughter's exhausted whining. The melody of a quiet siren formed in pleading. But this, to no avail, as the mother opens the big safety pin in quiet determination. Taking hold of her daughter's nipple firmly, pulling it forward. Placing the top of this metallic fire underneath, shoving the pin quickly into her daughter's flesh, this, to the sound of a woman's scream born anew. This, to the sound of a death scream.

The mother latches the pin with as much speed and strength as she has left. Taking up the other pin. Letting the daughter's screaming *no's* caress her inside. Letting them touch her inner self with a tingling from her soul and spirit. The mother pulls her daughter's other nipple far forward, pushing the pin up into the flesh. Hearing, feeling the second death scream vibrate at the center of her body down below. Understanding what pleasures there are to be wrought from pain. Pushing the pin through, latching it closed. Pushing her face to her daughter's cheek to cheek. Feeling the cool tingle of the pins at her own nipples. Perceiving the warm flow of life created from them. Imagining the drip, drip, dripping of this reckoning in red, to contrast the beauty of her daughter's tanned, fair skin.

The mother is unable to stop her own hands from rising up to her daughter's hair. To the long, silken black mane of glory fallen about her shoulders and the length of her back. Taking firm grip of her daughter's hair. Pressing herself against the front of her daughter without moving a muscle.

Without as much as a squeeze of the hips. Knowing that part of her is about to die. Feeling the approach of cataclysm. The third part of the truth.

As a match struck and lit wildly in the dark. As a flame touched to a reservoir of liquid fuel in waiting. The mother is powerless to stop the spark of this blast wave that slowly appears. Struggling to hold her voice in check. But hearing the energy push its way up into her body through her breath, opening her mouth with no effort of her own, so that the siren of this explosion may vent its way forth, until she hears herself wail the call of the motheress into the small space around them, taking a breath from it, then releasing a second and louder cry in weeping, as the rest of a lifetime of repressed energy explodes into every corner of her body. From this burst of energy released inside, she endures the quaking, the quivering of her hips and her thighs, passed upward to where her breasts lay pushed against her daughter's, enduring the Armageddon Quake, the shaking of her body from her shoulders to her feet.

In the wake of this teary eyed release come and gone. In the aftermath of this wailing siren and weeping passed into the countryside. The mother holds her daughter by the hair with both hands. Staring her in the eyes. From the place where pretense has gone to die. Where the knowledge of the forbidden is born. Where the proverbial box is opened, and the spirits of Pandora are released into the world around them.

In the summer winds of this reality. On the eve of the Second Coming. The mother lays her lips upon her daughter's. Kissing. Breathing herself back to sanity. Breathing a breath of resurrection.

A breath of life.

Julie Weinberg Rides the Wind

*J*ulie Weinberg rides the wind. On the eve of eschatology.

Standing in the swirling wind and rain. Her gaze affixed upon her daughter's grave. Understanding the end of days. Knowing when barriers are breached. Comprehending when end of the world devastation has come and gone. She remembers her time in the office of Magdalene St. John. When the third part of the truth revealed itself in cataclysm.

Julie Weinberg rides the wind. On the eve of eschatology.

Remembering the sound of her own voice in trembling. The sound of desperation, of annihilation born anew.

"Maggie, tell me you're not believing a single word that horny little TWIT told you. How the fuck can you stand there, with my work record, with my academic achievements and..."

"I'm not saying I believe her yet, Julie. But I'm saying that the fact that she even brought it up means..."

"Means what? That I locked the door? That I tried my best to spank a bruise onto her little fat ass? Huh? That I tried my best to get milk out of her big ass titties when nobody was looking? Is that what you want to hear? That behind closed doors I fucked a student in my office? You want me to suddenly become the psychological scapegoat for what these fucking men have been doing to these girls in their offices for a hundred years at this goddamn school? Well you can forget it Maggie because I'm denying every word that bubble breasted little CUNT says."

"She says you traded sex with her for good grades on all her papers. And when she didn't show up before the Christmas break, you gave her a D+ on a paper that was, literally, no worse than all the B+ papers she had been doing all semester."

"I had been lenient with her all semester and grading her on an incentive curve, hoping she would get better by the final exam, and she didn't."

"Julie do you expect me to believe that? I've read the papers myself. They're all mediocre at best, including the one you gave her a D on. All of her papers were graded too high and the last one was graded too low. A straight A student wound up with a C in the class because of this. What did you think was going to happen?"

Julie Weinberg rides the wind. In the rain at her daughter's grave. In memory of her own lust unbridled. In memory of her office victim at the edge of Thanksgiving cold. When the heavy hipped, long breasted girl was made to stand at Julie's desk bent over, her hands resting flat, her breasts hung long above it. Julie remembers the feeling in her own body, when she was forced to wield the extension of herself strapped on. When she pushed lotion into the girl's bottom with her finger. Julie remembers the tensing of the girl's body. The drawing in of her breath through her teeth.

Relax your bottom, Julie says, in the heart of this end of the world memory. Having commandeered this future blonde soccer mom. Having robbed her of what little innocence she had left in this life. Having taught the girl that there are *none* righteous, no, not one. That no one can be trusted to maintain morality. That the mask of hypocrisy covers a multitude of sins.

Julie Weinberg rides the wind. In the heart of this latter day memory. Hearing the voice of someone she thought she could trust. Someone she thought understood her.

"Maggie, I've won more literary awards than every other teacher in this whole goddamned school put together. I have TWO PhD's and an undergraduate Magna from VASSAR. You can't tell me that fat breasted little bitch has ANY power over that."

"And its exactly that... that's part of the problem. Everybody knows the depth of what you wrote in that controversial book. Things that frankly I would be afraid to mention out loud unless I were locked behind a closed door in the privacy of my own home."

"So this is it"... Julie says. *"This is what you're going to use to finally get rid of me isn't it? You've been jealous of me since my book became famous and yours was rejected by EVERYBODY..."*

"Frankly, Julie, that comment was so typical its pathetic. And I think its beneath both of us."

"Don't try to deny it Maggie, you and everybody else in this whole fucking school have been conspiring to get rid of me since I made the lists

for the two biggest literary awards in the world, for a book the critics DESPISE... I have felt it every since then... if you gave a damn about me, if you had even a SHRED of integrity..."

"Integrity? You low grade a student who's papers obviously never should have been graded so high in the first place, and you talk to me about integrity?

"I was trying to help that brainless twit maintain her GPA, could I help it if her last paper was so bad I couldn't in good conscience give her any more leeway? She did NOT deserve an A in my class so I gave her a C+. What is the big fucking deal?"

"The big 'fucking' deal, Julie, is that she claims you did exactly THAT to her seven times in your office back in the fall semester..."

"Seven... what..."

"That's right, Julie. And here's the kicker. Otherwise I probably wouldn't even have brought you in here today. Her and her LAWYERS... yes, her lawyers...showed me something. Something that legally I'm not even allowed to mention."

The types of fear are many, indeed. And uniquely distinguished.

"A cheap little camera pen. Laid on her book bag on the chair in the corner. She knew no one would believe her. So she made sure that if she ever had a story to tell, they would believe it."

Julie Weinberg rides the wind. In the wake of devastation come and gone. Mouth open. Unable to breathe.

"That's right. And I don't have to tell you what I saw."

The image of the girl moving this chair conspicuously to the corner. The image of the girl's clothes being draped upon it. The image of the academic looking felt tip. Pointed at her in the heart of memory. Like a pistol.

"The girl didn't ask for your resignation," Magdalene says. *"Although she most certainly should have."*

"You're going to stand there and judge me? After the conversations we've had in this very office? The things you've told me you wanted to do to these little bubble hipped, bubble headed, bubble breasted bimbos, every one of 'em here on Momma's honey and Daddy's money? Want to hear what pathetic is, Maggie? Self righteous hypocrisy."

"My job is to protect this school."

"No, your job is to keep kissing Lucy Albright's ass..."

"What?"

"You have been schmoozing with President LUCY for a year now, trying to set yourself up to be Vice Chancellor of this school, and this is the golden egg, baby, and you KNOW it. Why else would you be acting like this toward me? Taking the side of a bimbo SLUT over me?"

"Well, this 'bimbo slut' wants her final grade changed on the transcript. To reflect the grade that she believes her paper deserved."

"That plagiarized piece of shit deserved an F!"

"That's not the point. Nobody, Julie, and I mean NOBODY," she says, voice trembling, *"nobody wants even a HINT of this to be made public. But in the age of YouTube and Facebook... if she changes her mind somewhere down the road. God help us."*

Julie Weinberg rides the wind. In the lust and fear of memory. Remembering the height of desire born that particular day. The day before the Thanksgiving break. When the hallowed halls were devoid of life. Devoid of all life but their own.

Julie Weinberg remembers the girl's disrobing. The careful placing of her clothes on the chair. The book bag left so conspicuously uncovered. The fine and beautiful academic pen resting flat at the top of it.

She remembers the height of this academic lust. The stepping up to the girl leaned over the desk. The adding of the lotion to her middle finger. The pushing of it in the girl's rectum. The sound of her own voice in quiet, easy command.

Relax your bottom, she says. Taking the strap on member in her hand. Pushing the head of it to impossibility. Hearing the girl straining against an Amazonian yell. A cry of burning agony. A cry which twitches the buttocks of Julie Weinberg in pure shock. Prompting her to cover the girl's mouth as she pushes herself further in. Far in. All the way in. Until every long inch is buried between the girl's buttocks. Between the fleshy cheeks of her bottom.

Julie Weinberg pushes in. Feeling the girl's suffering. Feeling the gruff vibrations of it in the palm of her hand over mouth. Taking her other hand, delivering two of the hardest spanks she can conjure. Unable to resist the first wave of trembling flowed in full through her hips and thighs. In grunting. In deep, animal groaning. Having to take both hands and grip the girl's waist. Lust so extreme as to invite recklessness. Causing her to slam the message home in the office before Thanksgiving. Unable to stop the girl's gruff yelling. Unable to care.

Julie Weinberg rides the wind. The wind of blue and black fire. The winds of Vesuvian lust spilled over, that rams her hips like a piston. That slams them without mercy. Without ceasing. To make the girl understand that she is in her power. In her control.

Julie drives this message home in rage. In the dog style that pertaineth to the masculine. Channeled through the feminine. Hearing the whimpering of her own voice. Feeling the energy build up in her body.

Julie Weinberg feels the fire. The lightning strike from the center of her groin. A fire of reckoning shot out into her buttocks and thighs. Twingeing her nipples in unrequited pain that begs. That begs her to need them pulled. A lightning shot that convulses through her body in a hard, shaking quiver. A quivering shake, followed by a massive shriek buried deep within. A sound that terrifies her. Scaring her into containing another. Letting it out in long, deep grunting. Pressing herself up against the full hipped, curve waisted girl. Pushing her breasts against the girl's back for relief. For absolution.

Julie Weinberg rides the wind. The wind of a life crossed over. The sound of a former friend's voice in self righteous torment...

"Because of the choices you've made, in the hallowed halls of this institution. Julie... you're fired."

On the eve of academic tenure. At the gate of the promised land denied. Julie stands at the rainy, windy gravesite of her daughter. Remembering her return to the hallowed halls of East Lincoln. Remembering the casual stroll. The walk down the empty, late summertime corridors. Having returned the following day. After everyone had left, to clear out her things, it was understood.

Julie remembers her bold, stylish walk into the unlocked office of Maggie St. John. Stylish in melancholy gray skirt and matching storm gray blouse, offset by the thick, black belt in the middle, to match the black boots underneath. This, under a matching gray raincoat undone and laid aside.

"My decision is final, Julie. You might as well..."

Words cut off at the source. At the root of their self righteous complacency. Magdalene St. John can only stare, at the front of the black *pistol,* pointed directly at her face.

"Before I kill you, bitch," she says, *"I need to hear you scream."*

"I... I..."

Julie Weinberg steps in authority. Taking the few, slow steps around the desk to her victim. To the dean of undergraduates. The former friend designated to close the gate on her life.

Julie Weinberg steps up beside the statuesque, tight skirted beauty. Placing the gun under her chin.

"I said scream, bitch."

"I... I.."

The pistol is pressed harder to her neck, under her chin. The pressure breaks her wall of resistance. To elicit the flow of screams. A series of them. A wall of deep, woman screams.

At the peak of tears in Maggie's eyes. At the height of the bureaucratic mentality broken down. Julie Weinberg pulls the trigger. Shocked by the blast of gunpowder, and the splattering of blood on the ceiling and the wall.

Julie lets the beautiful zombie thing fall in a noisy, clumsy heap. Watching its sickening attempt at life. Its hopeless struggle to escape damnation.

Julie watches her beautiful friend lie still, a pool of blood forming at her head. Turning away, stepping over to her gray coat laid across the back of a chair. A chair in conspicuous, comfort cushion repose. Sliding into the long, gray fabric, then sliding the gun into the pocket. Walking calmly out of Magdalene St John's office. Strolling the empty corridors again. Intrigued by the absence of life. By the space she needs to walk away.

Julie opens the doors into the gray. Into the wet, weeping world. Walking through the rain without remorse. Without pity. Without fear.

Julie Weinberg rides the wind. At the gravesite of her youngest daughter. Standing undeterred in the lightning storm. Lowering the gray umbrella. Leaning it against her daughter's headstone.

Julie Weinberg puts the pistol in her lips. Lips red with a lifetime of desire. A lifetime of promises broken.

In a flash of sound. In a blast of lightning from the sky. The woman at the grave falls in an elegant heap to the ground. In the glory of feminine beauty in gray.

Julie Weinberg rides the wind. On the eve of eschatology.

"*olice are investigating the murder of the dean of undergraduates, at East Lincoln College near Spring Valley, New York. Forty two year-old Magdalene St. John was found shot to death in her office yesterday afternoon. Investigators are working to determine if the dean's murder is connected to the death of award winning novelist Julie Weinberg, author of the controversial book 'The Lesbian Mother,' a book known for its graphic depiction of mother-daughter incest and violence in a wealthy, suburban neighborhood. The forty six year old author was found dead at her youngest daughter's grave of a self inflicted gunshot wound, a day after she was fired from East Lincoln, for allegedly having an affair with a female student last fall. I'm Cora Leeds, the Associated Press.*"

Jonathan Lovejoy

The Last Taboo

The death of Julie Weinberg haunts me, as severely as so many other ghosts and spirits have these last several days, joining the spirits of birds and big breasted busen mothers at the core of apprehension, to remind me that there is no longer a place to hide from the coming judgment on this condemned world. If nothing else, it gives me an excuse to hug and comfort my grieving daughter as she sobs and weeps, grieving the loss of this feminist icon and her daughter Jenny, who was at the horizon of best friends forever with my daughter. And as I sit on the old, comfort cushioned sofa with her in my arms, I wonder if she really knows why she is crying, being that she didn't really have that strong of a connection with Julie, and her future friendship with Jenny would likely have been more one sided than not. Yes, she cared a lot about Jenny, but I always sensed a certain coldness there. A lack of enthusiasm or desperation on my daughter's part, noticing that whatever closeness they were developing was initiated almost exclusively by Jenny herself. And I always knew that my daughter was going to become an anchor and a refuge for her, a shelter in the storm of her life in private—someone that she could confide in and cling to, to confess the mountain of secret things to, of what tragedies that were between her and her mother in the shadows. Julie herself had used her as a psychological dumping ground for the unspeakable. A place for her to run to and squat a dump from her twisted soul upon, until I understood better than anybody what was going on behind closed doors, in the high class halls of Chappaqua, New York.

"That book you wrote," I used to say, shaking my head back and forth— *"if people ever got wind of just how autobiographical it really is..."*

"But they already know that," she would say. *"And that's why they can't get enough of it. And the other part of the crowd refuses to accept that something like this can even exist in the real world. Even in the world of pornography, for God's sake, they just opened the doors to this no more than about 10 or 15 years ago, and some of these movies force the actresses to recite a disclaimer at the beginning, that they are not really mother and daughter, that they are just actresses. As if we didn't know that for God's sake. Mother-daughter incest,* she says, *is going to carry us from here to the end of time. It is, literally, the last taboo. It is the final frontier, the modern day pinnacle of literary storytelling. There is NO relationship—across the whole of human history—with as much dramatic potential as that between a mother and her daughter."*

These words haunt me from the theater of my mind. As if spoken to me by some kind of end-of-the-world prophet, as some strange, apocalyptic warning that people just won't be able to process with ease, because the spirit of hypocrisy and denial are just too severe, as an ocean that is simply too wide and too deep to cross without sacrifice. I sit here in between the generations of this truth, holding my crying daughter while my mother sits quietly and respectfully on the other side of me, understanding that the truths told in Julie Weinberg's book are symptomatic of the Fall of Man, and the Mind of Eve passed down from the Garden of Antiquity.

Mother pats me knowingly on the thigh, sliding up from our comfort cushioned repose, walking up the staircase toward the upstairs hall, glancing at me once in a beckoning call. I kiss my daughter firmly on her forehead, confident that she can survive at least a brief absence from my side. I get up from our sofa of dreams, from our magic ride through dark destiny, strolling through the massive country livingroom toward the staircase, drawn upward as though adrift, along the current of her aura and energy left behind. I follow this Indian woman's spirit up the staircase, moving in apprehension down the long, darkened hall to her upper room.

"Is she going to be okay?"

"I think so," I say, moving over to the view of the gray, misty world outside her window. "There's only so much a child can take, Momma. Between what *we've* done to her, and what's happened to her friend Jenny..."

"What *did* happen?"

"I don't know. But the news said that her mother killed herself by Jenny's grave. We didn't even know Jennifer had died. And to tell you the truth, Julie Weinberg *was* my best friend."

"In all these years, you never mentioned her to me. Why not?"

The rumbling of answers from the clouds goads my sensibilities, until I am in no mood for pretense, nor any shadow of behind closed doors games of hypocrisy played.

"If you're asking me, if Julie and I were *fuck* buddies... then yes. We were."

The look of shock and awe I had hoped for in her expression is nowhere to be found. Only a quiet, hyperintelligent gaze of intense knowing and satisfaction. As if she were watching the unfolding of her own pre knowledge and prophecy.

"Even before both of our divorces, we were doing it. We took weekend road trips together. Cruises. Trips abroad. Leaving our daughters with their rich assed philandering fathers. Sometimes, the girls would spend a whole week together at one of their father's houses. I think it's starting to dawn on Kathy just how close she and Jenny really were. I think I'm starting to feel the same thing about Julie."

"Your...'*bed* buddy'...she says, "was a world famous novelist. I hardly know what to say about that. Am I jealous? Or just plain turned on by it?"

What questions do beg the rhetorical air? I turn away from the beautiful woman, from this exotic half Indian beauty, to see what new messages can be read in the streaks of lightning in the distance.

"I think I'm going to have to take a trip, Momma."

"Where?"

She asks this on an upswing of the syllable. Walking toward me with her head tilted, as if my audacity for even suggesting such a thing is unbelievable.

"I want to take Kathy back to Chappaqua with me. With what just happened to Julie and her daughter, I think we need to go back. Drive back through those damned birds. Maybe even visit Julie's other daughter up at

Yale. Try to put what's left of our lives back together. It's all too much for her, Momma. She can't handle the two of us *and* the end of the world anymore."

In the periphery, I see her struggle to suppress the sigh, the loss of control over her breathing.

"Do you think it's a good idea to just rip her away from the peace and quiet she's enjoying? Especially with what's happening in the world right now? To even suggest driving back through that migration..."

"Mom?"

I turn to see the quiet chirp of a voice flowed from two full little lips, from a face burdened by a beauty beyond its years, still colored by profound fear and naiveté.

"What is it baby?"

"When are you coming back downstairs?"

"I'll be there in a minute, honey. Are you okay?"

She opens her mouth as if to speak, but the words are choked by a sudden fearfulness unlike any I have really seen from her before, as if burdened by an anxiety deeper than any she has known before these strange, otherworldly events began. She tucks her full lips in, walking timidly into the room.

What instincts I have as a mother are suddenly shocked as if hit by a live wire in a wall socket, when my mother brushes past me aggressively, picking my daughter up bodily in near masculine strength, cooing: "come to Grandma Katherine, baby. Grandma's got you."

I watch my daughter wrap her arms and legs around my mother like a lady logger up a tree, draping herself onto her, laying her head on her shoulders with her eyes closed as if I'm not even there. I can only stand idly by, floored by my mother's bold statement of possession, by this act of aggression, watching my daughter float away in her arms, as she is carried away from me in the bosom of strength and power.

The end-of-the-world audacity of this woman plagues the theater of my mind, haunting me from the time I went to bed and far up into the night. I don't know if she cared or not that I heard her go into my daughter's room late last night, because although she certainly didn't announce it, she didn't exactly sneak in either. I clearly heard the heavy, barefooted steps going down the hardwood hall, stopping at Kathy's bedroom door. The loud clicking of the old doorknob had almost seemed for my benefit, whether she intended it that way or not, being that the spirits that govern this thing certainly *were* intent that I heard it, with the understanding that I may as well lie still and forget about it. As long as we are in this house, we are subject to this woman's sickness, which she wields over us like so much witchcraft, until either one of us at any time is cast under her spell.

Her beauty and sensuality is such that she could have any man she wanted, young or old. But her libido has done the Amazonian swing, to where the touch of a man's body could only bring bitterness and contempt to her soul. And as I drift away again in the storm, visions of my thirteen year old self haunt me in the night, to where I can see myself knelt down at her feet, tying one of her stockings tightly around her ankles as she sits on the bed, with her wrists tied already behind her back. It is the spirit of this sent to me from the present day, I know. As a warning, I suppose, that the reincarnation of opportunity hath blessed my mother's perversion, so that she is able to resume with another 13-year-old girl what she once did with me.

And I am hardly able to push the image away in the storm, of my naked Pocahontas girl, my naked daughter sitting astraddle my naked mother, bouncing up and down on top of her at her groin in bunny hop fashion, knowing already not to continue it to completion, as she is learning that it makes Grandma Katherine have to cum too quick.

From the squeaking of the bed in my dreams, I hear my daughter cease this bunny hop to her and my mother's oblivion, to rapidly, then slowly, pull my mother's giant breasts up into her mouth one by one, taking them both by the hand, wobbling them back and forth, where my mother's hands are tied behind her back underneath her. Every single pull of her nipple into my daughter's mouth pulls the stored energy in her libido up higher, until again, Kathy's learning instincts take over, letting her know that too many more of these will shake Grandma Katherine's body from head to toe.

She rubs both hands down the curve of my mother's waist, unafraid to squeeze the flesh of it, moving herself back onto my mother's legs, so she can follow the outline of her hips with both hands, while Mother's legs are still tied tightly together at the ankles. She massages Mother's hips and thighs to the rhythm of the rolling thunder in the night, until Mother's words finally come out on their own...

"Gag Grandma's mouth, baby... get the cloth and the stocking... when I turn over, massage and spank Grandma's bottom..."

And my daughter shoves the white handkerchief cloth in my mother's mouth to gagging depth, turning my mother over, breasts flopping heavily, mashed incredibly out to the sides from underneath her as she lays on her stomach, hands still tied, my daughter securing the cloth in her mouth with a tight pull on the stockings like a girl rider pulling on the reins of a white horse, pulling tight without mercy, in a twinge of sadism passed through her young body. Enjoying her grandmother's mild, soft grunting from the pain of the stocking pulled too tight, tying it around her head in a naively clever bowknot, so it can be untied easily when my mother's sickness has passed.

My daughter runs her hands down my mother's back slowly, down the back curve of her waist, down past her wrists tied tightly, down to where the great buttocks are spread to maximum width on the bed. A mischievous flash of energy raises both the girl's hands high, bringing them down hard on my mother's buttocks, bringing a deep, powerful grunt muffled in the cloth. As my daughter squeezes, jiggle, rubs and wiggles my mother's Jello hips with enthusiasm, the woman writhes with determination and awe, her eyes wide open in focused concentration on the task at hand. And she is grateful for her granddaughter's own instinct, feeling two very hard whacks on her right buttock in succession, making her close her eyes and grunt again, shocked by two more hard whacks in the same spot, to ignite the burning of the cerulean midnight flame.

The girl puts a fifth and sixth smacking down onto her grandmother's big bottom in this burning spot, then observes the caress of these Pandoran whispers in her young soul, lowering her head to my mother's bottom at the point of contact, biting the flesh with enough force to cause worry, then sucking the spanked flesh hard up into her mouth, releasing it once, twice, then three times for Our Lady of the Hips, releasing the bruised skin in the sound of a hard, kissing pull. And she studies the beauty of this red and blue mark created, lowering her head to the other side, beginning the sucking of this white skin to blood. With even less mercy, she buries her face into the flesh of my mother's hips, pulling the skin up in deep, hard suction over and over, interspersed by several hard whacks with the palm of her hand, until my mother's bottom is heavily bruised on both sides. The girl massages the woman's hips firmly, grabbing the tender flesh in both hands and squeezing hard enough to cause the woman pain, until she is satisfied that enough of this burning heat has passed through.

She now deeply wiggles and jiggles, rubs and massages my mother's bruised bottom, rubbing the outline of the woman's big hips from her buttocks to her thighs, obeying again the whispers of Pandora, sliding her hand down between my mother's thighs, higher and higher up, until her hand is where it needs to be to strike fire, rubbing inside the swollen warmth of deep moisture-cushioned heat of pink and wetness grown.

With tuck lipped, clear eyed focus, she gauges my mother's desperate grunts and groans, the up and down, side to side of her hips, until she knows to merely keep her hand still, and enjoy watching this woman's pitiful humping, her body's pleading search for a release from this plateau. The girl sits astraddle her grandmother's legs, her hand still between her thighs, watching the bound, gagged woman hump desperately now, burying the girl's hands in a tight squeeze of thighs and buttocks in steady rhythm, until the girl can feel the profound growth of the woman's desire in length and moisture down below.

The girl watches, until she sees the woman's squeezing take on a new power, a firm and forceful rhythm of otherworldly origin, where she sees this new tension in the woman's body break suddenly, hearing a loud, muffled sound of pure, bovine bellowing from the woman's voice, as her entire body quivers a jiggling spasm, shaking the bruised hips mightily around the girl's hand trapped inside.

And my daughter's obedience to these Pandoran Spirits continue, causing her to move her hand ever so slightly against the swollen *girl cock* she feels, to torture my mother in the after-tickle, making her grunt quietly again in disapproval, raising her hips up high and twisted away from my daughter's hand, to display the massive, heart shaped beauty of her bruised bottom to the spirits that stare.

The Witchcraft of Her Desire

he morning thunder rolls across the Oklahoma prairie, rumbling a deep, gentle reminder of its cataclysmic potential. I wake up in the aftermath of my mother's audacity, which still burdens and plagues my spirit with the witchcraft of her desire. The moaning cow noise I heard coming from my daughter's room last night haunts me as if I dreamt it. And truthfully, I have to run my hands back through my hair and think for just a moment... did I dream that sound or did I actually hear it? Either way, I know my mother didn't go to my daughter's room to read Bible verses or eat Butterfinger Bites with my daughter.

In my white, breast flopping t-shirt and tiny, white underwear, I slide out of bed in the spirit of apprehension, caused by the rising of a new warning in the storm. *Your mother is a perverted bitch...* and *...get your daughter away from her...* are the messages thrown at me in pure mocking from the clouds, as if the two things aren't already as true as peaches and cream in my spirit: I know she is a twisted bitch. I know she is corrupting my daughter.

But for God's sake, who am I to judge now? I allowed my lust for my own mother to get back into me so deeply that it cast a spell I couldn't shake, until it caused me to do something with Kathy I had sworn to the Holy Mother that I wouldn't do in a thousand years. As I look at my tired, blonde headed morning face in the mirror, I listen to another warning boom, looming at me from the gray world outside.

And so yes, it's something that I know I have to do now, for any number of reasons, my own lust surely not being the least among them. My breasts shake and tingle in this latest tooth brushing, while I consider how best to break it to my daughter that our time in this country paradise has come and gone. Sadly, the constant rainfall has kept us from enjoying a summer afternoon stroll to the nearby forest grove, or beyond it to the massive wheat field that stretches to the horizon.

Hopefully, Mother has already processed this inevitability when I mentioned it to her. But I know that I have to gather my daughter up from this place, and make my way back through the bird kingdom until we are in New Haven, Connecticut to see Jessica Weinberg, to inquire of her where it is that her beloved mother could have gone.

In heavy breasted, white t-shirted repose, I stroll from my little private bathroom back to the rather large bedroom, remembering that both my phone and laptop are somewhere downstairs. *I wonder if she's still in my daughter's bedroom*, is the thought wrapped around my brain as I reach for the doorknob, hardly able to process the fact that the door won't open.

Yes, that's right. This door actually will not open.

Maybe, its stuck, might be some kind of an explanation. If it had not been working perfectly the whole time I was here. And if the knob itself was not the problem.

It won't turn.

Part Three

Jonathan Lovejoy

The Italian Shore

51

$\mathcal{S}$omewhere inside the Italian Shore. Over the Mediterranean countryside. The flock rests in the calm of uneasy acceptance, that this journey is not done. Spread out over the Italian landscape in nearly every town, every city, every country province.

The people walk the summer, rain-soaked streets of Milan unafraid. Undeterred by the sleepy flocks of blackbirds, pigeons and the like. Acting as though they have always been there. Unable to care.

These opera lovers brave the weather in determination. More unsettled by the weather than by eschatology. Unable to hear the warning in birdsong. Laughing at the irony. The giddy, impish irony of it all. The devilishly appropriate exposition, the introduction to the future in snare drums. The irony of a title in feathered inspiration. In the rare summertime opera staged at La Scala, the red and gold brilliance of old. Décor surviving the centuries passing. The regal display of Rossini's laughing fit, of what happens when a magpie steals a silver spoon. When a calloused, judgmental humanity reveals itself to a servant girl named Ninetta. When she is falsely accused of stealing the royal silver. When she is sentenced to death.

High in the rafters. Above the thieving overture played. An overture that stole the opera house from German effort two centuries ago.

Amber eyes dipped in crimson. Eyes blinking with cold instinct. An unseen parliament of dying. A gathering of impending death.

The largest, strongest owls in the world. These Eurasian eagle owls. Horned feathers in a devil's manner on their head. Expressions evil with something beyond hunger. An impending rage touched by contempt. By hatred.

The great horned owls of the east look on. Listening to the screaming chords of manic ingenuity. Migrated from the northern forests. Joined with the flocks of every other species. Many dozens of them gathering in the upper darkness unbeknownst. Hidden from the musicians, the singers, the summer opera lovers unawares.

Waiting.

They listen to the first storm of melody come and gone. Hearing the magpie's arrival in the second quarter. This gathering of beaks and claws, attached to merciless instinct. Hearing the third storm of melody come and gone. Feeling the ruffle of nerves when the fourth melody arrives. The truest overture to the beginning of sorrows. The tragicomic laughter and pain from the throne of God expressed.

This secret gathering of eagle eyed devils. The great horned owls of the east. Sweeping in lines of predestiny from the darkness above the stage. One by one, in rapid succession, appearing above the dimly lit stage of props and paintings. Gliding away from the orchestral sounds, gliding on their own current of air to the smiling, laughing, giddy crowd, who thinks this is some carefully choreographed chaos. Believing this in stubborn repose, until one of the six foot wingspans settles above a little girl at the edge of a scream. Gripping her shoulders. Lifting her bodily in a massive whir of beating wings. Finally causing the outpouring of shrieks and screams from the surrounding crowd. From the girl's finely dressed, brunette haired mother pulling her down from the air.

From the growing chaos of the maddening crowd. The screams come in terrifying waves, as the gigantic owls swoop and swirl to the pathetic, upscale howls of misery. All of it done to the manic chords lifted from 1817, drifted into the clamour of the modern day. As a sign of the coming eschatology, as the theater of owls swoop and swirl—as they swerve down and across the latter day breakdown of civility. As the opera goers trample and claw one another to break free of the red and gold death room, the orchestra plays the end of this powerful overture with fever and precision, playing on without ceasing. Motivated by depression. Inspired by fear.

In the death of cultured civility, the orchestra plays on. In the performance to end all performances. In a power and precision unimagined since Rossini's ironic burst of inspiration came forth, a beauty and heavy depth of sound never before gleaned by the end of this age. To the whim of Fate, Destiny, and God, they play. As though ordered by a divine intercession, to play the chords of judgment over the unworthy, the melodies of condemnation over the unrighteous.

The song of damnation over the unredeemed.

Jonathan Lovejoy

Snowbird

$\mathscr{W}$hat good will it do me, to pound and holler at this door for another hour? All of my attempts to pick this lock with paperclips and hair pins have just assured me that it only works in the movies. It is one of those old fashioned, keyhole rust iron country locks that uses a skeleton key or either side, so that I am locked *in* instead of out. And I have gone through every range of emotion there is, from rage to downright pleading sorrow, until I am spent now, knowing I don't have the strength to try and tear off one of the wooden chair legs and try to pound a hole through the door.

As I sit in this old, comfort cushioned chair, gazing out this second floor window, I can feel what is left of myself drowning like a butterfly in the rain, as I suddenly realize that along with Mother, my daughter has also refused to help me. But at least, the clock radio has been assigned by pure Fate to see me through this latest bout with fear and despair. How many more hours, I wonder, before I finally hear the lock click, and then my mother drifts apologetically into the room? Standing there at the door with arms open wide, ready to accept my contrition for every wrongdoing? For every feeble attempt I made to try and escape from her? To try and escape her will? Waiting patiently to hear me say how sorry I am, and that *I'll stay, we'll stay as long as you want.*

And part of me refuses to process or believe that I am really locked in this room, that maybe the doorknob really did get stuck, and maybe because of the storm, my mother and my daughter just can't hear me. But even while I say this to myself in false hope and desperate delusion, I can see, I can feel the two of them somewhere along the timeline of this last hour, standing together in a fog of sinister sorrow, my daughter in tears, and my mother in stern commitment. It can only be symptomatic of what darkness that has come upon the earth in this latter day time, here at the end of the age, the end of the second world. *As it was in the days of Noah,* my brain feeds me over and over, a verse I'm vaguely familiar with somewhere in the Holy Scriptures, concerning the impending end of the world.

And I can suddenly feel it more and in greater fashion than ever, as though I have been pulled out of the dreadful reality I was in, and have been plunged into a dark fantasy. But as hard as I try to convince myself that this is a dream, I know for a fact that I am awake, and I am about to reconcile in desperate measure what comeuppance I am overdue.

In the wake of a distant lightning shear, the thunder rolls gently over the rainsoaked landscape, having enough power to rattle the two bedroom windows still. I'm learning exponentially the power of what is meant to be, as opposed to what we want, or what is righteous and fair in this life. Is this why I chose, above all things, to return to the cold of my mother's unloving arms? For what reason have I been forced back into the Hellish fear I have not felt since I was a teenage girl on this very farm? Why did I think that I had somehow outgrown the reach of her dark and cold spirit—the one who so callously was able to kill my father? I grew up being punished by this woman in echoes and shades of this, but nothing quite this completely fearful, beyond the fear of impending pain and humiliation. I was fortunate enough to have not had the terror of being locked in a closet or a shed, or held down and smothered to near unconsciousness. These were the flavor of what tragedies Katherine Hardwick endured from the time she was little Katherine Rose, little half breed Indian girl, daughter of Pia Rose Hardwick, whose white husband had left the both of them behind for an early grave.

In the heart of the earth's fervent memory, the widow Pia Rose is forced to live with her two Indian sisters for a time, on their little Carolina Mountain farm, where they scratch out a dreadful little living selling farm fresh vegetables, with Pia's older sister working part time in a local supermarket, lucky enough by sheer beauty to have a job in produce. Pia's bastard daughter Katherine is an angelic little *snowbird*, they call her, because her skin is so pale compared to theirs. And from her time in the crib aflat of her back, to her 13th year, to when she met the Carolina horse farmer Bryan Kidd when she was 21, and moved with her mother to Oklahoma, Katherine Rose was buried, ensconced, enshrouded in an aura of violence and perversion, a three pronged attack from mother Pia and her two sisters, an attack which begins in the crib at six months old on a visit to their little farm, when the "white mouse" will not stop crying, and Pia's younger sister turns her upside down by her ankle and spanks the daylights out of her until they are both exhausted, throwing her back down into the crib hard enough to break her arm. And for many hours, the child is unable to stop fretting and crying, being neglected until it is time for another beating, where the crooked little forearm is the telltale sign, that baby Katherine must be taken to the hospital.

This, by the mother of cold concern, the full blooded Indian Momma Pia Rose Hardwick, who is able to pass all the doctor's and nurse's instincts with truth, that her sister told her the child tried to climb out of her crib on her own, and fell down and broke her arm. These mountain backwoods doctors and nurses do their best fungalooga grinning, smiling to the Indian mother and her little half white doll, while the child's broken arm is set, straightened and wrapped in a little plaster cast, before the condemned little thing and her Indian mother are sent back through the twilight to their little vegetable farm.

And this cast serves as a reminder and warning, as a signpost unto them, that what tortures there are to come must not go much farther than skin deep, than into the muscle, than past the brittle bones and into the soul. This little white cast on Katherine Rose's arm, the barrier between her and the three pronged attack, which may have seen the child in a backwoods grave before she was two.

The necessity of this little white cast on baby Katherine's arm. Because this poor child is meant to be kept alive to suffer. The necessity of the little white cast on baby Katherine's arm. Where the danger of death is set in detour, to come where and when it will in some unknown future. Where the threat of broken bones will be replaced by the threat of broken skin, until the threat of a broken spirit is manifested in reality.

From the time the child is old enough to walk. On these visits to the little Carolina Indian farm. The spirits of true sadism descend in this three pronged attack, where Mother, First Aunt, and Second Aunt launch this war upon the girl's sense of hope, and all hope of feeling normal in the world. The switches and the wet cloths, these graduate and transform into the softness of the leather belt, which graduates to the wooden spoon, which graduates into the paddle and pieces of kindling wood, which settles into the noisy sophistication of the whistling cane, and finally to where the skin is cut to blood, by the snap of the short horse whip in tow.

My mind is burdened by the fear and pain of what I know, when the beautiful 13 year old is stripped from her brown dress and boots by the second aunt (the aunt of the broken crib arm), and from the repertoire of suffering is gathered the punishment stick, so that the mother and first aunt can watch the younger aunt take out her young life's frustration on the 13 year old victim; watching her wield the long, rounded stick in hard fashion, a stick in the manner of a mop or broom handle, brought down again and again over the girl's shoulders, thighs and back, as if crossing the barrier of the white cast into the future, bringing the stick down upon the girl's arms and ribs without mercy, without compromise, without remorse. Entertaining Indian Momma Pia and her sister First Aunt, who both brave the chills sent through their bodies by her screams. These are the screams of fear and rage. The screams of disillusionment. And despair.

In the wake of the earth's fervent memory. Upon the voice of doom rumbled from the clouds. I hear the impossibility of hope, the clicking of the country lock, and the turning of the knob. I wait with a breath unbreathed, gazing as the door swings open, in time to see the stern, half Indian beauty Katherine Hardwick, hurrying into my bedroom prison, with smooth and quiet authority, her navy dress ruffled elegantly against her leg as she walks, the midnight blue cloth in contrast to the white punishment stick held firmly in hand.

With me in my tight, big bosom white t-shirt and country denim shorts stretched tight over widened hips, my mother grabs me in the pain of punishment stick memories come and gone, and begins to beat me in the rage of vengeance, as if trying to beat back the spirits of the three pronged attack, and their revisitation of her misery in the present day.

53

The thunder carries me hopelessly along the hours, from the time of my deep, death screams in the early morning, through the rise and fall of hidden sunlight, across the rainy afternoon into the evening. And the gray twilight rolls without mercy into the fall of a rainy night, with nary another appearance by either my mother or my daughter at the locked door, with not as much as a bowl of soup to remind me that I'm human. And so, I retreat into the bosom of an early nighttime sleep, still haunted by the spirits of mother-daughter perversion, the beauty and the power of it passed down, of its vortex energy that pulls the unsuspecting in as victims, until the daughter's playful rolling over on top of the mother isn't quite so funny anymore.

A woman's body is a garden of secrets. A maze of twisted motivation, where everything from the washing of a dish to the driving of a car might have hidden orgasmic potential. And there are some who have been touched by the forbidden fruit upon the palate, who have learned that the taste of their daughter's lips is as sweet as wine, and the feel of the daughter's tongue in her mouth is nourishment to the soul.

"Your mother has to be disciplined," I can hear my mother say, as given to me by the spirits of what I know, ablaze upon the theater of my mind. This shapely woman is naked upon the toilet, as the earth turns toward the evening day, with my 13-year-old daughter straddled naked upon her lap, the two of them ready to engage the spirit of defecation at the precipice of depravity. And this woman pushes her thumb into her granddaughter's mouth, engaging the girl to a deep sucking of it, nearly twitching at the sight of the girl's anguished, sucking expression. In this, Katherine Rose must join in, kissing and sucking her own thumb as she pulls it out of Kathy's mouth, quickly pressing her lips to her granddaughter's for a quick but deep, pressing kiss.

"Why do we have to punish Mommy?"

"Because she was going to try and take you away from me. And I know you don't want that to happen, do you?"

The girl shakes her head 'no' in the glory of young naiveté, in the gullibility of youth commandeered and wrapped in chains.

"How long will she be punished?"

"Until she understands that you and I can never again be apart."

And upon this note, Katherine plays upon the melancholy D minor chord, the prodigious breasts of her granddaughter, pulling one deep into her mouth, nursing the girl's tit until she hears her granddaughter's breathing give way, staying upon it in expert instinct, rising this breath up and higher up to a vocalization, sucking her granddaughter's nipple until her breathing transforms into a high pitched squeal for the ages, and Mother finds that she is unable to unclamp her sucking lips from her granddaughter's breast, feeling what spirits that caress the libido go to work in her body, striking a fire in her groin that spreads to her waiting rectum, which is in grieving to release its burden, relaxing her body to a state of automatic undoing, where the feeling passes from her breasts and groin to her bowels, as she lets her nature's call pass through, in profoundly orgasmic flow as was hardly felt since her youth, grunting a long, animal groan, muffled by her mouth at her granddaughter's breasts as the softened defecation relief passes through.

And in this depravity, the two of them rest and bond in this end of the world revelation, where the buildup of the second flow causes Mother to say, *"I need you to suck on my breast...suck it like you're drinking milk..."*

This, the girl does, still straddled on her beautiful grandmother's lap, pulling the giant, bell hung breast deep into her young mouth, while my mother takes her other breast into her own mouth, feeling the second wave of pleasure pass through her rectum into flushing waters down below.

And of this too, she is unable to release her sucking, groaning another long, gruff exclaim, to acknowledge the waves of energy striking her groin with each sucking pull of both her nipples. Resting again the long building of a third and final pass, hugging her granddaughter tight, panting the long breaths to recovery, undeterred by the flowery stench of their new bonding, holding on to my daughter in tight hugging. Waiting. Waiting for the third buildup to complete itself, to gather itself to inevitability. Waiting until she is ready, her granddaughter studying with delight and awe what deep ecstasy this woman is held prisoner by, her face anguished to the point of pain and suffering displayed.

"Pull on both my breasts," she says. *"Pull both Grandmomma's tits... pull 'em both as hard as you can... pull 'em like you're trying to pull 'em OFF!"*

And Mother yells this syllable into the stench of her depravity, holding her head back in both agonies and of pain, as the third wave of dumping gushes through, undertaken by the heat of her granddaughter's hard pulling at her nipples, and the crashing of two bolts of lightning from both her breasts down to the center of her shaking, quivering body in the evening.

Jonathan Lovejoy

In the Hour of the Bird Kingdom

The fires of eschatology burn my spirit with revelation, over what souls are condemned in the hour of the bird kingdom. This, at the end of my second day of pain and misery, while I have spent the day marveling at the bruises and scratches all over my body. In the mirror, I have seen the one eyed doe staring back at me; the blonde in my reflection with one eye swollen shut and nearly blackened from a wayward strike of the punishment stick. As I gaze out into the evening storm, from high inside this second floor window, my mind is on fire with what I have heard on the radio, of the impossibilities that nature now seems capable of.

Migration

I am lifted upon the ungentle breezes of this stormy day, aloft in the flight ill advised, from Oklahoma city to 800 miles northeast, where the promised land of academia waits in gold and emerald green. The light skinned mall beauty I remember is shown to me—tall, shapely, nerdish beauty with her hippy mother in tow, I remember, from my mall trip to Oklahoma city a few days ago. This lovely, yellow skinned black woman, this middle aged display of modern sophistication, having her daughter's life planned out for the next five years already, moving through the future timeline painted the colors of prosperity.

This suburban Momma of privilege. Taking her daughter to see the campus of our Holy Mother, whose name echoes the Great Cathedral in Paris. This mother and this daughter board the doomed flight from Oklahoma City, rising high over the sight of devastation on the ground in Missouri, where every acre of the state is covered at least in part by this sign of the times. This mall mother and her beautiful daughter, the two of them holding hands in public defiance of secrets untold, telling it in their own way, of why they did not want to be driven to the airport by their husband and father, by the white surgeon too ensconced, too enamoured by his own career and busy phone on speed dial life to care.

We're driving up the night before, Momma said, *so we can get a hotel, do some shopping and go out to dinner.* And this was said in the confidence of a secret never told, in the shadows of a neglected husband's naiveté, who has accepted his beautiful wife's new found frigidness, and the alienation of affections to ice. A mother-daughter trip, told to the husband in two fold purpose—one, to produce the satisfaction of envy, to make him jealous that she would want to spend time with their daughter and not with him. And second, the hidden satisfaction of what churns beneath cultured civility.

This, the satisfaction of depravity, of flowers that bloom in the shadows, of blossoms in the shade of the forbidden.

This mother and daughter hold hands on their first class flight. Undeterred by the sight of great flocks of geese that fly in formation far underneath the plane. Undeterred by the news of the migration far below unseen, stretching through Missouri and into Illinois. The mother holds her daughter's hands undaunted. Unmoved by what curious stares have come and gone, where there rests a bewildered look or two. Still reeling, the two of them, from their night spent in the Four Seasons Hotel in Oklahoma City. Where the punishments completed what evolution there was, that begged its bringing out to fruition. This, where the pretense of punishment was finally put to rest. Born from the showers of a morning rendezvous weeks ago, where the mother's aggression in their argument led to a shower curtain being slid heartily open.

I have had it with your smart mouth, she had said, while removing her bra quickly, braving the daughter's rolled eyes in angry frustration, fully prepared for another bare handed, bare skinned bruising of her hips. But the mother steps in the shower in renewed purpose, this time, ready to go deeper into the well, grabbing her daughter firmly by the crotch. Holding the skin of it together tightly, oh, just so tightly enough, to put the seventeen year old girl on notice that this is a new day, and a new form of discipline born. Pushing herself firmly against the girl, pressing her noisily against the shower wall. Staring the girl in the face, the two of them breathing roughly, until the girl's anger is risen by the burning fire tinted blue, causing her to grab her mother between her legs in like manner, both women standing in the shower, soap fallen to the wet tub, breathing onto each other's lips, unable to let their hands go free.

As if on their own, the two of them slip past what barrier there is that remains, sliding their lips together in the wet, weeping world in microcosm, until their tongues touch in electric shock passed to both their breasts and beyond. In this rendezvous to the future, in this fateful meeting in the crystal fountain stream, the daughter pulls her mother's tongue into her mouth in strong sucking, in sucking frustration unleashed, unfurling this new power through her free hand onto her mother's wide and jiggling backside in the shower. Spanking this woman's bottom with extreme force, one slow, hard whack after another, suddenly shocked by the violent quiver of her mother's hips, and the throbbing of her arousal at her other hand down below. From this, the mother must cease the kiss, to capture her breath, to gather her reason from the edge of fainting, breathing in heavy, deep breaths of recovery, unable to move, unable to take her hand down from its grip in her daughter's wet hair, nor her other hand from between her daughter's legs down below.

And in this frustration born and bred, the daughter grabs hold of the flesh of her mother's hip with one hand, rubbing her feverishly with the other. The Oklahoma City daughter rubs her half devastated mother without mercy, watching her strain against the monumental loss of control, and the waves of Vesuvian groans that push at the surface of breathing. The mother returns this rubbing to her daughter in their new violence, their new confrontation in battle, rubbing the Amazonian figured nerd beauty, but to no avail.

From the peak of feminine sensuality, from the universal plateau of womanhood matured, the tension in this woman's body breaks, to send her trembling backward in a mighty attempt to escape her daughter's hand at her groin. But the daughter rubs her mother without mercy, to bring forth the deadly aftertickling, bringing up the mother's voice in deep, gruff, bellowing howls into the small space around them. These, the mother endures, until the shaking, the gruff howling, the cattle voiced moaning cannot stop the pleasure from rising into pain, causing her to grab hold of her daughter's hand firmly.

In the shadows of their memory. On the morning of a dynamic crossed over. The mother takes her hand down from her daughter's hair. Her other hand up from down below. Standing still in the crystal waters. In the upper class waterfall of their time.

Over the skies near Springfield, Illinois. These two ride first class luxury. Secure in upper class beauty. Brains. Breeding. Still reeling, the two of them. In the afterglow of the night before. When discussions of what must be are manifest into what is.

Weeks beyond the shower rendezvous. In the nighttime haze of luxurious dreams. The hotel of their fantasy come to life. The light skinned daughter stands nearby the mother of like complexion. Women of beauty, the two of them. Spurred on by the spirit of travel. Of fine and elegant surroundings. The daughter obeys her mother's whim, and whacks a powerful spank upon the mother's hips. Shaking the flesh. Burning it red. Spanking the mother's hips beyond the tenth blow. Until the reddening deepens to bruising. To ignite the flame. The burning of blue and black fire.

From the bed, the daughter lifts the nine inches of heat. Nine inches of Amazonian power strapped on. Sliding this up around her Mother's hips. Helping the woman tighten the straps in complex simplicity. In this simple complexity, the mother stands in the glory of herself. Wearing it for the first time. Seeing in the mirror the power of perversion. The apocalyptic vision of the masculine lust channeled through the feminine. The futanarian mystique. The future of woman to woman in the latter day.

In long breasted, curve waisted repose. The wide hipped mother binds her daughter's wrists in front. Tightly in black leather bondage. Her phallus hung down long and low. Bending over, breasts swinging free, black strapping her daughter's arms to her sides. Pinning them. Observing the lamp lighted glory of her beautiful daughter in the mirror. Bending down, taking one of her daughter's D cups into her mouth. Engaging the Nun's Intercourse, pulling it deeply in sucking. Sliding it in and out. Gauging the roaring of a new flame inside. A warning fire in repose. A warning combustion of desire.

From this powerful sucking, the mother releases the nipple in a hard, kissing pull. At the edge of a pissing pull down below. In a hissing pull of breath through her teeth, she takes the phallus in her hand. Holding the inches of nine strapped on. Sliding it deep and slow into the back of her daughter. Watching her daughter's pained expression in the mirror. Hearing the girl's loud, deep grunting come forth. Hearing in her voice, perceiving in her manner, the calm of uneasy acceptance. The embracing. Answering the Call of the Motheress in Predestiny.

The mother can only stare down at what she sees. At the fullness of herself grown. The expression of herself, sliding in, sliding out, sliding into her daughter's chastity from behind. Feeling the rise of the inevitable, but not heeding the warning. Unprepared for what must be. Grabbing hold of her daughter's waist. Glancing the bound arms and wrists, and the hang of her daughter's breasts in the mirror. Attempting to thrust harder. Faster. Shocked—by a sudden strike of lightning in her groin. Stronger than any she has felt in her years of living. A strike of lightning accompanied by a wave of feeling in both breasts. Responding to this strike of energy with a mouth open in awe. Eyes closed in aguish. Feeling a second, equal bolt of lightning. Lurching her hips forward into her daughter. Grabbing onto her.

Holding on through the shaking. Yelling a single, powerful shriek into the hotel room. Unable to stop her body's quivering. The earthquaking. The shaking of herself from the waist down.

The mother grabs onto her daughter's breasts. Onto her nipples. Unprepared again for what must be. For the sudden slamming backward of the daughter against her. Her breathing heavy with impending insanity.

To the mother's inner delight. In answer to a depraved prayer unknown. Her bound daughter wails a quick siren. Taking a breath, wailing a long, banshee call into the room. The mother looks at her daughter's reflection. To see if there is the echo of pretense. There is none. As though inspired, the woman exacts a painful revenge. Rubbing her daughter down in front. In the after tickle. Rubbing her firm. Deep. Without mercy. Listening to her gruff, hoarse yelling. The deep, woman's screams for mercy.

The mother and her daughter hold hands above the clouds. In conspicuous commitment. Having already decided to spend their lives in devotion. In private, behind closed doors dedication. Coming out, so to speak, with their newfound closeness in the public eye. To leave the public guessing as to whether or not their closeness is inappropriate. Whether or not it extends beyond the barrier. The line of what is forbidden.

At her view of the window, this middle aged, light skinned beauty breathes a sigh of freedom. Content. Complacent. Convinced that the flock of great, white birds passing by the plane are a sign. These majestic, great winged angels of the air, with their long necks and black bills, to match the jet black beauty of the legs and feet in tow.

This woman breathes her end-of-the-world sigh, absorbing the energy from her daughter's hand, already committed to the image of their rendezvous in South Bend, after their fruitless campus stroll among the spirits of gold and green. This rendezvous in her head impending, of two tongues pressed together flat, with mouths wide open, as their fine, fancy clothes are slowly removed down to their underwear—

And suddenly, the woman is shocked awake from this daydream, by the rapid flash of white by the window, followed by many more of them above and below the giant wing, until she sees the back of the engine flare into a burst of flame, marked by the sound of thunder, and the shaking of their world to oblivion. And what pin pricks and needles invisible on her skin are magnified, by the scream of a woman in the seat behind her, and the sight of this flame becoming a fireball where the wing used to be, and the cataclysmic sound greater than thunder in the air around them.

From this shaking, from this new quaking of their world emerges a cacophony of fearful screaming, including that of her beautiful daughter, who claws at her mother's arm with both hands in a grip of pure madness. From the view of the burning, smoking remains of this engine, the mother turns as in the haze of a slow motion dream, unable to convince herself that she is truly awake, staring at her lovely daughter's big, white teethed mouth open wide in what surely must be a scream, for is this is not the face of terror? The wide eyed gaze of the condemned, when the Godzilla monster of their judgment approaches?

From inside the vacuum of shock and silence, these dreams of hope awaken into a nightmare of hopelessness, as her senses are suddenly slowed down to lucidity, where the world around her is no longer in slow motion and quiet. She is a captive, a prisoner in the same Hell as her daughter, as the rest of the screaming passengers, with the reality of a sudden drop in the pit of her stomach, and a view of billowing black smoke and flame outside her window.

In the nightmare world beneath the gray clouds. Across a suburban landscape of fear and rain. The skies over Springfield, Illinois bear witness to the truth, in the message of a glowing cloud of orange vapour, illuminated by the flame of whatever it is appearing from deep within. This suburban landscape in Springfield is covered with this message of eschatology, as part of the nationwide strip in revelation which is the bird kingdom. In the fine, middle class neighborhood of underworked, overpaid souls in divine luck gone bad. The crows and ravens cover the streets in dominance, seeing their control spread to every yard and casual rooftop, covering the entire square mile of privileged real estate with flocks gathered from every other species known and unknown to the untrained eye, until even the strangeness of a pelican is part of the norm. And in the midst of this dreary afternoon rain storm, the eyes that look up from the ground, unprotected from the rain are not human, seeing a metallic silver bird of manmade flight burst through the cloud cover, traveling behind it a message in orange fire and black vapour of smoke. These soulless, black eyes that stare, do so in the heart of sacrifice, unable to honor their natural fear response to the approaching fireball.

These suburban skies over Springfield are alive with the remains of a swan song. Brought down from the heavens by an avenging angel in feathered white, as the burning sky chariot plunges down to the ground in the middle of this suburban paradise; exploding itself into a gigantic ball of liquid orange flame. Devastating the acres of privileged homes and property, laying waste to the fine glass and brick fortress of their delusion, and the departure of every condemned human soul burned and blasted away in the storm.

" *A* United Airlines flight from Oklahoma city to South Bend,
Indiana crashed in a suburban neighborhood in Springfield Illinois today,
leaving much of the wealthy neighborhood looking like a charred war zone,
killing all one hundred seventy nine passengers aboard. No word yet on how
many residents of this affluent suburb were killed in the crash. Radio
communication from United flight 22 revealed that the left engine exploded
at 20,000 feet, after the plane flew into what the pilot described as "the
biggest white birds in God's creation." The pilot later said that a passenger
on board identified the birds as trumpeter swans, one of the highest flying

bird species on the planet. Springfield is located in the heart of this massive migration, that is responsible for the deaths of an estimated 27 million people in the US alone. It is estimated the flock numbers range into the tens of billions, a number which the President says would make any attempt at a bird war, quote: "an exercise in futility." Cora Leeds, the Associated Press."

Jonathan Lovejoy

294

The Meaning of Pain

The pain of my Mother's youth has reached out to her, and broken her psychology. There can be no other explanation as to why I am still a prisoner in this bedroom. Since the day she burst into the room with the punishment stick and acquainted my arm and leg bones with the meaning of pain, I have been belt whipped everyday for two weeks. This, in various stages of undress for both she and I, though sometimes fully clothed for the both of us, or sometimes in the nude. And because there has been such a powerful and potent mixture of dress and undress between us, I have no idea which is her favorite; which one of them is the truest light at the end of her tunnel of misery.

I know that from the age of 13 until my mother escaped into marriage from Pia Hardwick, she endured a beating of some kind almost every day. And this is enhanced by a network of old scars all over her beautiful body, concentrated on her back, her buttocks and the backs of her thighs; the many light scars across her huge breasts notwithstanding. And these scars do nothing to diminish the extraordinary nature of her beauty, which seems to grow more exotic as she gets older. The Indian part of her blood is more apparent in her features than when I saw her seven years ago, when my daughter was only six years old.

But even though what we had then was steeped in behind closed doors violence, in secret aggression and forceful passion, it was not laced with the purity of this contempt, the no nonsense battle drone of a warrior's frown in her expression, which is no façade that could be cracked and broken, but a reflection of how she feels about me when I am being beaten. I have been given a glimpse into the twilight of her sanity; this, as she murmers almost under her breath, mumbling something unintelligible, ending with the clarity of "...*take my granddaughter...*" Then, after my clothes are stripped to where my lily white ass shines like chalk in the moonlight, she proceeds upon it with raw intensity, slashing, lashing a crash of lightning flashes to my white skin, unafraid to whip my swinging breasts as they may flop and get in the way.

It is a microcosm of the world at large in this bedroom prison, which is the breakdown of cultured civility, where the world will begin to crave the cutting of one another's skin to blood. Over the course of these simple whippings, I have learned that these are not under the shading of pleasure, but are in the shadows of pain. The cure for one's inner pain is to share it with another soul. It is why the world is suffering, why those who have are slowly but surely drifting further away from the rest, until there will soon be a great gulf affixed between them.

My mother has the power, and it is her goal, her craving, to use it to ease whatever pain it is she feels. I am fed generously three times a day, so that sadly, I now crave the coming of each meal like a lady thief on a prison work farm. And I know exactly why she feeds me. It is so my body will not lose the wiggle and jiggle she needs to see and feel while I breast flop and howl around the room in her strong grip, under the whip of folded leather belt pain and misery.

And which of the pains and miseries from her childhood will haunt her in this rainy afternoon or night, that will fuel the fires of what must be? Is it the simplicity of the young aunt's grabbing of my mother's hair after school, pulling the girl's head back, staring at Mother's then exaggerated features in her young face? Then laughing like drunk girl at a comedy club, followed by a sudden frown and quick smack across mother's eye? Or the complexity of this same little girl being held down by both her mother's sisters, in precursor to what was to come when Mother would turn sixteen? Is it the fear, still fresh a generation of years later, when the two grown women laid on top of her at once? Squeezing themselves down heavy on top of their niece until she could hardly breathe, listening to her call for her Momma to please help her because she couldn't breathe?

Which of the agonies in myriad, which of the many trials of Katherine Rose have reached out to her today, to make her have to cling to my daughter like a mental patient to a cloth baby doll with no eyes? All of it is confirmation of the look I suspected when we first arrived—a look that said from the start, *Hell will freeze over before I let you take her away from me again.* It was a flash of warning that I chose to ignore—a combination of lust and fear, that has held me prisoner already to my mother's will since I was a child of thirteen myself, when my mother shot and killed my father in the evening day.

In this stormy evening, as hope fades out into the twilight, I am still sore already from the fortnight belt whippings, wishing to just simply get this one over with, sliding off the bed and walking toward the center of the room, where they all seem to take place. These are not the calm, calculated blows with me laid on the bed on my stomach with my hands between my legs. No. These are the belt whippings of legend and lore. The wild, flailing expression of a woman's grief upon her daughter's skin.

"Momma... Momma, in the name of God and Jesus have mercy. I swear to 'em both I won't take her from you. I swear I won't..."

But this kind of begging is only fuel thrown on to the fires of the sadistic mind. The sound of a woman's begging is foreplay to a lustful soul. Truthfully, I'd be better off if I kept my weak, whining mouth shut, and just let her do what it is that a large *wooden hairbrush* is made to do, when the bristles are not called upon. Even while she slides out of her dress, then so nonchalantly out of the gigantic bra and underpants, I can feel my daughter on the other side of the locked door, her ear pressed hard up against it, listening to her forty year old mother beg in a wailing, weeping moan to not be beaten, that all lessons in heaven and earth have been learned.

And I am struck by the power of this imagery in my body, as she bends over to slide her underwear away, the view of her voluptuous, naked form, and the bulbous, elongated breasts that swing down from her body. I am truly amazed, that the mixture of emotion that flows through my body is a burning hot alloy of lust and fear, tempered in the fires of what love I have for this woman.

I am privy to the girl at the bedroom door, who presses herself against it in fear and mourning, to listen to the sounds of her own mother being punished to tears and blood. I am too weak to fight. Too weak to do anything but put my weakling arms around her neck in false hope, as she slides my pink t-shirt off over my head, leaving me topless in the glow of the twilight room.

"Take off your pants," she says.

"Momma, nurse 'em." I say, in full whining, teardrop repose. *"Nurse 'em until I can't take it anymore but please don't do this…"*

Outside the door, my daughter hears the rare sound heard, that of a grown woman in hopeless, tearful begging. As to what feeling this passes through my daughter, this, I cannot tell. Is it the cold breath of fear in her lungs and her blood, touched by the heat of an inexplicable desire in pissing twinge down below? What does it do to your young body, my poor Kathy, to hear the pleading wails of your mother in breathless sorrow?

"I said take 'em OFF, " she says sternly. In craving to watch me disrobe in helpless obedience, in total submission and compliance to her will.

"Momma, I don't understand. You never had to be like this with me, you know I always— "

The last syllable is cut off by a brutal slap from the naked woman, making me grunt a gruff, sickening yelp into the room.

"If I have to ask you again…"

" *I will. I will, Momma."*

I unbutton and unzip my blue jeans, my futile attempt at staying normal, as if I had somewhere else in the world I was allowed to go. I bend over in like manner as she, first once in slow, stalling fashion, peeling the faded jeans off. Taking forever to pull them past my feet, one leg at a time, knowing that if she were holding the belt, this insolence would have been striped across my back in response by now. But part of the Sadist's Call is in the whining for compliance; the slow, steady attempt by the victim to stall in hopes that some angel or demon will interfere on their behalf. But she stands there. Undisturbed. Unperturbed by my sluggishness. Undeterred from the crying face. And the breasts in G minor hung in like manner as her own.

"Stand up," she says, when my underwear cloth is down and away. Pulling my hair firmly.

"Do you realize yet, why I have to punish you?"

"No," I say. Shaking my head. Blinking the tears from both eyes.

"You're lying," she says. *"I know because you had plenty of time to think about it. Why is it that I'm punishing you?"*

"I don't know, Momma. I said that Kathy and me were gonna stay."

"But for how long?" she says. Her voice echoing the strong, *sane* depth of her easy command that I have known.

"I... I don't..."

"And there's your answer," she says.

"But I'll stay as long as you say..."

"Nothing you say now makes any difference," she says. *"Because in your heart, somewhere in the back of your mind, you'll always be thinking about leaving. About taking my granddaughter away from me. And you know... as surely as its raining 'til morning, I cannot allow that to happen."*

"But I won't leave. I SWEAR I won't."

"But when I'm through with you, you'll understand that the choice is not even yours to make. You'll understand that there IS no choice."

She walks over to where her bra lays on the floor, near the crumple of her dress fabric. Lifting her bra casually. Walking back over to where I stand unclothed. Waiting.

She kneels down to my thighs, placing her hairbrush briefly to the floor. Tying the white fabric of her bra as tightly as she can, clamping my legs tightly together above the knee.

Of these ties that bind, there is no escape. As if driven forward in sorrow. As though surrendered to the weight of predestiny. She grips the large wooden hair brush tightly in her hand. Holding me firmly around the front of my waist by the other.

"There are things...that you and I are called to do together..."

And upon this, comes the first note of an acid pain, a burning agony I only thought I had understood before, causing me to understand at once why my legs are tied immobile. But without hesitation, without remorse, she stares deeply into the task at hand. Slamming the wooden brush onto my skin in hard, fast paddling form, with full strength and speed displayed, with nary a single word of warning or support, driving the message home in burning heat, to cause my daughter to hear the wild screams of a woman in pain, screams that rise to heights of hopelessness, which is the depth of sorrow and pain.

She listens through the door. To the sound of despair coalesced.

The sound of a death scream.

Beyond the lightning shears over the prairie. Above the rains of a wet, weeping world. The cloud blanket bears the colors of a sun dressed in amber, as it lowers far beneath the line of the Western Gate, in a sky turned toward the fall of another hidden, starry night.

In the agony of a revelation shared. In the pain of dominance, and submission reborn. I endure the growth of a foundation of fire on the skin. Able to perceive the power of force that drives her in the paddling. The pain that she channels. The pain that she channels through the paddling wood. Battering. Bruising. Burning us in this blue fire tinted black.

Cutting her daughter's white skin to blood.

Jonathan Lovejoy

Su Ling Yin Was Twelve

These rains fall in grieving perpetuity. From the open fields of Oklahoma green, past the bird kingdom stretched from the Rockies to the Appalachians, to all points north and east. At the campus in New Haven, Connecticut, Jessica Weinberg rests uneasy in the arms of another, in the nighttime bedroom of an on campus rendezvous. Having invited her friend, her lover to stay with her in the luxury dorm.

Susan Yin. Su Ling Yin. Called upon to protect her friend from the ghost of a woman departed. To protect her friend Jessica Weinberg from the approaching hurricane. From the storm of madness that threatens. Madness caused by shock and grief, from the news story heard around the world, of the famous novelist from East Lincoln College. The novelist who murdered the Dean of Undergraduates, and then turned the same pistol on herself at her youngest daughter's grave.

Su Ling raises up in the nighttime bed. Laying on her side, head leaning on her hand. Hip curved to a monumental height, breasts milk bottled in double-dop flop to the bed. Breasts elongated enough for her to perform the self sucking her own mother had loved to watch. The self sucking her Jew Girl friend craves to see.

Su Ling lays still on her side. Not noticing the bed sheet damp with the flow of her milk. Seeing only the stirring of her friend laid on her back. Watching her begin to whimper, to mouth words from the dream world unspoken. Content to watch. Determined to see this nightmare drama played to its inevitable end.

Su Ling watches Jessica's movements grow more desperate. Watching her trying valiantly to break the paralysis of sleep. Hearing her break the veil with two coherent words *"oh, no,"* spoken in dark whisper. Then the breath of this last syllable rises to vocalization. The early warning of what is to come.

Su Ling, a.k.a. "Annette" Susan Yin, watches the leading edge of a storm. Watching it come rapidly ashore in her friend's sleep. Chilled and thrilled by the rise of an orgasmic siren, a sound born of pain rather than pleasure. A sound born of fear.

Annette, a.k.a. Su Ling, watches her friend begin to struggle. To push against the barrier of sleep. Watching her in a sudden, sadistic craving. An instinct to watch her suffer. To watch her struggle to wake up. To escape what devil or demon there is, sent into the dreamworld to torment her. To touch her heart with the true meaning of fear.

Su Ling watches Jessica open her eyes suddenly, to transform the pitiful, sleeping wail into a full bodied scream. A deep, woman's scream of pure energy.

Su Ling watches in fascination, as her friend, her lover, rises up in zombie coffin fashion. Able to pull herself up from the depths of dreaming somehow, now beginning to thrash around in the wildness Su Ling had been waiting for. The lightly trained, lead footed kickboxer grabs her naked, jiggle breasted friend carefully by both wrists flailing, until Jessica is able to see that she is not a nightmare *Ju-on* brought out of her dream, but is the girl she fell in love with nearly a year ago.

Su Ling hugs the sobbing, crying young woman tightly, feeling the tingle in sensitive breasts as she does so. Absorbing the energy of her friend's sobbing. Pressing herself together with her breast to breast. Cheek to cheek. Her body still abuzz from the sight and sound of her unique suffering. A suffering caused by the spirit of fear.

Su Ling shushes and hushes the crying girl firmly. Gently. Laying the wide eyed victim of Fear's touch back down on the bed. Sliding herself into place, into the comfort of their hidden dynamic. Into the private truth of their public relationship on campus.

Su Ling slides one of the snow white double dollops into the crying girl's mouth. Patient as she hesitates just a bit. Quickly taking one of the gigantic nipples into her mouth. Nipples naturally enlarged by heredity. Made larger by arousal.

Su Ling lays there. Barely able to fathom the flow of pleasure. The sucking flow of electric twingeing coming through in waves. Pulling through space at her groin. Making her feel the pissing twinge. The desire to wet the sheets, to relieve the new pressure down below.

Su Ling lays there. Propped up on her elbow. Watching her lovely friend take full comfort in the dynamic of who they are. Watching her cheeks sunken in full nursing form. Unable to block the image of her own mother, when Jessica suddenly opens her eyes and looks up at her. Gazing. Staring a quiet begging at her in the darkness dimly lit.

Su Ling is unable to push it away. To push away the image of her mother laid in this same position on her side, breasts heavy with milk when Su Ling was twelve. When Dr. Yin was away. When mother Yu Ling, a.k.a. Sarah Yin, was a housewife alone. The house mother of twelve year old Su Ling.

This kickboxing beauty closes her eyes in anguish. Wondering why the sucking pulls will not relieve her suffering. Feeling her hand move on its own. To her proper place. Her improper place. Touching herself. Barely moving her finger at all. Needing only to press her hand in position. To ground the flow of this current through her body.

The deep, sultry voice of her mother begins to torment her. To push her toward the precipice. To the place where her mouth must hang open so she can breathe. Gazing in the darkness, down at her friend upon her breast. Watching it being pulled deeply into her mouth.

Su Ling cannot push it away. The sight and sound of her mother, when Su Ling was twelve...

"Take the milk from your mother's tits, Sarah Ling says, English rich with her native Asian tongue. *"Your mother cum in her TITS..."*

Su Ling sees her mother's face flash in agony. Seeing the grimace of pleasure unleashed all at once. In this spark of memory, Su Ling perceives a pushing. A last, deadly sucking of milk from her own breast. A sucking that pushes her over the edge. That sparks a bolt from her nipple to her groin. Causing her to cry a yell in the dark. To yell a cry as her body spasms once. A violent twitch born in pain. The suffering of a connection established. The agony of energy exploded within.

As the deep suckling goes on, the tension breaks in her body. To sound a blast wave from ground zero, from her groin to her legs, up into both breasts with precision. Doubling her over in deep convulsions. In deep grunting that cannot cease to be. The energy passes through her in waves, pulled through her body by the force of each sucking pull at her breast. Swallowing as her mouth waters in the grunting. Her vision whirling into a dizzying haze in the dark. Hearing the deep, woman's voice of her mother in the storm.

Su Ling Yin was twelve, when the spirit came unto her. Su Ling is twelve, when the spirit of Sarah Yin hath come.

"That was some dream you had," Su Ling says.

"That was some orgasm *you* had. You went to another place. It was Sarah's Place again, wasn't it?"

Su Ling allows herself the Great Looking Away. The gaze somewhere beyond the ceiling, and the ceiling of grieving gray clouds, toward the spirit that rules the glory of the Third Heaven.

"We've been together for a year, Annette," she says, evoking her friend's chosen name, "and still I can't believe I met somebody whose mother was as perverted as mine."

"That stuff your Mom wrote in her book… how much of that is, well…"

"Autobiographical?"

Jessica answers the question with a quick, quiet glance into her distant past. When her mother gave pretense and behind closed doors hypocrisy a permanent dismissal.

"I'm sorry," Su Ling says. "I always wanted to ask that. I swore to myself that I never would. I guess maybe I shouldn't have. But Hell.. oh, what the Hell, it's the end of the world anyway. Did your mother rape you?"

"In some form or another," she says, "she raped me a thousand times."

"What do you mean by that?"

"I mean that every blow with her fist. Her hand. The belts. The canes. The wooden spoons. The paddles. Every penetration. All of it was me being raped. Being robbed of myself. Sometimes I feel like I'm dead inside."

"Still? After all these years?"

"The last time she did it to me, was right before she died. Half of me is devastated and scared to death. The other half is relieved. Exhilarated. Like I've been set free."

"I'll never be free," Su Ling says. "My mother's too rich. Too beautiful. Too sexy. I'll admit that I still crave her sometimes. It's a dark secret, Jessica. I've never told anyone else but you. And the only reason I even told you is because your mother wrote that book. I've read it twice."

"I think the whole world has. They say it might become the biggest selling novel of all time."

"It's why your nerves are so bad, I'll bet. Because of her. What you went through."

"But you went through it too," Jessica says. "And you turned out fine."

"Yeah," she says, voice rich with sarcasm, "I turned out great. I've slept with at least one different female professor every semester since I've been here. And you know something. None of them claim to be lesbians. Your mom was a prophet when she wrote *"every heterosexual woman is a closet lesbian underneath."*

"And all four of those women were married," Jessica says. That's what gets me."

"They were okay with it because I was a woman. Two of 'em didn't even consider it cheating."

"What do you do to these women? These 'closet dykes' of yours?"

"I like to get 'em all on their back. On the corner of the bed. Or the side of it. With me standing up. I raise their legs up. And then I fuck their brains out. It was Sarah's favorite strap on position. She liked it up the ass from that position. Only position she squirted from."

"What?"

"She would cum so hard she would piss a fountain when I did that. She trained me to do that from the time I was 13 years old."

"Jesus," Jessica says. "It's unbelievable."

"It's why if your mother's book had been a memoir, it would have hardly sold a few thousand copies, instead of damn near a hundred million. I hope you were in your mother's will. If so, you and me are rich, baby."

"I don't give a *fuck* about my mother's money."

"That's because you're already rich. You have the privilege to not 'give a fuck' about money. You don't need it."

"You're rich too," Jessica says, as if offended by the comment.

"Upper middle class rich. But you're Hollywood rich. Thanks to your mom's book. If they made a movie out of it, would they get it right? *Could* they?"

"When you came," Jessica says, "you said something brutally weird."

"What?"

"You mean, you *don't* remember?"

"Not at all. What did I say?"

"You said to me, '*suck the milk from your mother's tits*,'" as if I were your daughter or something. And then you said '*your mother's going to cum in her tits.*' Actually, you said '*your mother cum in her tits.*' You said it like you *meant* it. Then, you shot off like somebody stuck you with a cattle prod. I thought you were going to pass out."

"I almost did. But I swear I don't remember saying a word."

"It came out of your spirit. You sounded possessed anyway. Your voice was deeper. And more Asian."

"I didn't mean to scare you."

"Trust me, after the dream I just had, you didn't. You couldn't."

"You sounded like you were gonna die from pure fright. What the Hell did you see anyway?"

"It was…"

Jessica pauses for a moment, as if the memory were nearly too much to bear.

"It was merciless evil. Her eyes. Her eyes were white as moonlight. Her skin was pale and blue. She was standing at the edge of the bed, back in our house in Chappaqua. In my old bedroom. In the dream, I woke up and saw her standing there. She opened her white eyes as wide as they can go. The sound she made, Su…it was the deepest, most classic ghost moan in history. I swear to God. It filled me with a fear so deep I thought I was going to die."

"That's more funny than scary."

"That's because you didn't see it. I'll be afraid to go to sleep for three nights."

"It's because you didn't go to the funeral," Su Ling says. "You need closure."

"Sorry, Doc," she says, her friend's future in psychiatric medicine notwithstanding. "This time, it wasn't a guilty conscience. This time... it was real."

Jonathan Lovejoy

The Mormon Girl

This is one of the lonely places. Nearby the twilight of human history. One hundred miles east of Salt Lake City, where the Uinta Mountains rise in the nearby distance, above the green forests and fields of Northeastern Utah. Nary an acre of ground has been spared this latter day visitation, all around the Green River Basin south, bordering the heart of sister wife country.

This is one of the lonely places. Far removed from the hustle of the city. Where the chosen lifestyle in triplicate may prosper, these three. Three born and raised in Salt Lake City, Utah. These are called upon, to perpetuate a lifestyle in secret. Three intelligent, college educated women, having chosen to leave the chaos of civilization behind for a season. To perpetuate the whims of one they love. To bear the brood of his children, near the rise of the Uinta mountain range, north of Carbon County, Utah. A family of seven children, born of a single father, mothered among his wives, these three. Having moved his home away from the nosy suburbs of Salt Lake City, to better live in the secret of his calling. A suggestion made and insisted upon by the time his third wife was brought on board.

Ironically the oldest, and breastiest of the three. A woman unable to refuse the depth of what twinges sparked her both body and soul, when she was introduced to his beautiful, and sensual first two wives. Two twenty something chirpies, they had been, each more rich with naiveté than the other, with little daughters ripe for the future impending.

This is one of the lonely places. Nearby the rise of the Uinta Mountains of Utah. A place off the edge of the civilized world, somewhere north of Carbon County.

Seven children roam this house and property. Seven children born of the sister wives, these three. Two boys acquainted with their father's lash, but with sympathy and compassion from the mothers. Boys in love with their beautiful mothers. The eight year old boy, and his fifteen year old half brother. Mama's boys, in the latter day place.

The two boys have five sisters. Five girls born of the sister wives, these three. Five girls from twelve to eighteen. The modern mother-daughter dynamic in deep microcosm. Whispered exchanges between the women, since each girl was twelve. Mother-daughter exchanges between the women in private, unbeknownst to the naïve boys and their father. Where the girls are introduced to the unspeakable by the women. In the picturesque country house, nearby the forests and fields north of Carbon County.

As the girls get older, their punishments become more severe. More sadistic. And the eighteen year old girl bears the scars of this from a missed curfew. When her hands were tied to the chinup bar in the basement. When all three of the mothers commissioned themselves to forty lashes apiece. Lashes that cut the girl's white skin to blood. This, after the mothers found out that the girl was seeing a boy at the mall that night.

"Tell the truth, and you won't get in trouble," they had said. And the eighteen year old had crumbled in naiveté.

"The boys were there but all in a group, Mom. It wasn't a date or anything."

"It doesn't matter. You were told NOT to see boys at all and you got home thirty minutes late. And after that C minus you got on your report card, you were told what would happen if you got in trouble again..."

In the heart of the Earth's fervent memory. Somewhere in the Du Shane wilderness, above the back roads of Carbon County. The eighteen year old is taken in secret to the basement down below. Made to undress. Unbuttoning her sky blue blouse, to expose the C-cupped cloth underneath.

"Take your bra off," the older mother says. Forty nine years of lust in the making. Watching the daughter of the middle sister wife take her bra off. Exposing the spongy perfect breasts. A bosom played in the C Major key. Breasts that the three mothers have visited themselves upon ad nauseam. In the basement of this isolated house.

In the fall of a starry, moonless night. The eighteen year-old's hands are rope bound, and pulled upward, where the rope is wrapped around the chinup bar and tied immobile. With a shorter length of rope, she is bound at the ankles.

Boys. Bad grades. Curfews. In the motherline curses passed down, the big three. When the name of discipline is Pain.

"Bite her breasts," the older mother says. This, said to the birth mother. The woman takes hold of the firm, spongy breasts. Biting the girl at the nipple.

The girl jerks and screams angrily. In the full strength of a woman's hold.

"Hold on to her," she says to the other woman. The other wife. Watching the girl's birth mother bite the girl's nipples with fire. Watching the other woman hold her tight from behind. *"Bite 'em good,"* she says. *"I wanna see a bite mark. You wanna whore your tits out to boys? Hmm? Well, not in this family, little girl. Bite her right on the nipple. Bite it hard!"*

This, the girl's mother does. Until the naked eighteen year old can only comply. Shaking her head back and forth. Babbling her promises of obediences. Of boys that will never be seen again.

"Now, suck her nipples," the woman says. *"Suck 'em hard enough to hurt."*

This, the mother does. As the three of them listen to the girl's screams transform to a wailing. A long, pitiful howling. A siren of weeping.

"Keep sucking those tits," The older woman says, handing the leather belt to the other wife. *"Now, whip her across her fat little ass until it bleeds."*

This, the youngest wife does. Obedient. Compliant. Intimidated to action. Bearing the folded leather belt across the girl's buttocks over and over again. Raising new welts on top of the old. Knowing already that each blow is delivered in full strength. Without reservation. Without mercy.

The two women trade places. The birth mother taking the belt. Taking the girl's bottom to the second stage of injury, as the younger wife sucks and bites new marks onto the girl's breasts. Both sides delivered with new energy. A rhythm set to the melody of new, louder screaming. Breasts red and blue with bites and bruises. Buttocks darkened from the dozens of blows.

The spot of skin chipped away is the sign. The cue for the older mother to take over. Forty nine years of lust unbridled. Taking the belt firmly in hand, bringing it across the girl's bruised breasts. Doing this repeatedly, to the music of new, wilder screams.

"Hold on to her," she orders. *"Both of you."*

This, they do. While the older woman burns stripes across the girl's breasts from top to bottom. Returning to the girl's backside, motivated by the spot of skin chipped away. Whacking the belt across this place of discovery. Where the mining of this gold takes the form of trickling blood.

The last welts are created on top of the first ones. Cutting the eighteen year old girl's white skin to blood.

The girl stands there. Straining to stand upright. Wobbling. Pulling down against the ropes tied around her wrists. And the metal bar above her.

The pretty brunette girl sobs quietly. Tears streaming down her face. Feeling the fire upon her wrists. Her breasts. Her bottom.

Burning.

This is one of the lonely places. Replete with pain and misery. In the days just before the latter day rains, on the eve of the rise of a bird kingdom.

The mother of the eighteen year old has a sixteen year old. A girl filled with mischief. Possessing a tiny rose bosom, little balls of jiggle in the A major key. In contrast to a wide, rounded bottom. A set of sixteen year old hips from Kardashia. Hearkened from the Isle of Lopez.

The mother catches the girl texting in her bed. Texting when she should be sleeping. The mother rushes over to her sixteen year old's bed. Grabbing the phone shoved quickly under the pillow. Finding the last message typed and sent. *I want your cock in my mouth,* the message says. In response to the boy's message of like vulgarity.

The mother of the sixteen year old shares this message to the matriarch. To the third wife on paper. The first wife in spirit.

This mother stares at the matriarch's eyes. Gazing every twitch, every shudder. Feeling the hidden deep breath taken. Watching the woman's lips part, that the breath may pass more easily in.

These two wives show the text to the other wife. Anger. Lust. Envy. The three of them.

The older wife takes a picture. A close up of the girl's phone. To record the message in perpetuity. Evidence of why she must be judged. The reason that the girl must suffer.

They let roll the River of Time. To the turning of another day. As the earth turns toward the evening, over the mountains of northeastern Utah. With the father's permission granted, for a private "talking to." To an overnight rendezvous, two hours away. West to Salt Lake City, nearly a hundred dollars spent on the hotel. Driving the girl in silence as the condemned. Quiet in silver SUV comfort, strapped in tightly in the back seat.

And this is the rise of fear in the soul, that affects the mind and body to pain, causing the heart to flutter at the edge of life, until there is a murmuring of shallow breaths in the body, and the flow of icy cold and pain in the soul and spirit.

The sixteen year old girl can only lower her head. Unable to suppress the sobbing squeak in her voice. The squeaking sob, accompanied by the single tear fallen, and the loss of clarity through the haze of watery vision.

"You may as well save that, little girl. 'Cause I can promise you you're gon' get somethin' to cry for tonight. And you know why? Because I read somewhere, that you want to put a boy's cock in your mouth... or so you put it."

"I don't," the girl sobs. *"I swear to God and Jesus I don't."*

"Takin' the Lord's name in vain's not gon' help you, girl."

"I didn't...I ... I'm sorry."

"I know," the older Mother says. *"Sorry you got caught."*

In the hotel lot of high aspirations shattered and torn, the three of them disembark their rolling chariot in the twilight. The older and younger mother walking briskly out front. The middle mother walking behind them. Gripping her daughter by the arm.

"Momma please... Momma..."

"Shut your mouth," the woman hisses. *"You're in enough trouble as it is so just shut up until it's over."*

Through the lobby, into the elevator. The mirrored doors close upon a drama played in secret. Three grown women. A beautiful, wide hipped 16 year old girl in black jeans and a tight, purple t-shirt. A girl whose face is already twisted in crying.

"If you don't shut up I'm gonna start right now."

The crying girl does her best. Holding the rest of the sobs in check. Staring at the women in the elevator door mirror. The three of them.

One, the younger mom. Blue jeans, button down sky blue shirt, white t shirt underneath, blonde hair in loose ponytail. In golden, silken sheen.

The middle mom. Her mom. Long, dark skirt in unintelligible hue, with flowers decorating it down to the floor. Brown hair long and frizzy. Pretty face somber with worry.

The older Mom. Mature, beautiful. Stern faced, voluptuous in dark blue jeans and lavender collar shirt tucked in. Earthen blonde hair done up in tucked-in fashion in the back, hanging loose in front, to frame her mature beauty in false youth. Curves bequeathed from a motherline unknown. Hips more extraordinary than even the sixteen year old condemned.

The elevator door opens into solitude. Into the corridor of shadows. Into the hall of secrets hidden from public view. The girl disembarks the elevator to nowhere. Walking down the hall of hotel doors. Dreading the arrival of room 722.

At the door of destiny. At the conduit from the past to the future. The girl stands in the midst of the women. Watching the older woman make quick work of the door in swiping. Clicking and beeping. Moving into the hotel room with the sister wives.

The three of them.

61

This is one of the lonely places. At the twilight of human history. Where a Mormon girl rides the wind. On the eve of eschatology.

The Mormon girl is made to disrobe. To take off every stitch of her clothing in front of them. Made to stand there, as the three women mill about in nonchalance. In the power of their easy command. Watching them slowly reveal their underwear in pieces. Until the three voluptuous figures are equally exposed. Watching in horror and fascination, as the older woman and the younger in their underwear, slide a harness of leather straps up the thighs of the naked middle woman. Up the thighs of her naked mother. Sliding the straps up to her mother's hips. Tightening them securely.

In one of the lonely places. At the twilight of human history. This girl is forced to her knees before her mother. Told to take in her mouth the realistic member hanging down. *"Go deeper,"* the older woman says. *"You wanna put cocks in your mouth? Suck your mother off then. You wanna be a little slut, then choke on your momma's cock..."*

These words spoken, in the heat of anger, lust, and envy. In envy of the girl's youthful beauty. The curves both athletic and fully formed. The tight, smooth skin of a bottom both fit and feminine. A bottom as big as their own, untouched by time. Untainted by knowledge of the truth. Uncorrupted by the knowledge of good and evil.

"Push your momma's cock into your MOUTH!" The woman yells. *"Push it down your throat until you choke on it!"*

This, the girl tries. Unable to comply. Gagging on it too quickly. Too timidly to satisfy them. In frustration, the older woman kneels down beside the sixteen year old, taking the member roughly in hand. Sliding every inch times eight down into her throat. Holding it there until she chokes. Sliding it out again in a wet wretching. Letting the spit fall heavily down. Down to her exposed breasts. Sliding it down her throat again. Coughing. Choking. Then sliding it out in wretching a second time. Her mouth aglow and wet with her effort. Grabbing the Mormon girl by the hair. Pushing her head down onto the mother's member strapped on. Watching the pitiful young girl gag to near vomiting. Holding her head down upon it without mercy.

In the periphery, the younger mother watches the inevitable go unnoticed by the girl and the older woman in kneeling. Which is the quick and violent quaking. A shaking spasm of the standing mother's hips unseen. Unnoticed by the choking girl. Unacknowledged by the older mother deeply engaged in her committal.

At the end of the girl's new choking. In the aftermath of tears fallen in trauma. The girl is escorted to the bed. Made to lie down on her back. Her mother sits on the girl's legs. The younger mother on her arms pulled straight. And the older mother takes the folded leather belt, and brings it down onto the girl's front down below. Bringing the belt down on her groin. On her chastity. Bringing the belt down across the front of her thighs as well. Burning a lightning pain through her skin. Watching the girl scream and squirm on her back. Striping her from her naval to her thighs.

In the agony of lust tempered in anger. The older mother retreats to the extension of herself waiting. Sliding a new harness of straps about her hips. In admiration of her reflection, of the glory of the masculine channeled through the feminine. Telling them to flip the girl over onto her stomach. Telling the younger wife to hold her hands. Telling the girl's mother, *"Hold her feet."*

The older woman climbs on top of the voluptuous young girl. In lustful envy. Gazing at the rise of the girl's backside in beauty. Spreading the girl's bottom with her fingers. Letting the spit fall to her rectum.

In the pain of lust. In the agony of envy. In the torment of anger. This sensual older woman pushes the head of the member into the girl's backside. Sliding it in deeply. Listening to the girl howl in misery. Laying down on top of her. Daring not to squeeze her hips even once. Knowing what tragedy it would bring.

"Do you still want a boy's cock in your mouth?" she says, her voice trembling.

"No!" the girl screams. A gruff, hopeless yell into the room.

In this lonely place. In this latter day space of grieving. The older mother lowers her head in worry. Looking up again into the eyes of the younger mother holding the girl's hands. Looking to the younger woman for absolution. For a reprieve that can never be.

In the pain of lust. In the agony of envy. In the torment of anger unleashed. This woman opens her mouth in anguish. Her brow wrinkled in suffering. Trying not to allow it to pass through. But in the depths of her womb. Somewhere beyond the suffering of her body. Predestiny ignites a flame inside. To combust a roaring blaze that spreads from her spirit, into her groin. From her groin, the flame erupts a blast wave, to explode ten years of repressed desire for this moment into her body. A desire she barely knew. A craving she barely understood. An instinct born from the motherline. An explosion of blue and black fire.

In the hotel of high aspirations. Of every dream tattered and torn. The woman hears the truth rise in her voice. Hearing the seeds of a yell planted. Listening to it grow louder. Hearing herself scream a battle cry into the room. The call of the motheress in the twilight. The cry of the banshee in the evening day.

This is one of the lonely places. At the twilight of human history. Where a Mormon girl rides the wind. On the eve of eschatology.

Blue Eyes

From the lonely place nearby the mountains of northeastern Utah. They cruise the road west, the three of them. Rolling in sky blue mini van repose, in the company of men. Driven by the father across this dreary Saturday afternoon, with the two sons they love in tow. Having left the five wayward girls at home in the throes of waiting. In the fear of anticipation gone mad.

"... and I am getting sick and tired of all y'all's pissy, disrespectful little attitudes! And I promise you tonight it is going to stop! Now the five of you are on punishment until we say otherwise. And as God is my witness the five of you are going to get your little fat bottoms BLISTERED when we get back home..."

This, having been said in the arrival of a new storm. The storm outside their home, which had flown in on the latter day wings of a bird kingdom.

"Every time we turn our backs on you we're having to break up a fight. How many times have we TOLD you, you are not to fight one another in this house!"

And upon the syllable for the world "told" is a massive, undeserved slap to the eighteen year old girl's face, which shocks her into an anger deeply suppressed, raising her hand to her face, staring at the oldest mother in open mouthed pain and disbelief. And in the agony of her own amazement, she grabs the 18 year old's wrist, thrusting her hand down to her lap.

"Put your hand DOWN," the woman says. *"Let it BURN!"*

The girl looks at her real mother, the middle mother, hoping to be rescued from the fear of pain risen again.

"You ca himme, cause ur nom addreeel mother?

"What did you say?"

"I said you can't hit me because you're NOT MY REAL MOTHER!"

The works of this storm flash in the hearts of their memories as they ride. As they ride in minivan comfort through the bird covered streets of Salt Lake City, toward their time of shopping leisure, to escape their lonely calling in brief, and full replenishment of these energies necessary for it all.

"Janice," the older mother says, holding her slapping hand still in the air. Shaking her head back and forth. *"Janice, do I have permission... to physically discipline your daughter?"*

"You have my permission," the middle mother says, *"to literally beat the HELL out of her if you have to."*

*"Mom?"*the girl says, eyes teary from the sound of betrayal thrust through. *"Mom you said this was going to STOP."*

"Girl... the only reason I'm not all over you right now, is because you're gonna get it later. And honey I promise that by the time its over you're gonnna need medical attention. Because we're gonna take turns on you with that wooden paddle until it turns as blood red as your backside is gonna be..."

In the midst of these storms impending. In the shadow of gray clouds that gather a weeping mist over the great western city. These three women give the signal in veiled command to the husband and the two sons, to leave the three of them alone and go into the huge, mega mall paradise without them for now.

"We've got something we need to talk about," the older mother says, the words *'the drama with those girls'* staying well tucked away in her mind. *"We'll be along later."*

In the light mist, and rising wind of this storm impending. There is a sudden *crash* on the passenger side window, where the older mother sits in bleak contemplation of cutting their oldest daughter's fair and white skin to blood...

At the moment of this contemplation, at the flash of the spot of blood that stains the future paddling wood, this *crash* splits the small space of air in their minivan, where the vacuum is filled suddenly with a shriek and a scream. This, followed by a second quick and powerful crash at the window, sending the shards of glass flying into the older woman's face, and the sudden stench of feathers in her nostrils, and the beating of wings in her eyes.

In her periphery, is the realization that the thousands of birds lining the buildings and nearby streets are there to be fed, that the meat they crave is that of Creation's former masters, and the breaking down of their control to nothing. Pain is scratched into the eyes of the three women in claws and beating white wings, in the rising cacophony of thunderous sound; though not of a rumbling, booming voice from the clouds. The sound they hear is that of their own screams, joined by the voice of the maddening crowd of human victims in the parking lot, as every wayward soul is attacked by the spirit of fear in razor sharp fashion, to where running is only a proposition for falling, and to have bits of their flesh torn from their faces, from their necks and from their backs exposed to the flock.

The small space inside the minivan is alive with two-fold screaming; that of the gigantic white gulls packed inside by way of insanity, where every attempt at opening doors is met with the pointed tips of beaks speared into their hands, sending bolts of lightning through their hands in epic burning and misery.

Even in the midst of this fear and sorrow, the older mother tears her way through the flapping and clawing whirlwind of pain, pushing herself out into the gray mist, eyes both already pecked to blood, tasting the metallic flavor of it already on her tongue and in the back of her mouth to her throat. Her vision is such that there is only sound to hear in a new, worldwide darkness she feels, made more real by a determined beak pushing through her closed eyelids to her eyeball inside, until the woman is not spared the pain of a hard fall to the concrete, and the pressure pushed into her skull through one of her eyes, until there can no longer be sight where this eye used to be. The woman raises her head from her place on the pavement near their rolling chariot of dreams, gathered and eaten in the mist and rising wind of eschatology born.

The three women are not privy to the sights and sounds of masculine screaming nearby the door of the mall, as their husband in triplicate is cut down, and devoured as his sons look on from false hope, behind the glass of the doors and windows being dived into by raptors gone mad in suicide bombings against the glass, cracking it just enough to provide a way, through which a greater crack is formed and breached, raining a shower of broken glass down onto the hopeless inside the mall, opening a space between safety and Armageddon.

Inside the mall, the uncertain quiet gives way to the screaming of women and children, with nowhere to run from the clawing and beating of wings, driving them hopelessly into the open spaces of stores exposed, where every unlucky onlooker, every unfortunate shopper is confronted by death from the skies, and the arrival of it in squawking, and screeching feathered beaks and claws to infinity. Many fall up and down escalators, tumbling over second floor railings when the birds fly into them at the proper speed and angle predestined.

One stubborn beauty waif stands in pleading, screaming in the midst of chaos, holding her baby, enduring the endless clawing and pecking at her back, until she is knocked to the floor, and her child is slowly, gradually, and completely torn away from her arms in bleeding and flesh carved to ribbons. This mother and child are descended upon, until their attack is akin to being eaten alive.

From the end-of-the-world running and screaming in the gigantic mall space, to the crashing, rolling cars and rain soaked victims outside, the arrival of this storm of melancholy is complete. From the floored car speeding hard into a gasoline truck nearby the highway entrance—from this apocalyptic explosion brought to pass, to the calm of a sky blue minivan on the other side, where the faces of two women inside are already picked down to blood and skeleton bone, and the eye sockets of a dead woman nearby are devoid of sight, life, and the blue eyes that made them.

Jonathan Lovejoy

The Queen's

Orgasm

63

$\mathcal{T}$he winds of eschatology flow the Oklahoma Prairie without ceasing, to infuse the landscape beyond every horizon with a dreary, oppressive mood. From every isolated bird attack in places from Pamlico Sound to the Bay over San Francisco, energy is a concentric whirled outward in every direction, until even the cities and countrysides north and south of the migration can feel the spirits of approaching doom. *They're just birds,* and *what the Hell can they do* are words that have been vanquished in the rain and wind, until the entire earth is at last convinced that whatever message it is they have to deliver, is done so on the platter of death and dying.

Around the world, no less than one hundred million souls have seen fit to departure, to move on to their eternal reward beyond the stars. What was glorious at first has become ghastly, a nightmarish echo of the reality that once was, where nature's beauty has been transformed into nature's horror, and the insistence that this tragedy is more real than the world had thought possible. Every two footed and four footed animal on earth has finally given itself over to the spirit of fear, and the acceptance of the truth in feathered terror and beauty.

I rest in my upstairs prison in uneasy tranquility, knowing I have no strength to try and break through the two big window panes, discovering that at some point in our visit, these windows had been *glued* shut. When I first tried to open them in curiosity (knowing that I was *not* going to climb out and break my legs jumping to the ground), I noticed after just a moment the spots and lines of dried glue all around the windowsill and up the sides. Filling me with a sense of the macabre and the sinister.

Was it done as an insurance policy for herself? Before she ever suspected that I might soon be leaving? Was it something that hit her mind from the moment she saw the two of us together—something she was going to do regardless? Or did I cause this with my audacity, with my insistence upon having hope of a normal life beyond her beckon call? As I drift over to the window, where I see my hopes of escape sealed shut for all time, I can't help but blame myself for my stupidity, for believing that I could return to my mother's unloving arms, for protection against the beaks and claws descended from these end of the world skies of grieving.

My presence here can only be another prime example of fate in microcosm, because I had first hand knowledge of this woman's psychology already. But the truth is, something inside me reached across the miles, across the years of deep, dark memory, to pull me through the landscape of what has visited destruction on this latter day world, as a sign of what tragedies are yet to come. Sometimes I wonder, if part of me didn't realize that I was headed for trouble, considering the childhood I suffered in private, and the Hell that she grew up in…in Cherokee County, North Carolina. Part of me must have known, that the years I spent apart from her had not tempered her resolve, the behind closed doors truth of who and what she is.

What still brings a chuckle to my aching body and soul, even now, is when I think about the middle class, mom-ish church and schoolboard crowd, who cannot believe that a woman like this exists in private and in real life, despite what they see and hear about on the news every so often, about when a child is held prisoner and raped to ruin by both the father and the mother alike. And these are women who hold no claim to lesbianism, so many of them having never actually been with another woman. But still, a lust for the innocence of their own daughters pervades their spirit from top to bottom, until it may manifest itself in the most charming ways in public; i.e. the control of the neighborhood sleepovers and all girl carpools, so that the woman may satisfy her cravings through contact—some of them becoming seventh and eighth grade teachers by necessity. With a few of them picking and choosing who to plant this motheress seed into, if they have not done so already with their own daughter.

My mother was lucky enough to have had at her disposal, a ready, willing, and able bodied young chirpie in myself, which the death of my father cleared the way for her to have full access to. And so, from the time I was thirteen years old, I have understood what so many other daughters have also in secret, that the lusts that control women often run wide and deep, and carry no allegiance to sexual orientation whatsoever. I know for a fact that my mother is not a gay woman, nor can she be easily called bisexual, as the definition encompasses. She is as heterosexual as any woman, I suppose; at least she was to my father until she killed him. But curiously enough, there were absolutely *no* men, nor other women for that matter, after I grew up and left home for college. Maybe, she just simply had found what was that seed planted by her own mother, that begged to be nurtured and grown, that drew her into itself like the force of gravity draws one world into another, where there is no hope for escape.

As the rains of this end of the world storm continue to fall, I am a prisoner of what I know of the modern mother-daughter dynamic hidden, and what there is of it behind the walls of this isolated castle home. I have already heard the howlings of this woman's depravity unleashed, knowing that she has given herself over to the depth of it, this, as it burdens the theater of my mind in my upstairs prison.

I can see her embracing the fullness of her primary lust, which is her extreme breast sensitivity, a gift passed down to few women in these heights of severity. And upon this is merged with her incestuous craving for conquest, the instinctual and unfathomable desire for the young female bodies at her disposal. I can see what unearthly bliss she bathes herself in every time, and in greater measure with her present love and capture. I can see, I can feel her full exploration beginning in this very hour, as my daughter lays on her back with her legs back and open, as my mother looks down at the growth of her own anomaly, at the top edge of a fourth inch into being!

Of what unseen depravity this is! Oh God, who can know the nature of it revealed! For this is a secret flown from the mind of Eve, where the women have abandoned the natural use of the man, to partake in fullness her part of what is forbidden. I see this woman on her hands and knees in the dimly lit, twilight bedroom, in full control of her world at the edge of tomorrow, pressing the fourth inch into the front of her granddaughter's chastity, holding it there, in grieving to resist the shudder that threatens to overtake her mature, voluptuous body. But in the strength of her calling, my mother holds her ground, with every pink and powerful inch of her clitoral self inside my daughter.

As to the depths of this new desire my daughter feels, she does not know. She only knows that she must take the woman's breasts that hang, to touch the mountains turned down toward her, to guide them into her mouth in deep sucking, as though to draw the phantom milk from these Vesuvian mounds of J-cupped flesh swinging in her face. And from this exploration of who my mother is at heart, an Amazonian Breast Goddess, she rests in the fullness of her calling, feeling sparks of energy from the girl's touch alone, which is the foreplay of what she must do, her clitoral self resting inside my daughter down below, while the pulling of her nipples into my daughter's mouth are the Queen's Intercourse; where every deep, hard sucking draws energy from deep inside her body, where it passes through her groin on the way up to the nipple in question.

Of this unique feeling that passes through her body, she is at a loss, not knowing whether to stop or keep going, whether to move or stay still, whether to breathe or not to breathe, that is the question she must endure. But as her beautiful granddaughter lays there, her young legs up in desperate missionary to serve her grandmother, my mother's instinct, her ingenuity tells her that above all things, she must not move, she must not speak, but only pray to the spirits that govern her perversion, that every touch, every squeeze, every sucking the young girl does is toward the breaking of the apocalyptic tension built up in her body.

And of this, to this woman's awe and amazement, the girl nurses in sensual instinct, staying upon a single breast, sucking at a single nipple without even the hint of ceasing, her legs up and wrapped around her beautiful grandmother at the sides, her eyes closed, her young face anguished with her own unendurable craving, knowing that she too, must not deviate this course, this deviance, and that she must nurse her grieving grandmother to completion.

And as this woman looks down in wonder of what suffering her body must entail, there is a rise of energy in her groin that spreads, that causes her voice to whisper the beginnings of a wailing, a pissing twinge of energy multiplied, pulled into greater being by each sucking pull from the young girl's lips and tongue, until this feeling rushes in at once in every direction in her body, causing the wailing to grow into a siren of hopeless pleading, where the name of her Lord is evoked in desperation for a reprieve. In this, the tension in her body refuses to break, but only sustains the unendurable plateau, which is a fearful place of wailing and whining, both coalesced into outright weeping, where the sound of a woman's torment is spread out into every wall of the house, into every wood and glass particle of shelter therein.

At this extended plateau the woman weeps, as the suckling passes this flow of energy smoothly from her womb and bowels, into both legs and feet, up through where her naval hides in the fleshiness of her curves, into both arms weakened by trauma, and finally through both breasts where the energy settles, drawn by the pulling of one nipple hard and long in the girl's hand, and the other sucked and nursed deeply into the back of her mouth. In this female superior, the Amazonian missionary pose, this woman weeps the Queen's Orgasm, where the plateau is heightened to where the woman must howl and weep to the gods for mercy, before the energy settles her mind and body again to renewal, as it passes so smoothly and violently through.

In the aftermath of this weeping, the woman lays down heavy on the little girl, so that the girl must turn her head to escape smothering under the mountain of breast flesh, her legs still up and wrapped around her grandmother, suddenly having to grab the woman's fleshy hips hard, to anchor herself from this energy transferred, making the granddaughter have to hold her head back and writhe against the wave of explosive energy trembling both legs, and every other inch of her young body it passes through.

Part Four

Jonathan Lovejoy

The House on Ashley Elizabeth Drive

At the foot of her mother's grave, Jessica Weinberg's tears are two-fold. This, in the heart of her brief memory, as she cruises through the apocalyptic gray, driving toward the lonely and abandoned streets of wealthy Chappaqua. In the heart of memory, standing at her mother's grave in the rainstorm, Jessica's tears reflect the double tragedy of her recent days.

"Jessica... Jessica please don't do this, you KNOW how much I love you, you know what we mean to each other..."

These words echo the theater of her mind, as she allows the rain to pour on top of her with the umbrella lowered, to feel the cold revelation of reality beckon. To drown her. To torment her with the third part of the truth that no, no one in the world is left that can truly be trusted past the end of the day.

No one can be trusted. No, not one.

As Julie drives toward the dead streets of privilege, she remembers the rainy repose at her mother's grave, and the burden of her two-fold tragedy.

"What am I going to do if you leave me Jessica? I gave up my apartment to move in here with you. I don't have a job, I don't have any money. I don't have anywhere else to go..."

"Then you should have thought of that before you started fucking Bethany Breeland behind my BACK!"

"You're always accusing me of fucking somebody, Jessica. She was just over here for a visit..."

The Asian eyes of Susan Yin play the theater of Jessica's mind. Traitorous, treacherous eyes. Eyes that had been able to look Jessica in hers, as blonde, big breasted Bethany Breeland had hopped up off the sofa like she had been stuck by a pin, and hurried out of the apartment with an embarrassment that she tried so hard to hide. Jessica had not bothered to pretend, had refused to give Susan even the slightest opportunity to slide past the moment unaccused.

"Don't even waste your time," Jessica had said, holding her hand up in 'stop' form. *"Because between the two of you, there's not a human being in the world that wouldn't fuck BOTH of you. So don't insult my intelligence, Sue."*

"I swear to GOD we are just friends, Jessica. I SWEAR it."

"Look at me, and tell me you didn't fuck her."

And true to her Asian lover's nature, there is barely a lie that she has the strength to tell.

"Even if I did," she whines. *"I swear to God it meant absolutely nothing."*

"Do you have any idea at all what this feels like? It's like being stabbed in the GUT. It is a cold, DEATHLY feeling. And I know what you did to her too. I guess she's a cheerleader for a reason, isn't she? Did you enjoy laying on top of her? Holding her down? Pinning her arms to her sides? Sucking on her tits?"

"Jessica, I didn't..."

"Save it Sue... because if you haven't don't that to her yet... I know you will."

Jessica drives onward. Remembering her tears at her mother's final resting place. Remembering that the pain of them was two fold. One, the burden of an unfaithful lover, and the sword of infidelity thrust through her body.

"And this is gonna shock you, Sue. A bigger end-of-the-world shock than that goddamned bird migration. I stood at the door, listening for as long as I could stand it before I came in. And I heard the bitch moaning into your mouth like she was gonna get off..."

Jessica's tragedy is two fold. One, the sword of a lover's infidelity. Two, the sword of a mother's depravity. Forged in the heat of lust and hatred. Tempered in blue and black fire.

Jessica Weinberg drives on. In the two fold burden of her brief history. From the cemetery at North Pineview, to the rainsoaked streets of New Castle. Cruising through the pain of loss, to the privileged roads of

Chappaqua. Feeling somehow drawn adrift, not to the upper class halls of her childhood, and the secrets that roam and lurk among the shadows.

From her mother's grave at Pineview, she is drawn to another house she knows. In the wealthy neighborhood, where she and her mother spent many a day and night in fungalooga smiles and laughter. Whirling in silver Cadillac luxury into the black asphalt driveway. Rolling smoothly past the golf course green stretch of property, and the row of cedar trees that decorate the entrance ride to prosperity.

Jessica disembarks her rolling silver chariot, walking through the mist up the walkway deeply familiar, then vaguely, then deeply familiar again. In the pristine, picturesque presentation of privilege and form, there is the curious anomaly in the rain, that of a bay window completely shattered, with nothing more than a tropical blue, flower made cloth secured across the top, blowing in honor of the beautiful lives that have come and gone.

Jessica tries the knobs at every door, wondering if she will obey her compulsion as she walks back to the front. This, to climb like some desperate squatter through the shattered window, into the livingroom of the abandoned mansion home.

As the mist of weeping continues to fall from the clouds, Jessica carefully climbs into the house on Ashley Elizabeth Drive, into the daytime darkness of a life left behind. Standing bewildered in the midst of a world of luxury scratched and clawed to oblivion, wondering where it is that the Indian girl... and her beloved mother could have gone.

Jonathan Lovejoy

Amazonia

Mother-daughter perversion is real

Across the landscape of human psychology

Modern day suburban witchcraft

On the eve of eschatology

The reality of who my mother is has settled upon me in tragedy. I have not spoken to my own daughter in the three weeks I have been locked in this room, in a dreary, dragging along of the timeline, with me as a genuine prisoner, too spiritually and emotionally weak to do a damn thing against my mother, who comes into the room as my bruises and welts try to heal, and straps upon herself that which pertaineth to a man. If there is a place of love and compassion left in our relationship, it has been abandoned for now, as she endeavors upon my training, to teach me that to be born is to be cursed, and to live is to suffer.

The world is unaware of people like my mother, except in the power of pornographic fantasy. Women whose loins ache with penis envy, the craving to feel the lightning energy grown big from their own clitoral power, and the desire to exact this punishment upon a female victim. Some could call it lesbianism, I suppose, but the truth of it is Amazonian, Amazonia, Amazonianism, where their sexual desire simply is, and what they desire is the physical and spiritual erotica of another woman. They neither hate men, nor are necessarily repulsed by men, but are merely indifferent to them sexually, as their desire for other woman burns them both body and soul.

And the seed of this truth lies dormant in all women, though unexplored by most, having not been provided the light of the right female attention, nor the nourishing waters of woman to woman opportunity. And my mother is the female antithesis of the man who hath left the natural use of the woman—Katherine Hardwick having left the natural use of the man half a generation ago. My mother's lust is that of the serial rapist, who can feel the tiding of a new craving over the next horizon. It is the perverted lust of the rare woman who is caught, of those women who have captured a little girl, tortured her, and then smothered or stabbed her to death. It is the pain that drives the young, sexually charged mother to beat her nine year old daughter to bruises from her neck to her knees, so the bruises are not visible to her third grade classmates. It is the same lust that drives the mother to strip her clothes off in front of the nine year old girl, then strip the girl naked, then beat the girl everywhere upon her body, including the head, until when the girl does not wake up for school the next morning and there is a stream of blood dried from her little nose, the mother calls 911 in terror, to have them come by, and pointlessly shock and press and pump the girl's heart and lungs, but to no avail. These are the little girls declared dead on arrival; in the shadows of hypocrisy and disbelief from all involved, that what bruises and scars there are on the child's body were put there by clumsiness, by school fights, by the careless echo of violence whispered, brought upon the child by a ghost of the unknown. These are the mothers of the dead, who stand at these girls' graves in solemn weeping, broken down by the sorrow of abandonment, and the tragedy of mistakes made east of Eden. These are mothers who hide comfortably in public, who have acquainted their daughter's body with rape, with the pain of an anal reaming with the phallus of rage, as with the sword of their own pain and suffering passed down. It is the tragedy of human existence, which is Fate, that insists that mankind cannot cease from sin, and that since the angel at the garden gate—that points the flaming sword of Nod—woman is wayward, and is heavy laden with sin.

As I lay dying, though my body is still curved and well fed at the bosom, the door to my prison clicks and creaks open, causing me to raise up to sitting, not bothering to hope that my handcuffs at the black iron head-railing will be undone this time.

I hear the clicking of the lock. This time apart from my mother as she stands there. The two of us locked inside, though her key is hidden somewhere in her dress or underwear cloth, so I would have to overpower her and try to steal it, which I know is impossible, as this former horse farming woman possesses the strength of a man. It is a strength and power that I can feel when she is heavy upon me in either form of violence, be it done in pleasure or pain.

She places her roll of beige packing tape, and her tangle of leather straps onto the bed beside me. I can only sit still, in my bra and underwear, looking up at her to see if the woman I know is there at all. And perhaps the scariest thing about this is that yes, the woman I see is my mother, in full sanity and presence, but so dramatically unafraid to turn on this dime, and watch the tear fall from my eye without even a spark of compassion.

"Take off your bra," she says, "and your underpants."

This, I do slowly, but without hesitation, my lips tucked in, my expression heavy burdened with sorrow, which begs me to beg her, to try and take this opportunity to ask her to please... to please let me see my daughter.

But I know better.

"Lie down," she says, looking down at me not so much as my captor, but as my mother, in full command and control of me from my mind, to my body, to my spirit, to my soul. She watches me lay on my back, breasts flopped in the G major key, but still so much smaller than her own. On my back, I watch her strip her navy dress cloth from her underwear exposed, letting it fall to the floor nearby. And she need not slide the black bra and underwear fabric from her body, to establish her as one of the most powerfully curved women of all time, but hidden from the world, as such a thing is hardly meant for the world to see.

She takes the tangle of straps, sliding them up her hips in requisite form, to where the member hangs Amazonian, in every inch of Sapphira's Sword times nine. This ninth inch of mother's lust hangs down from her, having already caused a shudder from her hips that she did not bother to hide, swallowing the desire, closing her eyes once as she retrieves the roll of tape and climbs on top of me astraddle, wrapping the tape at the base of both my breasts, to stand the gargantuan things up in wobbly possibility.

Here I lay on my back, both my breasts wrapped with the beige tape, to where the fleshy front of them can still be seen. She slides me to the edge of the bed, confident in my immobility, my paralysis; though my wrist is uncuffed from the bed railing. I watch this woman in the depth of penile lust strapped on, holding the member, rubbing the head of it at my arousal, to torment me, to test me, to tell me without a word that yes, I am little more than her slut, laid here for her pleasure, and that this is the end of the age, where all pretense behind closed doors will be dropped, and female perversion will see its full flowering on the eve of earth's final departure.

In this prophecy unfurled, in the beauty of uncurled depravity, she slides the member into me, standing at the edge of the bed, gazing at my breasts taped, reacting as though the member were somehow nerve attached to her body. And the sight of me laid helpless on my back, pathetic, my legs up and propped on her arms, the sight of my taped, wiggling breasts, the feel of my helplessness drives this woman forward, to where I know that she is engaged in one of her many sexual gifts, which is to drive her message home in masculine power, channeled so smoothly and violently through the feminine.

I watch this woman possessed, unable to hold down my own arousal, which I feel being pounded into me as I am raped by my mother. I watch her lose herself in this, driving the member up into me in total feeling, her breasts jiggling mightily in mountainous cleavage, the flesh of her hips wiggling in the underwear cloth, as her beautiful mouth hangs open in white Indian squaw, her cheekbones especially high at this moment, so that I can see that this white woman is half Indian, and all Amazon.

I watch her brave a feeling passed through her in greater power than that achieved by a man, who feels only the physical, and the touch of it in his pathetic human spirit, while this woman feels the member as though it is an outgrowth of the very soul she carries. I watch this woman lose her breath to a whimpering, a whining she cannot suppress as her hips drive like a piston, as she gazes unflinchingly at my breasts taped up and wobbling, until suddenly her entire body jerks mightily, which shocks her expression, which she is unable to pound any further through, her mouth hung open in total awe of the lightning strike, braving another spasm of her body that convulses her hips and both her legs, causing her to yelp an unearthly shriek into the room. I watch her strain to resist the passing of it a second time, which convulses her body again, this time from her hips and legs up to her waist and arms, jiggling her breasts mightily, moving through her voice in a pitiful, mournful wail.

Outside the door of this prison. There is a face of beauty pressed to the wood. A face of sorrow. Of weeping.

Of fear.

Mother of the Bride

In the heart of the earth's fervent memory. At the twilight of history. I see the judge's wife at her daughter's wedding. In the land by Washington D.C. These are stubborn in upper class misery, on the green lawn of prosperity. I see the judge and his brunette, beautiful wife, on the eve of eschatology.

In the wealthy suburb at Washington D.C. At the wedding of white lace audacity. A daughter at the smiling edge of her second marriage, in the aftermath of her own adultery. A woman divorced from her first husband at the behest of her mother's depravity.

This wedding in white cake and white lace beauty, in end of the world audacity. I see the judge's wife in the throes of victory, at her daughter's second trip to matrimony. Having ridden her daughter's marriage like a witch in the wind, twenty four years come and gone again. Watching her smiling daughter marry again, in these end of the world rains of misery.

The swans are a blessing from God above, they said, when they erected the tent without fear or dread. Rain soaked property of the judge and his wife, their lust for the pride of life bears grief to be fed. Marrying, and giving in marriage, at the height of latter day hypocrisy. Family secrets landscaped and hidden away, at the twilight of human history.

At the wedding of this privileged daughter, in the wealth of Washington D.C. These great snowy owls look on, from the branches of every nearby tree. *A sign sent to us by God,* they say, *for all of us to see.* That all of us are meant to be happy, from this day until eternity.

White on white is his judgment right soon, in the wedding suburb at D.C. When the white snowy owls spread their wings in the rain, in the branches of every nearby tree. Gliding in hunger and instinct, to the wedding in white audacity. Flying violently under the massive tent roof, through their barrier of protection in the rain. Flying at least a dozen strong, over the screaming guests they see. Digging razor claws into their faces and eyes, causing every one of them to flee. Screaming in chaos from underneath the tent, in terror and calamity. Stumbling in agony through the rain, in white washed debauchery. Dominating the judge's wife, who is the mother of the bride, clawing her to blood and bitter agony. Sending every beige cloth bridesmaid stumbling through the rain, in grieving for another place to be. Knocking the pretty girl chorus all to the ground, as the rains fall without ceasing to be.

At the wedding of Laodicea, in the latter day suburb of D.C. The white swans flap and honk in the rain, across the lawn of their prestigious property. While the great snowy owls find their way to the weeping, wailing bride. Running for a place to hide. Stumbling in her audacity to be dressed in white, slipping on the wet grass in stride. Tripping when the great owl slams her in the cloth of the veil, causing her to hit the ground and slide. Standing up again by help from the faithful groom, clawed by razor talons in tow. Covering his eyes in blinded agony, unable to see now where to go. Unable to see his wife fall again, flat on her face to the ground below. Unable to see his bride covered again by feathered wings as white as snow. Unable to see the judge's wife run to her daughter, stumbling to the ground with a thud. The judge's wife stumbles down to the ground in the rain, while talons cut her white skin to blood.

In the wedding suburb of prosperity. In latter day Washington D.C. A mother and her daughter lie dead on the lawn. In the aftermath of hidden debauchery. Having left a trail of blood, bruises and broken hearts behind, along the timeline of upper class pain and misery. A mother's secret strapped and hidden underneath her dress, after the rendezvous with her daughter in her wedding dress, a secret carried by them to their grave, no less, at the twilight of human history. A mother and daughter taken in the aftermath of passion, in the wedding suburb at D.C. An apocalyptic secret in an early grave. In the rains of upper class misery.

A mother-daughter secret in an early grave. On the eve of eschatology.

Over the Golden Gate

As the invisible sun sets over the Golden Gate. Somewhere beyond these clouds of grieving. The traffic flows casually from east to west in the gray twilight, every soul in grieving to be free. Gazing at the infinity of large, exotic birds perched along every inch of red railing from top to bottom. Gazing at them with a renewed hatred and contempt, as if mankind were never acclimated to what beauty they once provided. Now, the sight of these migrating flocks, the smell of their woodsy, feathered dominance in the air brings only a question of hatred, and whether or not millions of human lives need to be placed at risk to kill them.

Migration

These bitter souls drive on in the late afternoon gray. Unimpressed by either the majesty of the red bridge over the bay, or the legions of buzzard hawks that gaze at them from the great heights. These ride on in false complacency, in the adaptation of the human spirit, ready for the world to turn away from this part of the timeline, where this migration will fade into a dark and distant memory.

And in the tranquility of this late afternoon travel and commute, there appears at the windshield of the eighteen wheeled truck a lightning quick break before the driver's eyes, shattering the driver's nerves and visibility, causing him to swerve unbeknownst into the oncoming lanes, shocking the cars and trucks across three lanes into slamming their brakes, beginning the line of crashing and flipping cars behind them, as the big truck squalls into the blonde mother and her blonder daughter's silver Camry, which acts as a ramp for the lifting, sending the truck high and wide over the bridge railing, slamming in noisy metal clamour halfway between hope and Hell itself, the trailer balanced but a moment, metal creaking a death call to the terrified passers by, as many sets of wings take flight away from the doomed truck crashed over the railing, the fuel tank split and spraying fuel toward the raging waters of the bay down below.

And at least one of the buzzard hawks must pay for its bravery, in the flash of bright orange flame and booming noise from the truck cab exploded, the outpouring of fuel igniting in a line of fire down toward the water. From the center of the bridge at this ball of fire over the railing, the cars crash and flip and swerve in stubborn audacity, by drivers who refuse to believe that the cars in front of them at 65 miles per hour have suddenly slowed down to ten miles per hour, until at last every car on the bridge from east to west is stalled, with every driver and passenger awestruck by the exploded 18-wheel truck hanging over the railing.

And these are unaware, unbelieving, unaccepting of a new fact, that their cars are no longer protected by the cushion of speed in motion, and are now subject to the whims of speed in feathered adversity. One by one, multiplied by one dozen, and then two; the hopeless windows of the cars are crushed and broken, so that the men, women and children are fed upon by the hawks, gulls and blackbirds great and small, as the buzzards soar their great heights above the bridge, circling slowly the inevitable future of their craving, and the bodies of the hundreds of souls that will soon be killed and fed upon.

"*The latest major bird attack took place on the Golden Gate Bridge today during late afternoon rush hour traffic, where over 700 people were killed, after a tractor trailer crashed and exploded near the center of the bridge. The accident caused cars to crash into one another across all six lanes, stalling traffic bumper to bumper, allowing the birds to attack the estimated 4000 passengers trapped in their cars with no means of escape. The governor of California spoke briefly about this latest attack, calling it a 'declaration of war.'*"

Governor quote:

"This is NOT Alfred Hitchcock. This is a Kubrickian nightmare. And this latest attack is nothing short of a declaration of war. The death toll around the world is apocalyptic. And it is now clear that the entire earth's population is being threatened. This latest attack is a sign that if left unchecked, this 'bird apocalypse' will continue to grow, until it begins to threaten more towns, more cities, more states and more countries around the world...."

Despite the governor's call to action, the President reasserted his position that an attack on this worldwide migration would be like, quote, 'trying to drain the Gulf of Mexico.' I'm Cora Leeds, the Associated Press."

The Fear of Death

$\mathcal{I}$ am resigned to my Fate. Along with the rest of the world, I have come to accept who, what and where I am, understanding that there will be no war against the inevitable. I have stopped eating the big meals she brings, satisfied now in her displeasure, as she takes one tray out and brings me another later, with her pulling hard at temptation's trigger, trying to kill my despair diet with every southern delicacy and delight she can think of to make me hungry, everything from breaded deep fried chicken and pork tenderloin to macaroni and cheese, even mocking me with a giant New York style pizza, which caused her to nearly laugh when she left it on the bed nearby where I was handcuffed, being that I had not eaten any of her cooked food for two days.

But to spite her, I know that I cannot eat, lest I keep these bosoms of mine blown up for her twisted, wicked pleasure.

"Aww..." she says, touching my chin in mock compassion. "Don't cry, baby. It has to be this way. How do you think it makes me feel, having to punish my own daughter?"

I raise my head up from my crying repose, gazing at her in near epic disbelief, at what apocalyptic audacity she displays.

"Momma... why are you *doing* this?"

With a look of genuine pity, she touches both hands to my face, leaning down, kissing me lovingly on the mouth. As to what feeling that my trembling lips and tear stained face does to her body...

I do not know.

"Because you think you actually have a choice in life. And you chose to take my granddaughter away from me."

"But I won't. I *swear*."

"It's too late for that," she says, her face somehow burdened with concern. "It hurts me," she says. "And it scares me to death to think about what has to happen."

In the pit of my stomach, there appears the butterflies of legend. To remind me that still, in my life, the types of fear are many...

And uniquely distinguished.

In tears, I watch the tallish, shapely, beautiful woman turn and walk slowly toward the bedroom door, opening it in slow motion flair of elegance, leaving me alone to my misery. Truthfully, as I gaze at the unopened box, and as I breathe in the air of culinary art, I am aware that there is hardly a hunger barrier born stubborn enough to resist this. But *who the Hell does she think she i*s, I say to myself, refusing to open the box and even look, as my hunger begins to take a life of its own, spreading out into every part of me, aching me to muscle and bone.

What form of punishment is this! Where I am fed Old and New World delicacies for the taste! A banquet of healthy and unhealthy food, from watermelon and sugar cookies to chili dogs and cheeseburgers, none of which I dare eat beyond a taste or two. She is, at heart, a farmer's wife. Who has fattened more than one sow for supper in her time, having fed far more than one horse back to strength and good health. But as I take the pizza box and toss it to the floor, wishing to throw the two 20oz bottles of Mt. Dew out the window glued shut, I am suddenly hit by the memory of just *who* it is that I call my mother, and the confirmation of it by what she's done.

As the thunder gently rolls in revelation over my resolve, as I sit at the edge of the bed handcuffed to a chain I cannot break, my mind is burdened with the truth, that perhaps the blood that flows through my mother is touched with something beyond perversion, and that maybe, the depth of her motivation is evil.

But what fault is it of hers? Is she to blame for the insanity that was put upon her by her Indian mother, and her mother's two sisters? The way she was starved and beaten like a dog, the way they took her out of school for long periods of time, locking her away like an animal in her back bedroom, sometimes for as long as a week before they let her out? The power of these tragedies cannot be denied, for here I am, a living testament, a forty year old woman held prisoner in her mother's home like something out of a dark fantasy, or even a darker reality, reported in documentary form. I have seen and heard of such things happening to children and abused wives, but I never really understood it before, never allowed it to sink in that the people they talked about were real, and not the substance of some depressed soul's imagination.

If I ever again see the light of day, will anybody believe me when I tell them? When I tell them what the horse rancher's widow Katherine Rose Hardwick, daughter of Pia Rose Hardwick, has done to me and my daughter behind closed doors? Will they believe me, when I tell them that the windows of my prison were boarded up like a beach house before a hurricane? I had been awakened from this dream early this rainy morning, long before the seven hundred souls died on the Golden Gate bridge. Awakened from the sight of a man boarding up the windows of a beach house in an approaching storm.

And when I woke up this morning, I saw that the daytime dark I had grown accustomed to was about to fade completely to black, as she nailed the pieces of plywood over the two second floor windows while I sat chained to the bed, never glimpsing at me once, engrossed in the spirit of her farm girl's labor, wearing her jeans and button down denim shirt in the break between rainstorms, placing pieces of plywood at each window then nailing forever upon each one, until even if I could have broken through those old style window panes, I would hardly have been able to push or kick my way out.

By way of the new permanent nighttime, I am now acquainted with the reality of my starvation, and the revelation of what she meant, when she spoke of what it is that 'has to happen.' But why should I be surprised, considering what she is? That even into her late thirties, before her mother, the Indian Pia died, my mother was taken to the horse stables on this very property after she widowed herself from my father—and was bound by her wrists to a post, and her mother literally 'horse whipped' her, until her back and her buttocks ran with trickles and streams of blood.

What can I expect from a woman, whose pleasure was to tie me up when I was sixteen, and lay a leather belt across my bottom and my thighs, as I lay flat on my stomach on the bed, my wrists bound underneath me, my ankles tied tightly together, my mouth gagged with a cloth and a thin black leather strap around my head? What can I say to the crescent moon scar at the bottom of my back, when I believed that just because I was a senior in high school, I could snatch away from her and yell *"leave me alone!"* What can I say to the way I was wrestled to the floor like a steer and hogtied with my clothes on, with my shirt cut and ripped open in the back? What can I say to the white heat of agony itself, as she stood over me with one foot on the top of my back, while she pressed the hot brand into my skin at the bottom?

Outside the boarded up window, the thunder rumbles in sorrow, in grieving for what truths it must tell. I am suddenly unable to stop myself from stretching as far out as I can, to reach the pizza box I so foolishly tossed only inches away from reachability. Having to reach out with my feet and grab hold of it, sliding it over to where I can pick it up, and place it on the bed. I notice that somehow, it is still warm to the touch as I open it, seeing the substance of Italian American perfection in thin crust glory, white cheese melted and tinted with just the echo of brown from the oven, over the slices of pepperoni, and the hint of red sauce scattered in places all around and about.

As I pull a slice with both hands, raising it trembling to my mouth, enduring the chime of sweet twang from my mouth to my soul, I can better feel the torment of nerves at the pit of my empty stomach, and the confirmation that yes, the types of fear are many, and uniquely distinguished. And among these—

Is the Fear of Death.

Kathy Van Scoy Rides the Wind

*K*athy Van Scoy rides the wind. On the eve of eschatology.

Having been witness to the death of sanity. There to usher in the newborn depravity within.

I had to beat the truth out of your mother, her grandmother says. Standing tall and naked, in front of her naked thirteen year old granddaughter. *I got your mother to admit to me why she wanted to take you away...*

At the edge of this truthful lie she must tell, the statuesque woman of curves stands with her arms down, gazing at every inch of the beautiful, fair skinned Pocahontas girl. Knowing not to dream of the girl's nipple in her mouth, lest she tremble prematurely.

Your mother was always stubborn, she says. *Stubborn as the devil himself. That's because she has always been wicked inside. I'll show you the grave of the little dog she killed when she was your age. And your grandfather,* she says, gazing at her nipple nearby her granddaughter's breasts. *I took the blame for what she did... to keep her out of jail for the rest of her life...*

In the candlelight of the dark'ned room. The heavy breasted, naked woman gazes at her nipple hung down low, as it crosses the electric barrier toward her reprieve, at the puffy areolas of her granddaughter's half developed young breasts exposed.

Your mother wanted me all to herself, even then, when she was your age. So one night, she took a pistol from your grandfather's gun collection... she started screaming in the livingroom. But when I arrived just before your grandfather died... I saw your mother standing there crying, holding the pistol with both hands. 'You're always hitting my mother,' she said. 'And you won't let her spend any time with me...' and even though I screamed, she still pulled the trigger, and she killed her own father in cold blood...

In the wake of this, in the power of this manufactured memory of the mind, she brushes her nipple across her granddaughter's, grunting once in full, involuntary sound.

Don't touch me, she says, stopping her granddaughter from raising her hands to her breasts.

But I want to touch them Grandma Katherine.

Please don't touch me.

But why not?

Because I don't want to cum yet, she says, in sultry, deep voiced desperation. *If you touch me anywhere on my body I'm going to cum. My body wants to cum. I can feel it in my tits. But I can't let it happen until you know the truth about your mother…*

The beautiful, Indian braided girl stares tucked lipped and humble, up at the exotic, curve waisted woman. Unknowing as to the feeling that begins the pissing twinge at her groin.

Kathy Van Scoy rides the wind. On the eve of eschatology.

I've been afraid of her all these years. Afraid that she would snap and kill me, if I didn't do with her in private all the things she wanted. When she was fifteen years old in the ninth grade, I had to let her strap on a big penis, and while I was standing up in front of the mirror, she stuck it deep into my bottom, until I had to scream from the pain. And then she twisted and pulled on my nipples so hard I h ad to beg her in the name of GOD to stop…

And the girl watches her grandmother's eyes roll upward upon the divine syllable, as if in prayer for him to release her from the Divine Plateau, wherein all must abandon hope, all ye who enter therein.

Because I know how evil your mother really is, I knew I would have to trap her and punish her before she did it to us. I had to strip her clothes down to her bare skin… I had to strip your mother naked, and whip her until the blood started to trickle, until she told me what she was going to do to you…

Kathy Van Scoy rides the wind. Watching the beautiful woman at the throes of what cannot be fathomed. At the edge of what cannot be endured.

She told me that she was going to drive the two of you north until she found a thick, dangerous part of the migration… and she was going to open the door, and throw you out into the storm…

The girl watches the woman's face anguish over in frustration, tantamount to anger, as she rubs her nipple across her granddaughter's without touching her breasts at all with her hands, without moving her arms from their place against her sides, her hands gripped tightly at her own thighs in anchored misery.

And it's this evil inside her, it's this evil I have to protect us from, It's this evil that I have to send from our midst. So that you and I can live. So that we can be happy.

And the girl is suddenly a prisoner at the base of this mountain climbed, where she can only stare down at the woman's gargantuan breasts, observing the nipple grown so big in knowledge, so sensitive in carnal wisdom and craving.

Tomorrow night, the woman says, *I will lie underneath her and hold her arms, and you will take the rope tied to a stick, and you will twist it around your evil mother's neck... until she has been judged by GOD..."*

And upon this divine syllable again, the woman feels the explosion sparked at the nipple, spreading through her breast and to the other, spreading down her flesh, past her waist to her groin, where it doubles her over, choosing to bypass her body's convulsive power, to express itself through her voice, causing her to grunt and bellow like an animal in throes of death, as a cattle in the torture of branding, as the energy passes through her voice in waves of deep, Amazonian grunting—gruff, hard sounds that betray her inner Estros, touched by Testros' unmerciful hand, to cause a woman to lose her sanity upon the fall from the Divine Plateau.

Kathy Van Scoy rides the wind. Holding on to her trembling, grunting grandmother tight. Picturing the rope in *garotte* at her mother's neck. Feeling the strength of tomorrow's pull in her body.

Kathy Van Scoy rides the wind. On the eve of eschatology.

Jonathan Lovejoy

Divinity's Call

From Washington, D.C. Down to Cape Hatteras. To the Golden Gate over San Francisco Bay. The skies resound in an apocalyptic cry, heard from east to west, in a network of lightning shears unknown, and millions of blasts of endtime thunder unbestowed. These are the volleys of morning thunder unleashed, to awaken the flock from coast to coast, to infuse them with this ultimate instinct to lift as a single force of doom, and take to the skies again. Gathered upon the four winds, placed here for a single purpose, these untold billions of feathered things take to the air in mass, to blacken these stormy skies across the horizon east to west, in the form of a mass of screaming death that approaches. Every soul above ground can only sit in their cars and houses in terror, still unbelieving that these creatures have been gathered together in apocalypse, to deliver such magnificent and mocking deaths to every soul unprepared.

Airports and bus stations, hospitals and hotels, every house and habitat for a lost humanity, every forest and field in their path is burdened by the spirit of nature's wrath, by the determination of predestiny's whim, to visit upon the earth a spark of its unknown history, of its unknown prophecy fulfilled, as this dark cloud of fear moves onward, to complete the earth's journey toward a billion human souls stripped of this life, and sent into the netherworld to be judged for lives lived apart from Divinity's Call.

From the Great Basin of Nevada, across every square mile of the Las Vegas city and countryside, east above the Grand Canyon, and the winding waters of the Colorado River. Over the mountains of Colorado and New Mexico, across the rolling sea of golden wheat. Beyond the wind blown fields of the Kansas prairie plain, these creatures move in the form of what has not been seen by modern man, nor hath been imagined in his wildest dreams of divine retribution. From the northern tip of Texas, across the landscape of the Oklahoma Prairie, the skies are dark'ned with the beginning of sorrows, to precede the endtime trumpet call, on the eve of the Second Coming, and a generation moved beyond Redemption.

Jonathan Lovejoy

The Woman in White

$\mathcal{T}$his is one of the lonely places. A place replete with pain and death. Where Katherine Hardwick rides the wind. On the eve of eschatology.

Having awakened in the spirit of renewal, in the dark glow of a decision made. After another night of depravity upon her granddaughter. Katherine Hardwick stretches and smiles to herself. Sliding into the softness of her white cotton nightgown, to protect her bare skin from the bite of this deep, late summer morning cold. Kissing her granddaughter gently on the forehead, at the tip of her nose, upon her lips. Making sure to imprint upon the girl's tragic soul on the morning of this dark decision made.

Migration

Katherine slips her granddaughter into her own cotton cloth. Enamored by the beauty of her Indian doll. Looking like a prairie girl ghost to her. A ghost hearkened from 1888.

At the behest of the thunder rolling, Katherine pulls the beautiful girl by the hand, gently as a lady groom enamored by her bride, escorting her through the house enlivened by thunder, as rich with power as that of an earthquake, and the returns of a violent and fervent rain. Katherine glides the young girl through the house, opening the front door into the storm, held enraptured by the powerful line of blackness across the prairie horizon. Wondering what manner of black twister clouds are these that have gathered together, to slowly move toward every living thing in its path. Until the thunder is quieted enough to allow the echoes of the truth to flow toward her in sound, as though a scream were multiplied a million times, and spread out in an approaching blackness from east to west.

In this brackish burst of thunder screeched from the clouds, accompanied by the cacophony of light streaked across the bottom of these same gray clouds of doom, the woman breathes a sudden breath of deep revelation, feeling in her country soul the coming of the truth, and the arrival of her life's predestiny in apocalyptic form.

"Grandma Katherine, what's *that?*" the girl says, in the painful bliss of ignorance, as Katherine opens the screen door, escorting her out onto the porch. The girl nervously, fearfully, obediently follows her grandmother closer to the wild storm outside, holding onto her on the porch, holding her arm tight, asking her again as to the line of black from east to west, and whether it is moving toward them. But the grandmother is unable to speak, unable to loose her tongue, unable to tear them away from the most amazing sight in human history, causing her to shake her head in quiet shock and disbelief. The young girl stares up at the beautiful older woman, further unnerved by the look of awe and worry in her expression, until she begins to hear the strains of familiarity under the lightning, and between the blasts of rolling thunder.

"Oh, my God," the girl says. "Grandma its *them! Its them!"*

And the girl is inspired to take over in fight or flight, pulling her grandmother along, from the porch back into the house, pulling the woman toward the safety of the basement door. The girl opens the door, moving first into the basement darkness, her hand slipping from her grandmother's as the door closes suddenly behind her, imprisoning her in the basement dark with the clicking of a lock, and the silence she strains to hear from behind the basement door.

Outside the locked door, Katherine Hardwick presses her head quietly against the wood, to listen to her granddaughter pounding and hollering, enjoying the sound of terror in her voice, and the aura of hopelessness that feeds her soul. Katherine lowers her eyes in the calm of uneasy acceptance, suppressing an inner smile as she turns away from the screaming girl in the basement, walking slowly through the house back to the screen door, and out on to the porch in the storm.

In the lonely place. At the house on the Oklahoma prairie. The woman in white stands ready. Watching the black line take on the form of a moving, black mass, in the company of a sound unlike anything that the modern world has ever known.

Katherine Hardwick rides the wind. Into the apocalyptic arms of predestiny. Holding her arms out to the sides, to embrace this judgment and reprieve sent to her from the stars, written upon the heavenly parchment a thousand years before she was born, when the end of the age was foretold already, and delivered to her in a lifetime of pain and suffering.

Migration

In the house on the Oklahoma Prairie. Imprisoned in the lower and upper room. A mother and her daughter listen in a fear that rises beyond terror, as the house is filled suddenly with the end of the world in a screaming, a screeching never before gleaned by man, interspersed by the occasional sound like that of the voice of a bird or two in the storm.

This is one of the lonely places. Replete with pain and death. Where Katherine Hardwick rides the wind.

On the eve of eschatology.

Jonathan Lovejoy

The Little

Prairie Doll

The streets of Stillwater, Oklahoma bear witness to the migration having come and gone, as Jessica Weinberg drives through Payne County, looking for the home of Katherine Hardwick. Along these country roads of isolation, cars are flipped and wrecked among the infinity of bird carcasses scattered about, as the remains of a light Oklahoma twister passing through. Jessica drives onward, in the aftermath of this storm of eschatology, and the storm of devastation in her own life as well.

What barriers there are to the future are raised suddenly at times. In Jessica's life, they have kept her from spending another day in summer classes at Yale, withdrawing near the advent of her senior year. Whether or not Susan Yin's betrayal, or the death of her mother were truly the obstacles in her path, she does not know. It is the culmination of two years of wondering, two years of struggling with whether or not she wanted anything else to do with school anyway, her relationship with Susan Yin being what had kept her at Yale in the first place.

Before the first bird attack on Chappaqua weeks ago, she had already considered that she was possibly done with academics, needing to retreat back to her mother's unloving arms, to cushion the blow passed down to her sister Jenny, of the many perversions and depravities therein. She did not want to spend the rest of her life being the daughter of *the lesbian mother* in public anyway, carried along on the current of phoniness and jealousy that such a thing would facilitate in the world around her, being the daughter of the woman who wrote the biggest selling novel of all time. Having every one turned toward her in secret longing, every ear tilted in the selfsame craving, to ask her the question that begs the lips of every soul who knows she is Julie Weinberg's daughter:

Jessica, did you fuck your mother?

And she has felt in her heart for the longest time now, the need to answer this question in solitude, in the pages of her own memoir, to twist the title of her mother's novel *The Lesbian Mother,* to call her memoir *My Mother the Lesbian,* to deliver the truth in nonfiction, which is stranger than that of even the most perverted fantasy.

Jessica Weinberg drives on, touched by a sudden regret, the sense of loss that she has avoided until now, that she will never again see the little sister of her memory, and that she must carry the burden of grieving, and forever wonder where it is that her beloved mother could have gone.

Jessica Weinberg drives on. Past the miles of cars and carcasses strewn about. Finally coming to the picturesque property of prairie green. Rolling slowly down the long dirt road to the big, white farmhouse in the nearby distance. Parking in the grass close to the house, Jessica steps out into the cooling prairie wind, perceiving in the air the lightness of a crossing over, in the aftermath of earthen trauma.

Jessica climbs the steps to the front of the house, knowing somehow not to bother with knocking. She opens the screen door, touching her hand to the main doorknob, not surprised when it doesn't move at all.

A strong breeze swirls her hair over her face, whispering loudly through the nearby grove of trees, as if to try and speak in desperate warning, to knowledge of events come and gone.

Jessica Weinberg steps back into the yard. As if afraid to take the walk around the big porch, too close to the realm of the unknown. She strolls through the blowing prairie breeze, her gaze affixed to the big, white house, watching the back part of the porch come into view. As if to acknowledge the revelation of the truth in her sight, the breeze blows harder across the prairie, as she notices boarded up windows on the second floor, along with blood stained rags and tatters laid across a body stretched out on the porch below. And this breeze is colored by the heavy, gentle rumbling of thunder from the clouds, to acknowledge the second part of the truth in her eyes that yes, this is the body of a dead woman on the back porch of this property. And she is suddenly shocked to the core of her soul, when a streak of lightning arcs from the top of the sky to the bottom in the distance, to blast the message home in apocalyptic doom, that yes, this is the devastation of the truth, that the woman's body is half eaten down to the muscle and bone.

Jessica steps past the woman's body laid half bare in the torn, bloody nightgown, opening the ripped remains of a screen door into the house, amazed by the level of devastation and chaos present inside, as if wild deer had been trapped and terrified, slamming against everything in sight while trying to get out.

And suddenly, in the midst of roaring rumbling thunder from the clouds, Jessica is startled by a lonely, ghostly voice from somewhere in the air around her, as a spirit trapped within these walls of isolation. Jessica is suddenly struck by the spirit of fear, trying to turn her instantly about, and cause her to flee for her sanity. But this lonely, pitiful little voice holds her captive in the return of the rainstorm, as the lightning sparks in places near and far.

The word *'please'* drifts at her from somewhere nearby, in the voice of this little girl ghost, followed by a light scratching, and gentle knocking against wood.

"Hello?" Jessica says, suddenly realizing that maybe, this is not the voice of ghostly fantasy come to claim her, but is a voice of reality somewhere nearby. And the voice becomes less phantasmal, less ethereal in purpose and intent, as the pounding and the pleading grows louder and more desperate. Jessica turns from the livingroom, towards a door she passed in the hall, where she hears the pounding and pleading clearly from the other side.

Jessica undoes the old, click switch lock above the knob, then slides the deadbolt latch away, unprepared for the sudden opening, and the beautiful little Indian braided girl in a white nightgown that bursts free from behind the door.

Jessica hugs the little prairie doll in total bewilderment, overwhelmed by the spirits of grief and compassion. Jessica hugs the little girl tight, a child she barely remembers from years ago, as the thunder recalls days of the earth's most recent past, with dreadful warnings of an apocalyptic future unfurled.

Dawn is the Morning Twilight

I rest uneasy, on the bed in the upper room. Sitting in my underwear against the iron head railing bound and gagged, my legs roped together, my arms tied behind my back, my neck roped to the iron bed rail behind me. My mother's stocking is tight around my face, pushing the cloth deep into my mouth to choking, where it seems that the cloth will be eventually swallowed. For some reason or another, these are the ropes bestowed in the wee hours, as she fell upon me like a lady cowboy over a runaway calf when I was half asleep. Straddling me, tying my uncuffed arms behind my back first, then roping me immobile to the railing.

Somewhere in the world, the dawn is the morning twilight, nearby the edge of night. As I imagine the nighttime fading to dawn's early light, I cannot stop the well of sorrow as it overflows into my eyes, and down both sides of my face. Somehow, I know that the pizza was my last meal, and I don't dare imagine what sinister intention these ropes entail.

I had listened to the end-of-the-world bird attack with little more than apprehension, resigned in my heart that if they had decided to get in, they would peck and claw their way through the edges of the bedroom door, and slowly, painfully put me out of my misery. And ironically enough, I know, the wood boards at the windows were the barrier between me and certain death.

I rest uneasy. Listening to the footsteps and shuffling sounds at my door, my body flooding with a greater terror than what I felt during the migration, feeling in my spirit that my days on this earth have come to an end. The door opens quickly, and I see my little Indian cherub, my Indian braided doll rush into the room in an angelic, white nightgown, rushing over to me in tears, hugging me around the neck and kissing me all over my face, untying the stocking and pulling the cloth from my mouth.

And while my daughter hugs me in sobs and weeping, I notice another figure walking slowly into the room behind her, a glimpse of something from the modern world, where at least there is a fleeting hope of living, and the chance to find tranquility, at the end of this age of twilight and misery.

Our delivering angel sees to it that my ropes are cut, helping me off the bed to my feet. The two of them anchor me on either side, the modern girl, and the ghost girl from 1888.

"Get something to cover your mother," Jessica says, to where I answer sharply *"no..."* and "let's go." Walking between them in my bra and underwear, every bruise and welt visible, to strengthen my resolve to walk in victory toward my freedom.

I step gingerly between them, helped along by what feeble strength they have, escorting me out onto the porch in the rising rain and wind. Though the older girl, this younger woman tries not to let it happen, I step with determination nearby the corpse, nearby the thing of beauty transformed, to where the ugliness of the motherline is coalesced, and descended upon her physical body. I stand still for a moment, gazing in disbelief at the thing that lies there face up, where the queen is dead, her eyes plucked from blackened sockets in her head, where the skin of her face is nearly picked clean down to the bone.

From this grisly revelation, my two angels turn me away. Walking me through the rain and rising wind, to the safety of her rolling silver chariot that awaits. Our deliverer sits us comfortable in the back seat. Glimpsing at the heavy breasted woman in wet bra and underwear in the mirror, being hugged by the weeping girl in the white cotton nightgown. Having the presence of mind, and the strength to not speak a word to the two traumatized souls she rescued from one of the lonely places, nearby the twilight of human history.

Birds of Paradise

Jonathan Lovejoy

$\mathcal{T}$he seven birds of paradise, as they burden the heart and mind

A robin redbreast and redbird cardinal, in the garden of grief sublime

Nearby the goldfinch and black capped chickadee, the woodpecker
*   marks the flow of time*

As the mourning dove and bluebird sing this melancholy heart of mine

$\mathcal{D}$ays come and go. As do the seasons. Until the earth has made another journey, and it is summer again.

Gone are the days of upper class mediocrity and misery, along the privileged streets of Chappaqua. I stand on the balcony of our new white mansion built, overlooking the lawn of our new prairie green, east of the Blue Ridge Mountains of Virginia. A grand, New World paradise bought and paid for by a mother's money, from the legacy of an end-of-the-world book left behind.

My daughter and I rest here now. At the home of the angel who delivered us. From the balcony of my bedroom, I watch my daughter, who is a year older now, walk the length of this grand scale property with our deliverer hand in hand. One with the younger sister she lost, returned to her by divine mercy. The other, with the older sister she never had.

I watch the two of them walk under the calm of these gray skies, protecting one another from the pain of memories, and from the spirits that haunt them from days long gone.

A breeze reaches out to me in determination. A wind touched by winter's chill, though the world rests at the edge of another long and dreary summer of fear and discontent.

In the first days of June, the weather is cold.

ABOUT THE AUTHOR

Jonathan Lovejoy is a graduate of the University of North Carolina at Greensboro, with a B.A. in Religious Studies, and a graduate of Liberty University with an M.A. in Theological Studies. He currently lives in Winston Salem, North Carolina.

For more info on the author's life and career, visit jonathanlovejoy.com